Dedicated with love to my mother SHAHLA
and my father JUERGEN.

"There are roughly three New Yorks. There is, first, the New York of the man or woman who was born here, who takes the city for granted and accepts its size and its turbulence as natural and inevitable. Second, there is the New York of the commuter—the city that is devoured by locusts each day and spat out each night. Third, there is the New York of the person who was born somewhere else and came to New York in quest of something. Of these three trembling cities the greatest is the last—the city of final destination, the city that is a goal. It is this third city that accounts for New York's high-strung disposition, its poetical deportment, its dedication to the arts, and its incomparable achievements. Commuters give the city its tidal restlessness, natives give it solidity and continuity, but the settlers give it passion."

—E.B. WHITE, "Here Is New York"

☾

New York City
—the collective belief in unlimited possibilities

In a minute, New York City makes itself known. Its knowledge is transmitted as a feeling—a golden hunch that we are among our fellows, that we have found like-minded friends driven by passion. And passion is a liquid that flows along the thoroughfares, seeps into the subway corridors, fills the warehouses and delis, boardrooms and bars. It pumps through the veins of a community that believes in the immeasurable truth that Life Is Good. So as the sun rises and illuminates the skyscrapers, the eyes of New York City are not seduced by the magnificent cityscape—great hunks of manicured stone and girder sheared at incredible angles, pointed spires shooting into oblivion; instead, they see their brethren walking in the shadows. For the skyline is not New York; it is a dream, imagined and actualized. And within the unnamed faces that carom in and out of the city's maze, there are collective visions of unlimited possibility—from bartender to banker, artist to architect—millions of cities within a city.

This is PEYMAN AZHARI'S New York.

New York City rushes to nowhere—a massive splurge of humanity unified in the daily recklessness of 1440 minutes. A clown in full regalia rides a motorcycle down 32nd Street as if nothing could be more ordinary. A cabby blares her horn and delivers a dissertation on Chinese economics before cursing fluently in six languages. Joe the banker becomes Joanne after midnight—the starlet of the cabaret. The Metro cards are swiped and throngs of commuters push through the starting gates, bursting forth like liquored stallions to catch the trains. They dive into the darkness of the subway, politely but aggressively sidestepping until falling into cars and hurtling through tunnels while they sip cups of coffee and check their hair in the reflective glass. These are details that veterans of the city have become immune to. But it is in these moments that the universality of the day is revealed. In the time it takes for a lens to open and close, a tale is told in a single frame.

DAVIS wears sunglasses and thump, thump, thumps on a drum he bought at a pawn shop in the East Village. He plays underneath a staircase, beside the heavy rattle of subterranean trains. And his audience comes and goes in harmony with arrival and departure times. He doesn't care. He continues hammering out some untouchable beat with his eyes closed, delivering the soundtrack of the subway that is his song, his dream.

FREDERICK taps out the rhythm on a briefcase full of fake watches and sunglasses while he looks for gullible tourists on a train car, tabulating invisible profit sheets in his head, devising a way to get by. The train stops, the doors fling open, and FREDERICK is shot into Grand Central Station, and it's humming with performers who bang on buckets, antique keyboards—anything that can be played.

PEYMAN ambles in between the movement with a camera at his hip. EDWARDO hangs over a piano that looks as though it has played him. His neck hangs like a broken stem while FREDERICK flashes his wares to the growing crowd. PEYMAN sifts through the masses, capturing the secrets on anonymous faces. He pauses, he points, he shoots—PEYMAN moves. He has found his home. His quest has begun in a place where the day unfolds in minutes, connections are continually forged and severed, and photographs prove there can be authenticity in fakery. FREDERICK grins and the crowd continues to stream through Grand Central Station like ghosts in transit.

CAROLINE has DAVIS' song in her head and a pair of bootleg Ray-Bans in her purse. She quickens her pace, climbing out of the subway and up the stairs, looking back and admiring the simplicity of the long, lonely corridor—a vein that empties and fills with the blood of a thousand beating hearts. But her musing is interrupted when she receives a glare from a madman hauling a mattress and wearing Mardi Gras beads. LEONARD was a professor of literature until he became habitual with the bottle and obsessed with the idiom "let sleeping dogs lie." CAROLINE says a Hail Mary and walks to a human-rights demonstration while donning an American flag on her shoulders. She protests injustice in Tibet, but cannot forget the destitute image of LEONARD and wonders if he found a place to sleep.

LEONARD walks shirtless down Broadway and GERALD spies him while gazing out a 6th-story window. His curtains are broken. They haven't been fixed and he doesn't care because he enjoys the light in the afternoon. He plans to smoke a cigar inside and remember what his wife looked like. And when it begins to rain, his sadness deepens because she always took pleasure in storms. His mind drifts to a place where his wife still laughs, and Professor LEONARD still inspires freshman to appreciate the beauty of a well-constructed sentence. On the street, LEONARD feels like he is being watched and drops his mattress and darts into an alley.

GERALD finishes his cigar, turns away from the window, and walks into the rain. The wind pushes him, tired and wet, into the oldest deli in New York where the ghost of the 19th customer stands in a line that never forms. And as he eats a Spanish omelet, GERALD understands what haunts the cook: JERRY looks wearily out of the kitchen, feels the weight of eternity, and waits for the next order. SHAYNE is an artist from Texas and as she fills GERALD'S coffee for the third time, she sketches a tribute to his sadness in her mind. She thinks of the blank canvas in her studio and plans to buy paint after work. Then she conjures two scenes: a mother and daughter dashing through the shower of an open fire hydrant on a hot day in Spanish Harlem, and a couple walking through a snowy landscape, feeling the small fire between their gloved hands. SHAYNE imagines both images hanging in a gallery and decides to paint GERALD'S portrait between them. But her epiphany is interrupted when more travellers enter the deli and she begrudgingly pretends to be a waitress.

It is a deal SHAYNE has struck with the city—she brews the coffee and New York tips in inspiration, her sacrifice a bridge to happiness.

Outside, RODRIGO loads crates of onions and potatoes into a truck. His neck is bent forward and his shoulders arch as the storm's deluge continues. Each delivery brings him closer to a daughter who lives in a city across the Atlantic. RODRIGO imagines her sitting in his wife's lap, thinking about New York and dreaming of her father. It is just an afternoon shower, a rainy day on 101st and Broadway. And in the delis and boardrooms and warehouses—the collective of New York City—all minds float to a vision of Central Park on an impossibly beautiful day in spring. The blankets are spread, the picnic baskets are open, a child laughs, a lover is kissed on the shoulder, and the soaring skyline breaks the blue sky into pieces.

And then the rain stops and NICHOLAS, mohawked and lovely, struts down the street with a hand on his hip. He winks at a child whose dream of riding a bike without training wheels has finally been realized. NICHOLAS loosens his collar and pushes against the current of the street, dodging traffic as a fashionable couple bursts past him, hails a cab, and disappears. And then New York disappears and its song is all that is left. A ghost of the jazz age is blowing so hard on his rusty saxophone that one of his eyes is rolling into his head. BOBBY'S song is undeniably true, like the goodness of warm bread. And the street is BOBBY'S stage because he lives there and his lovers are the cigarette butts he picks out of the gutters in between performances.

They are all kings of the city, all emblems of diversity, strength, and love; all bound together by the string of possibility. PEYMAN contemplates this feeling as New York swells like a wave, swirling paper and dust into the darkening night. He closes his eyes and prays for purpose. When he opens them, like a spark igniting into flame, he has direction. He cannot see it, only feel it, and there is a breeze in New York. It is at his back. Suddenly, he is compelled to sprint and Amsterdam Avenue recedes in his wake. He follows the squawk of pigeons for two blocks and notices crows swooping down from their rooftop perches. And when PEYMAN arrives at their destination, he finds a beloved king holding his royal court on the sidewalk. BENEDICT'S audience flies for miles to pay their respect and looks up at him in awe as he shares gold from a plastic bag. The pigeons are floating and thrashing in the sky, buzzing around the castle, praising the king's kindness. Now PEYMAN can feel the goose pimples begin to rise. His heartbeat quickens and the rest of the city is gone. There is only the spotlight on the stage and the whole world bearing down upon him—all the sadness and joy, triumph and defeat, unified in a single frame. Then, in a whisper lost in the steel, glass, and raging gears of a city that feeds him, he says, "What an honor it is, to be a witness."

—DONOVAN ORTEGA

1440 Minutes New York City — Peyman Azhari

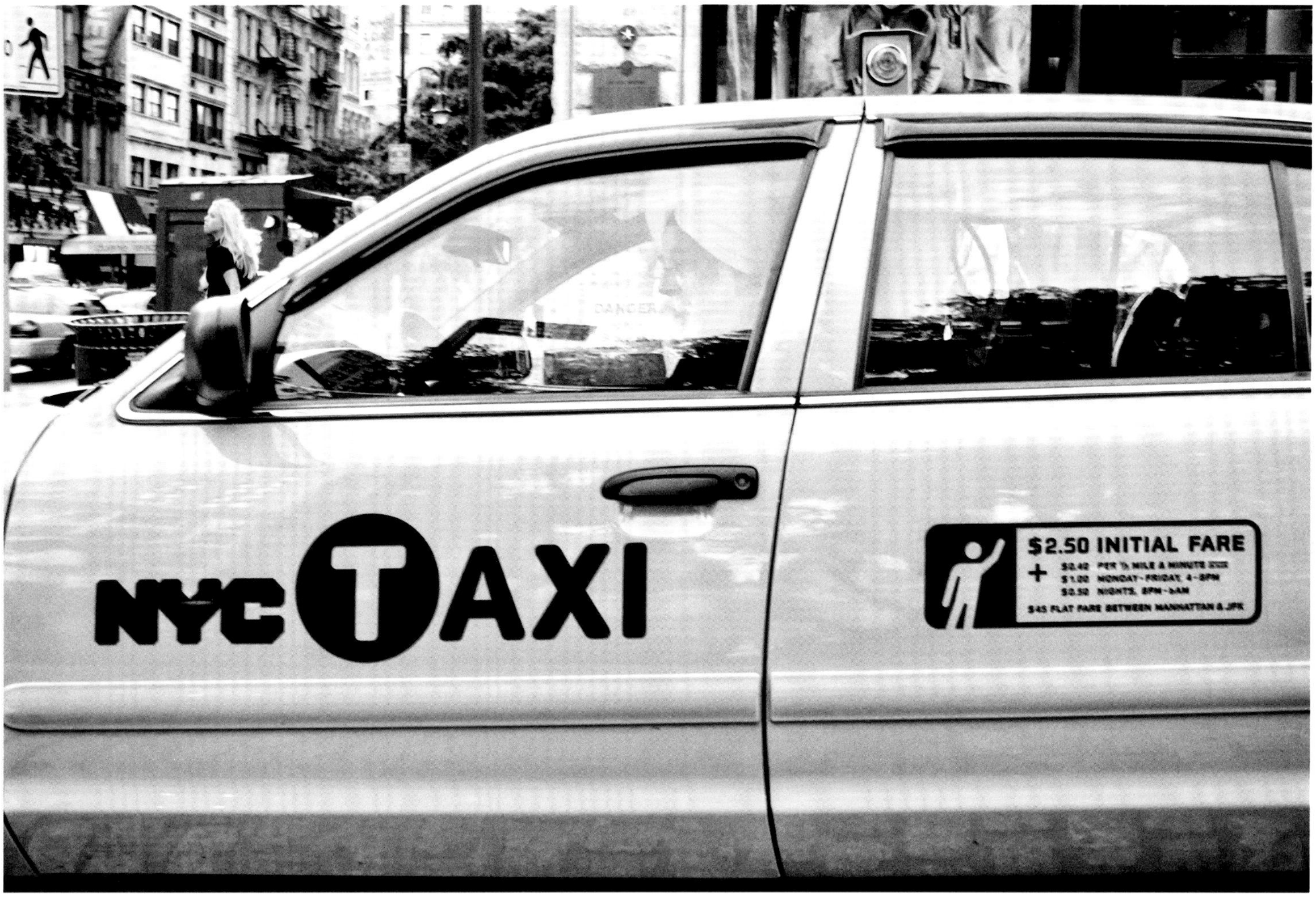
NYC TAXI
$2.50 INITIAL FARE

SLICE
CORN ON THE COB
HOT DOGS
SHISH-KABOB
FRIED CLAMS
FRIED SHRIMP
ONION RINGS
LEMONADE
CANDIES
FUNNEL CAKES
HAMBURGERS
AREPAS
SWEET CORN WITH MOZZARELLA CHEESE
HOT SAUSAGE
ATM
24 Hour
SHISH KEBOB
GAMES
FOOD
TATTOO
GAMES

GARAGE
HIGH
SPEED
INTERNET
ACCESS
copy
shop
INTERNET
DESIGN
STATION
MALL
CHABAD

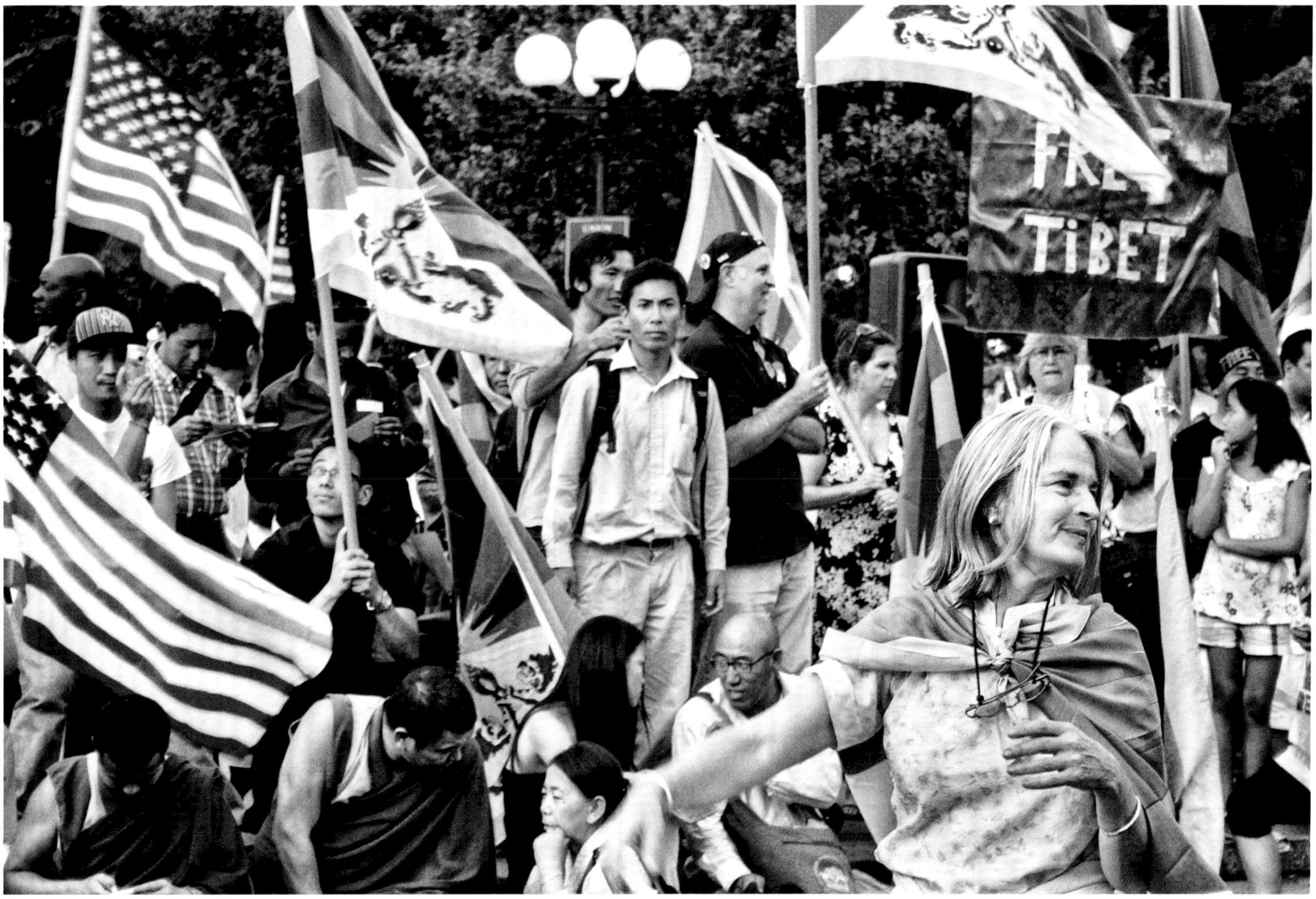
FREE
TiBET

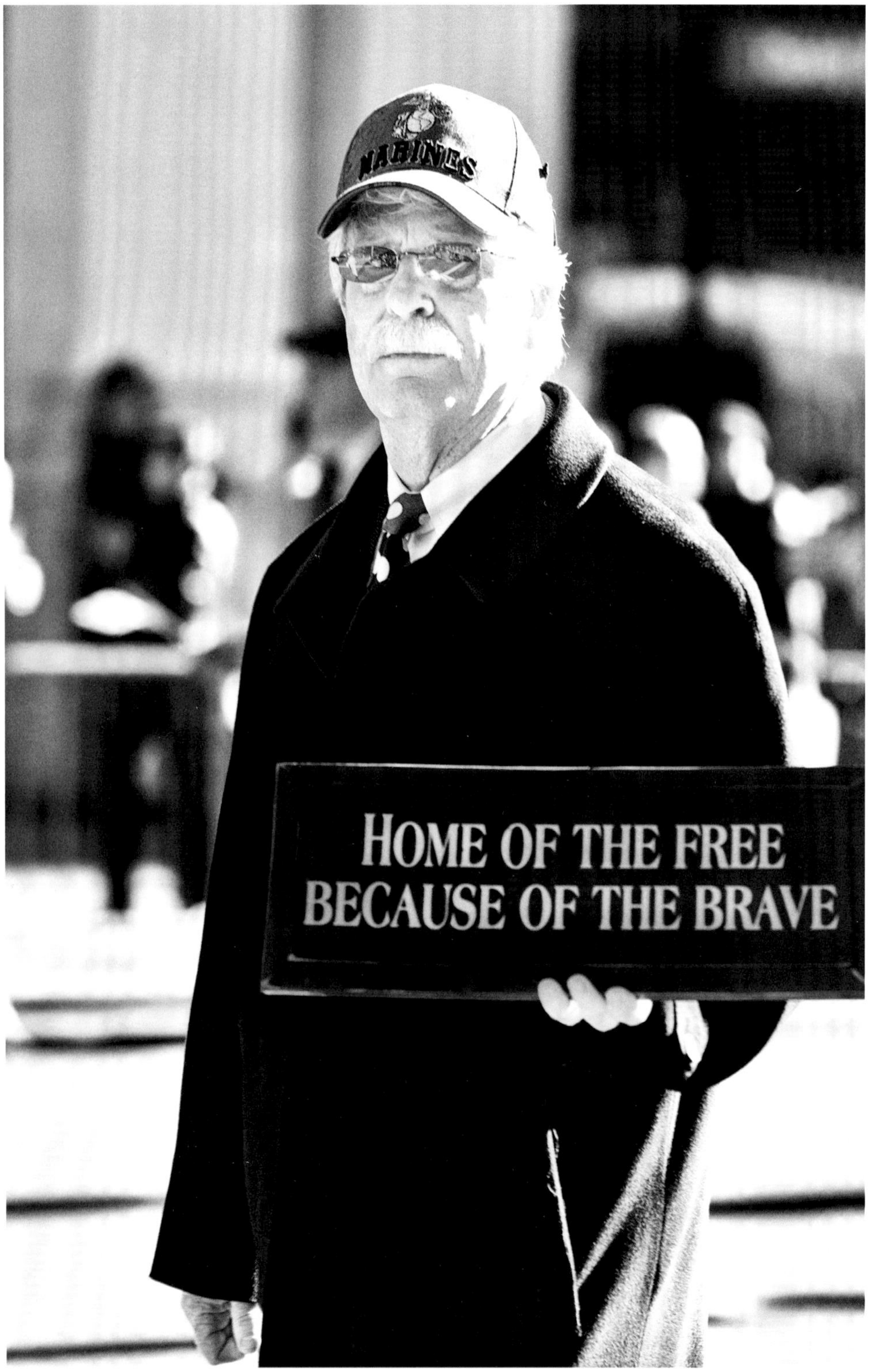
MARINES
HOME OF THE FREE
BECAUSE OF THE BRAVE

43

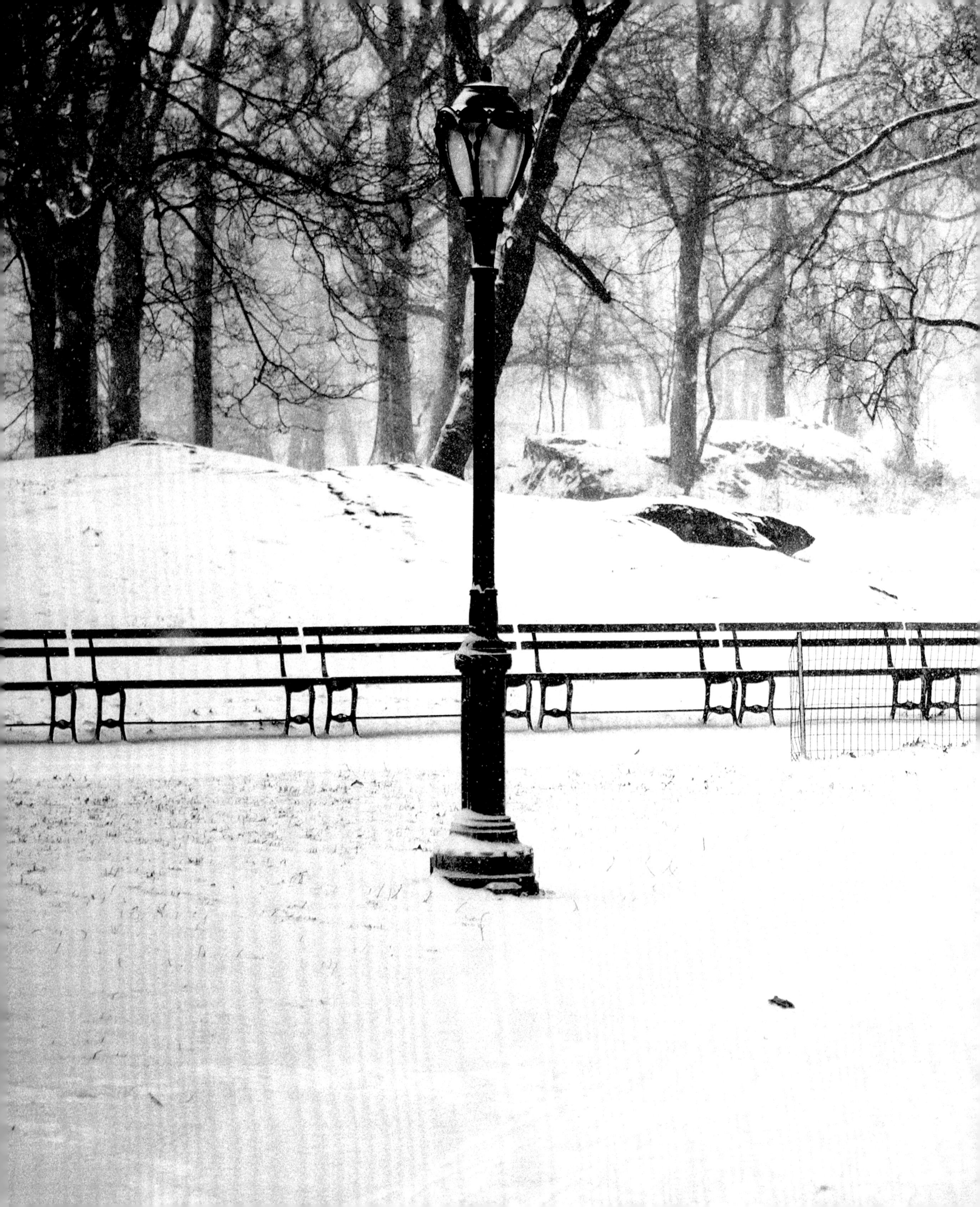

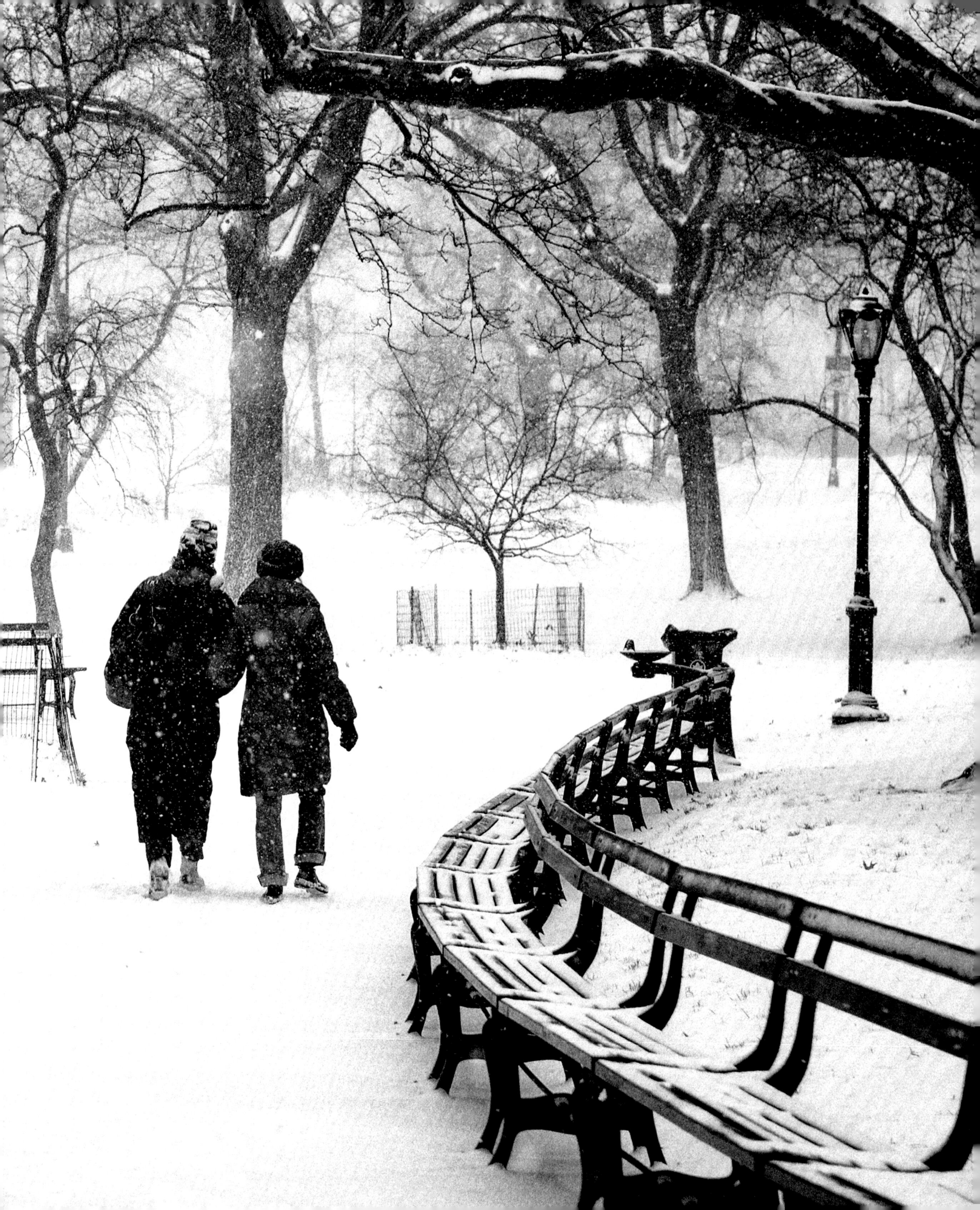

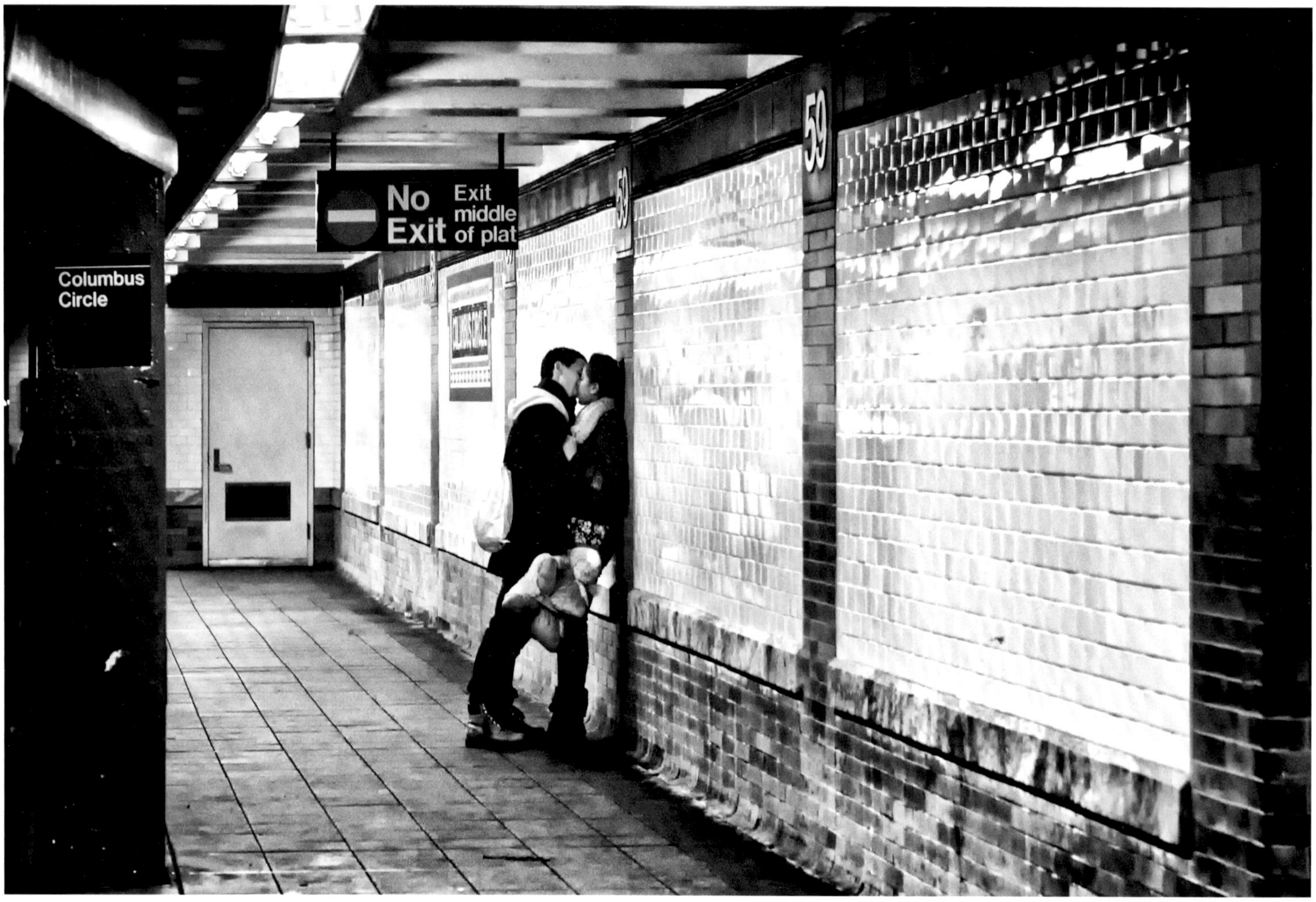
Columbus
Circle
No
Exit
Exit
middle
of plat
59
59

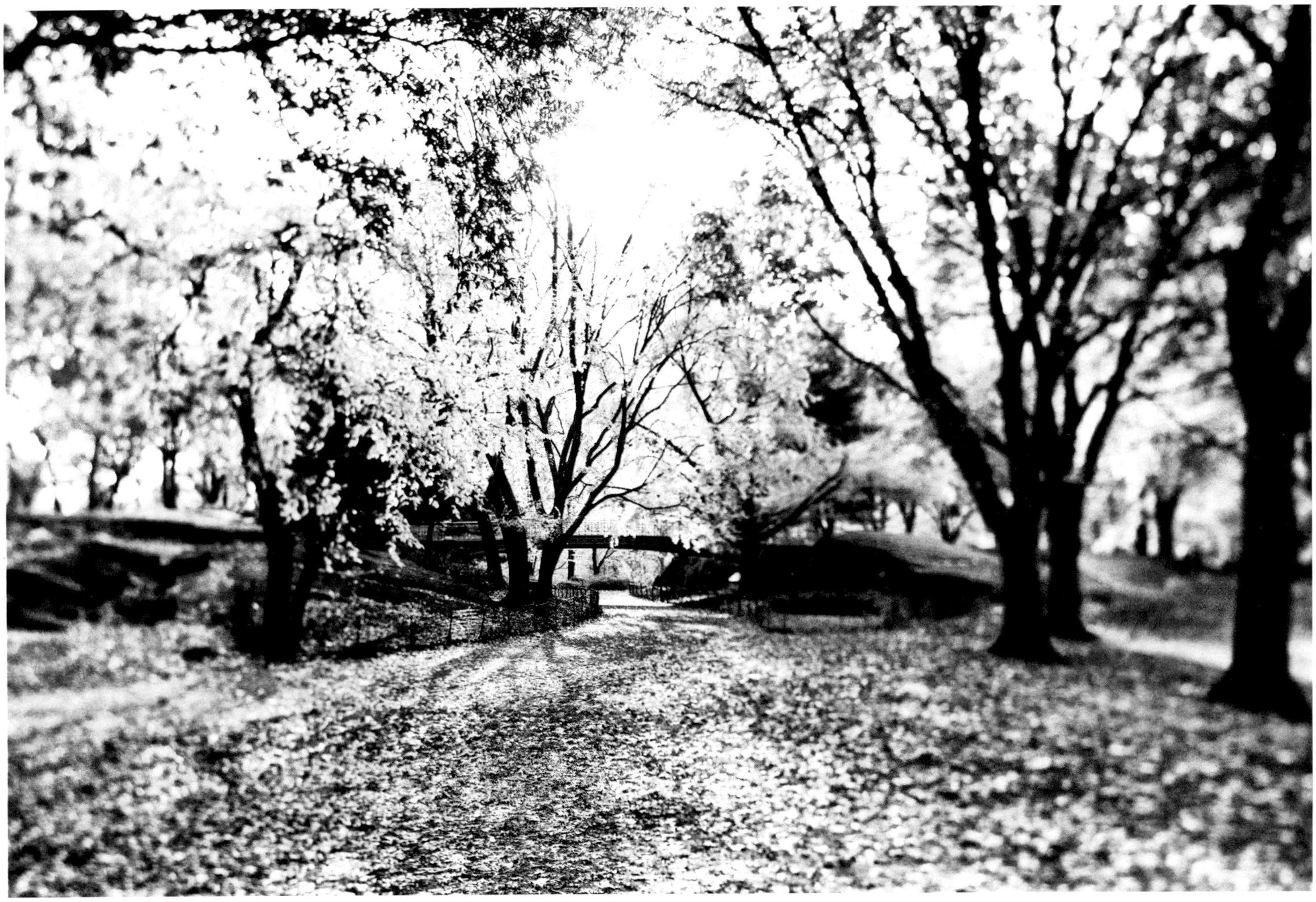

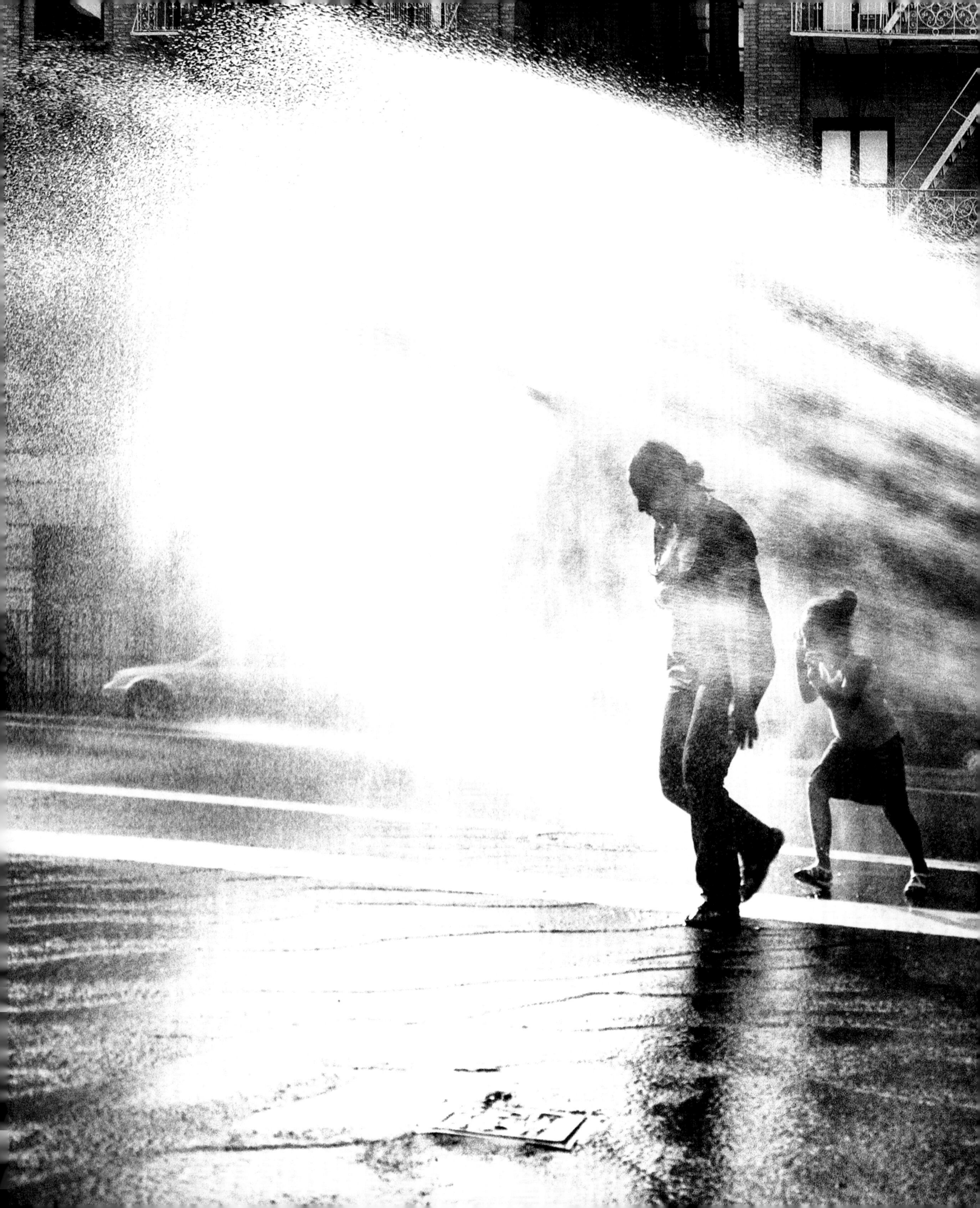

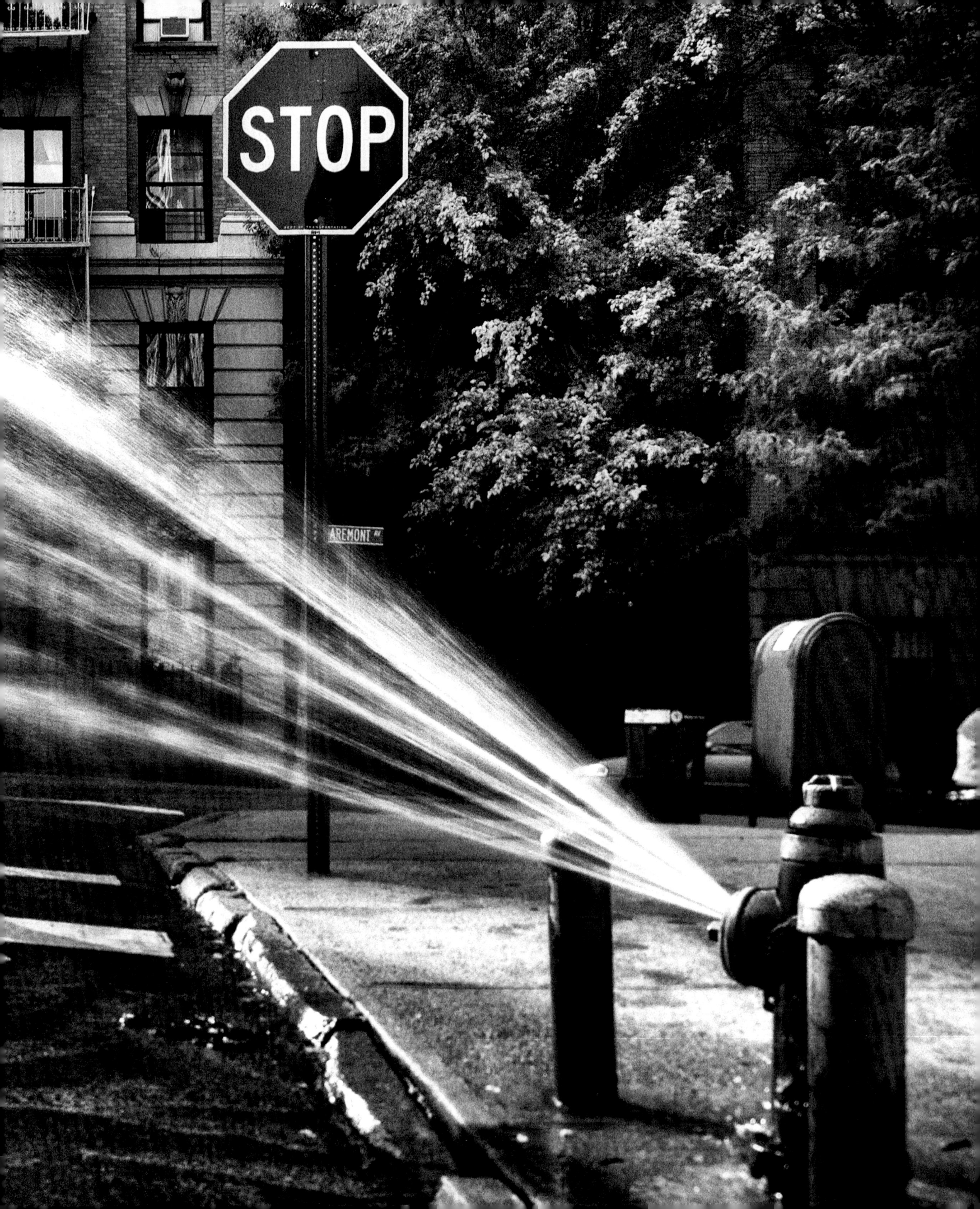
STOP
AREMONT AV

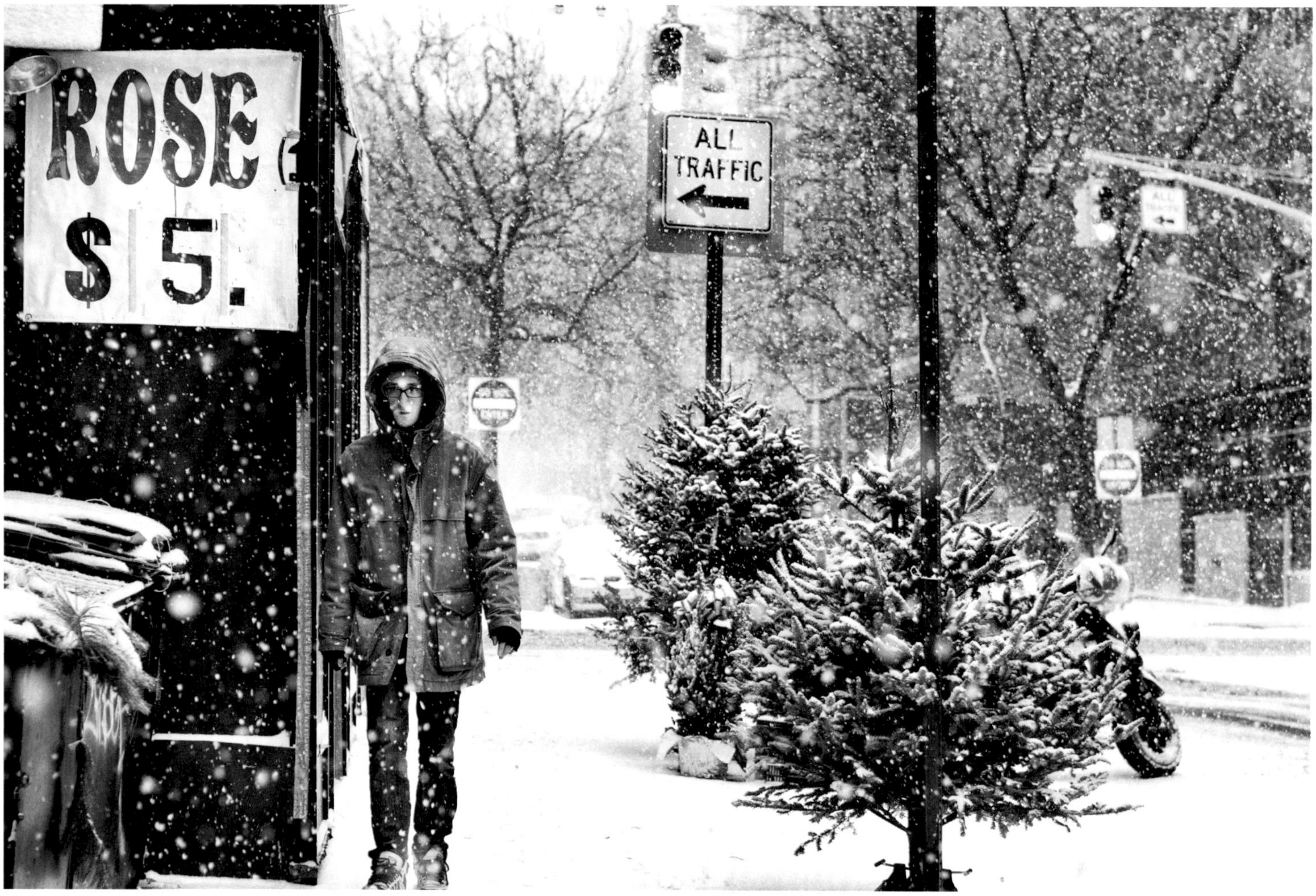
ROSE
$ 5.
ALL
TRAFFIC

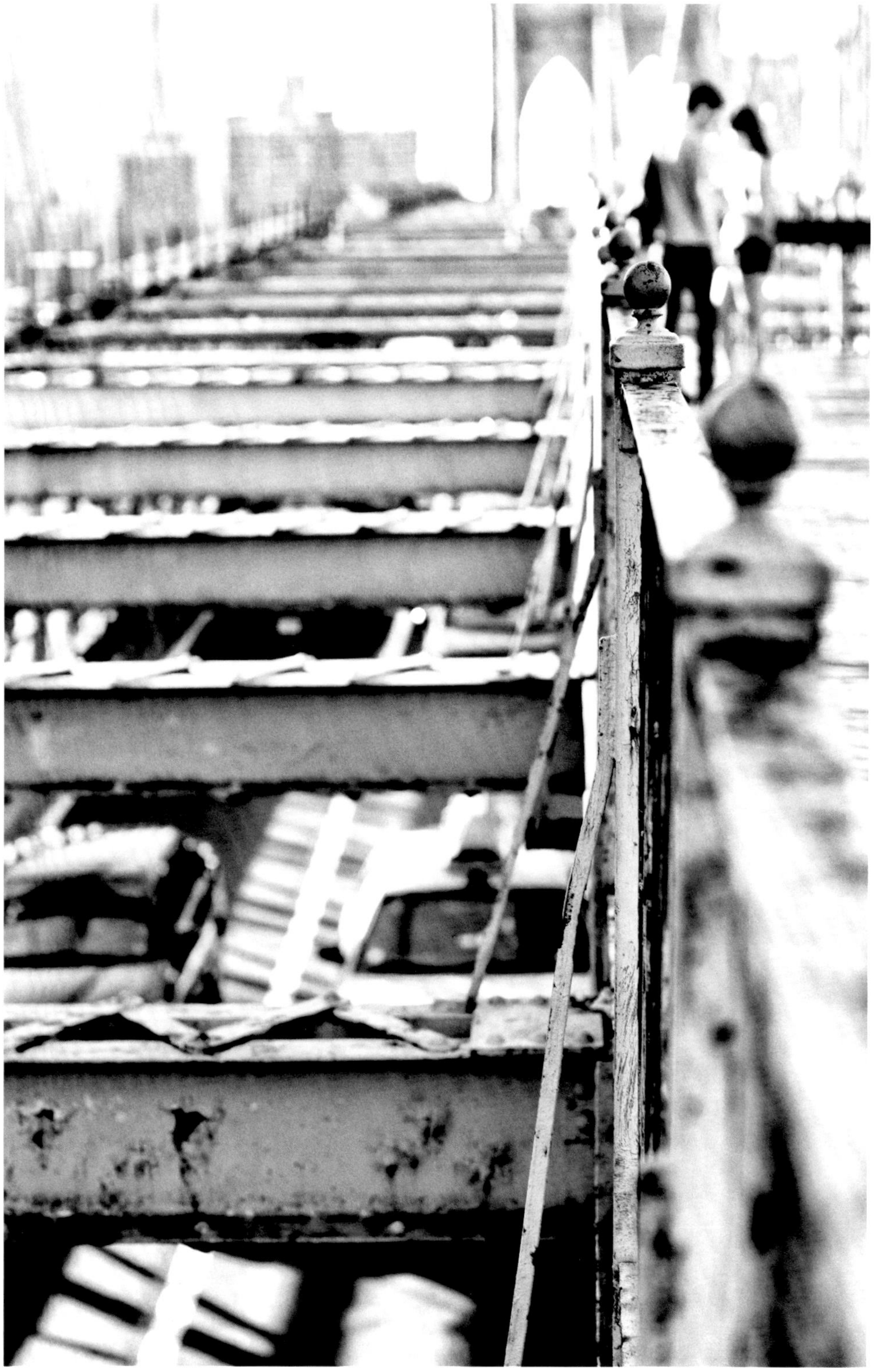

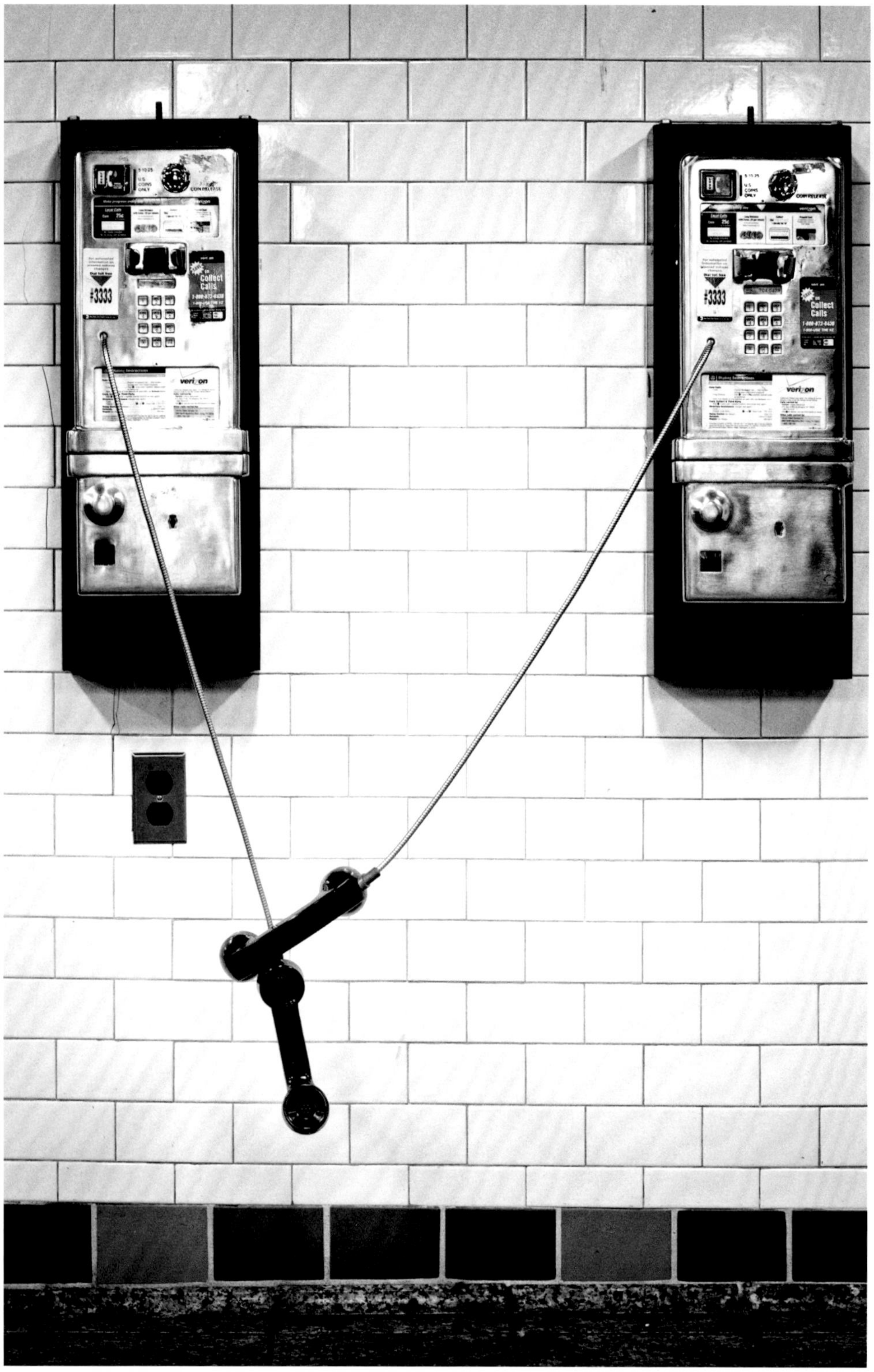
#3333
Collect Calls
verizon
#3333
Collect Calls
verizon

STILL A VIRGIN?

FOR HELP CALL
888-743-4335
TOLL FREE

THEVIRGINITYHIT.COM

GET FORTUNE BELOW
WHAT · DOES · GRANDMA · SAY ?
GRANDMA'S
PREDICTIONS

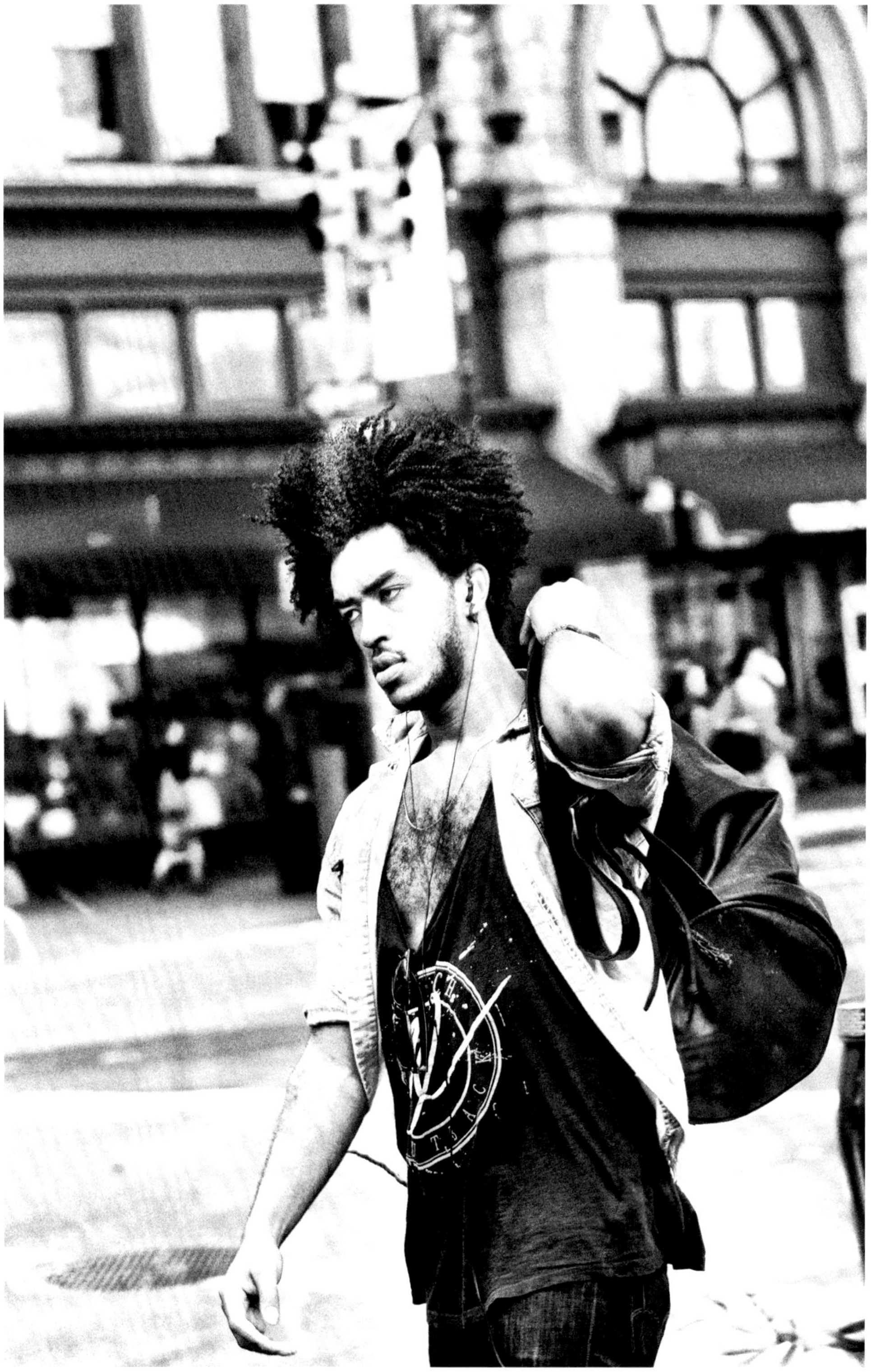

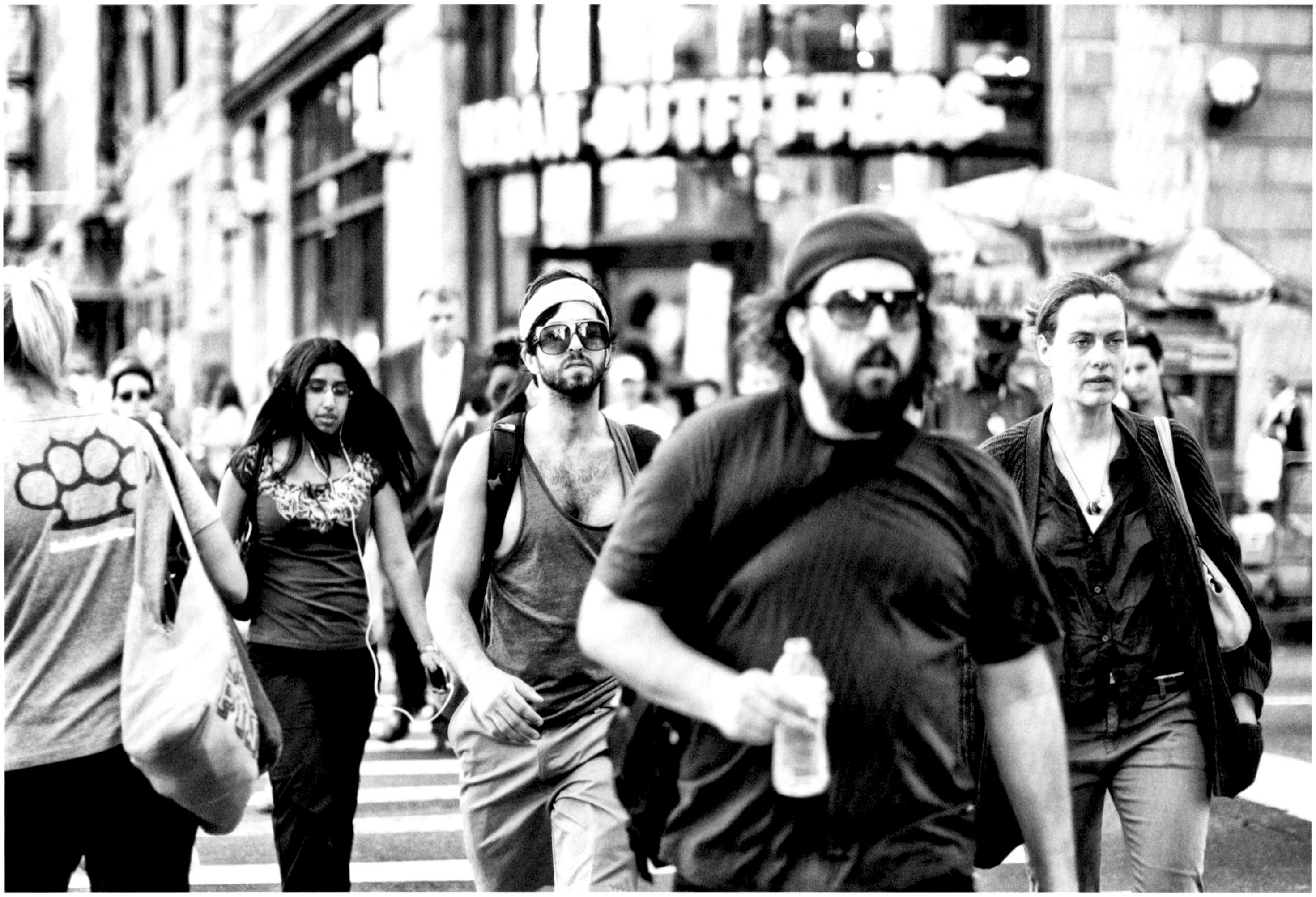

Levi's curve ID
HOTNESS
COMES IN ALL
SHAPES AND SIZES
GO FORTH
25 W. 14TH ST.
Van Wagner
M-710

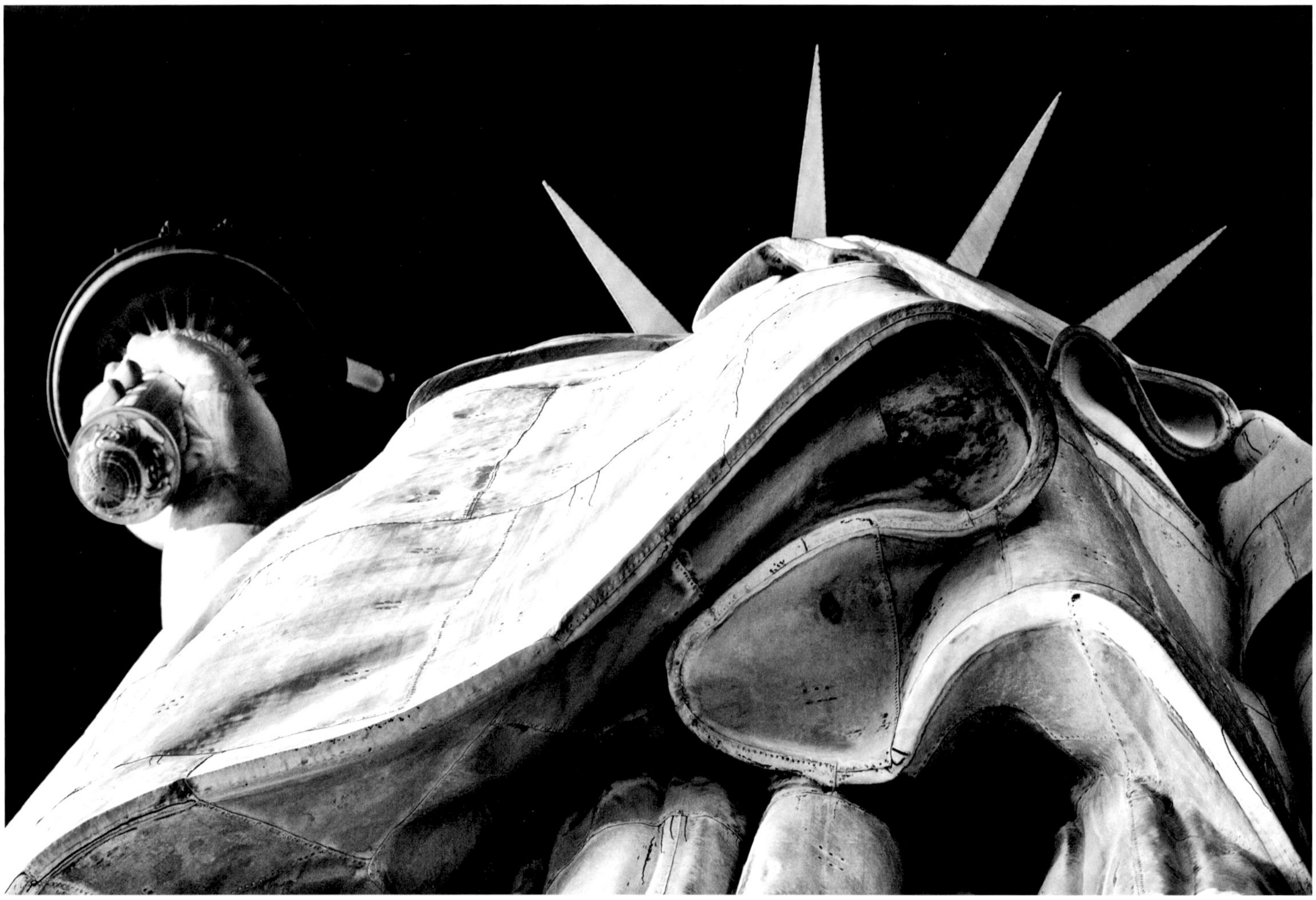

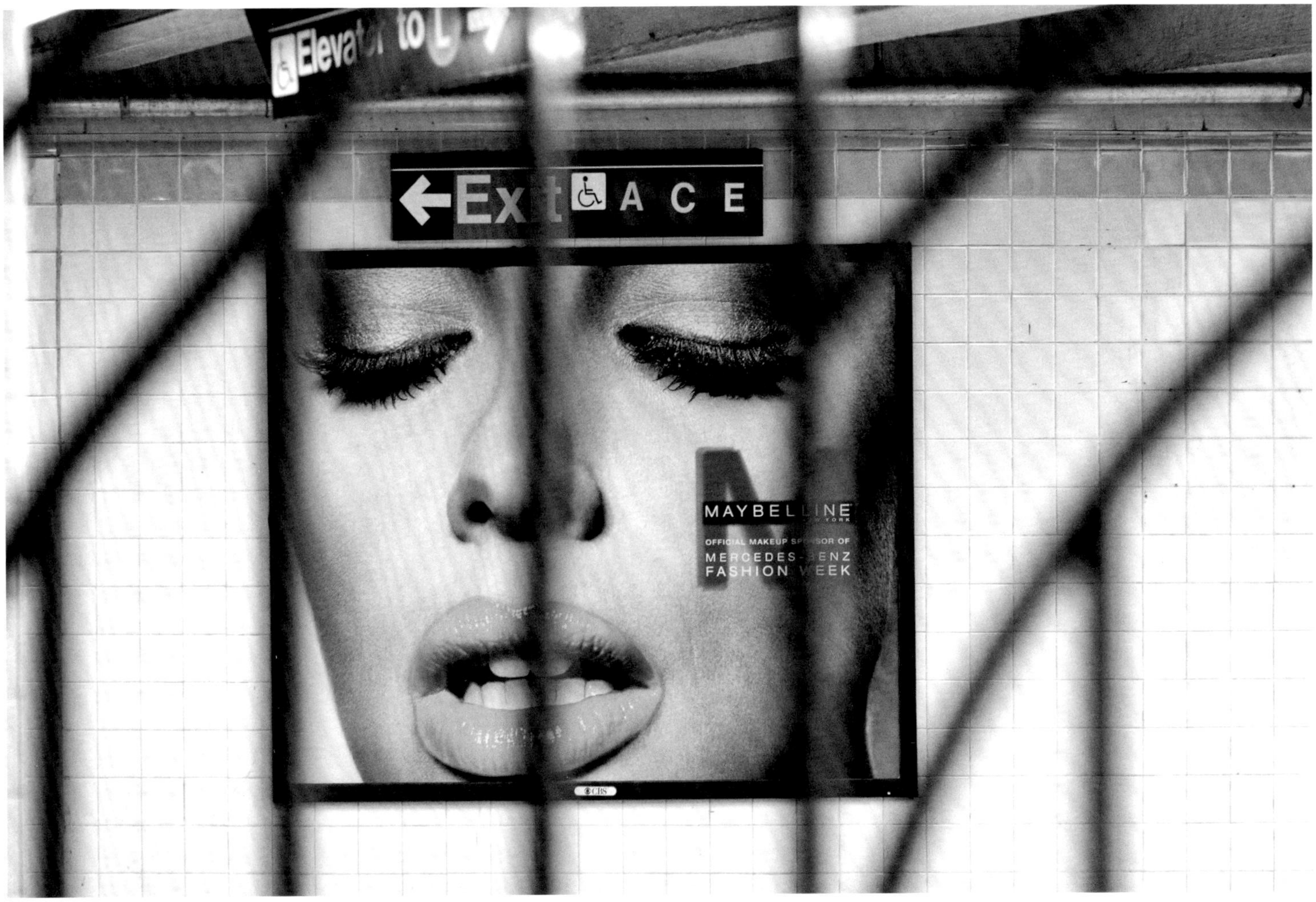
A C E

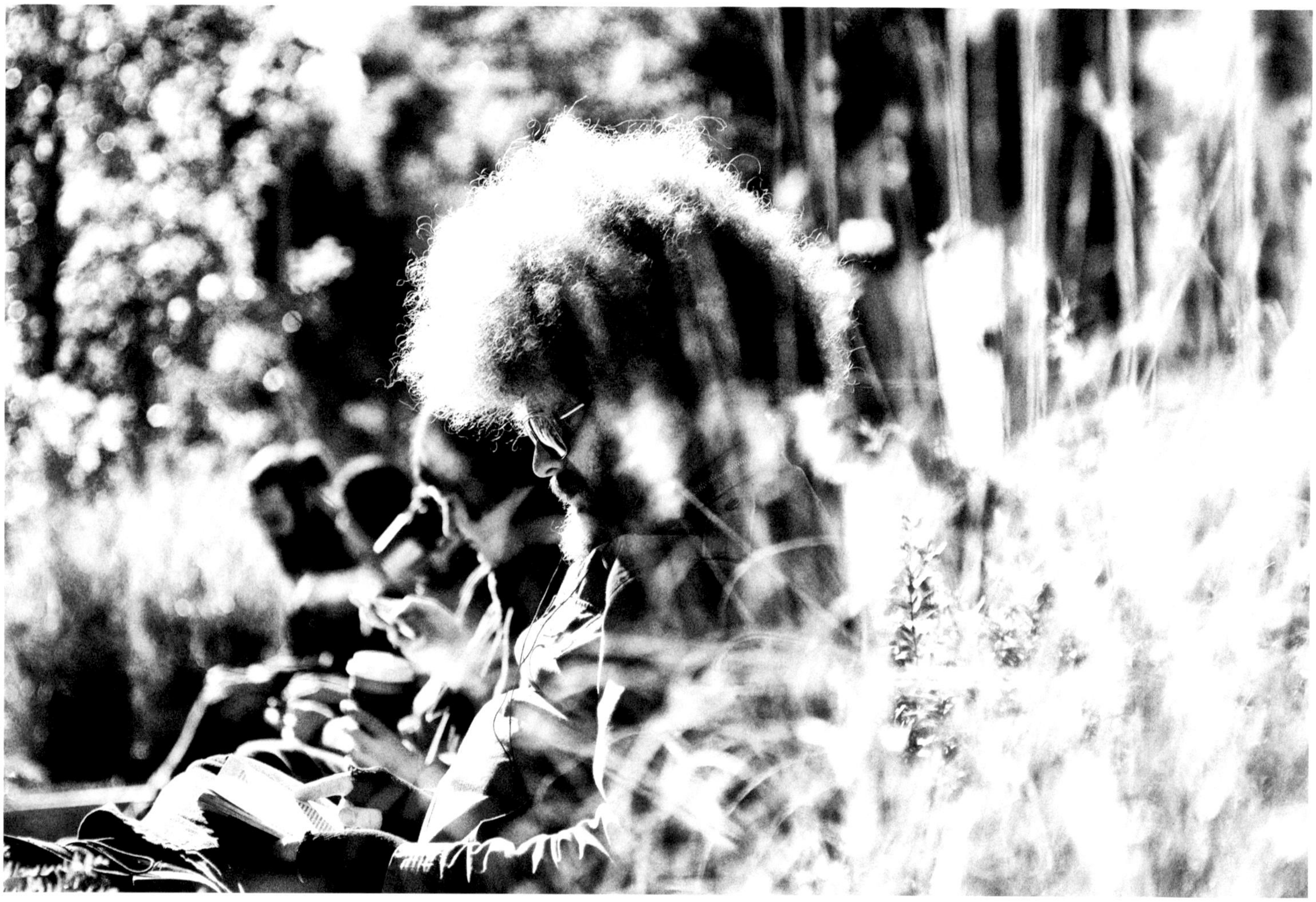

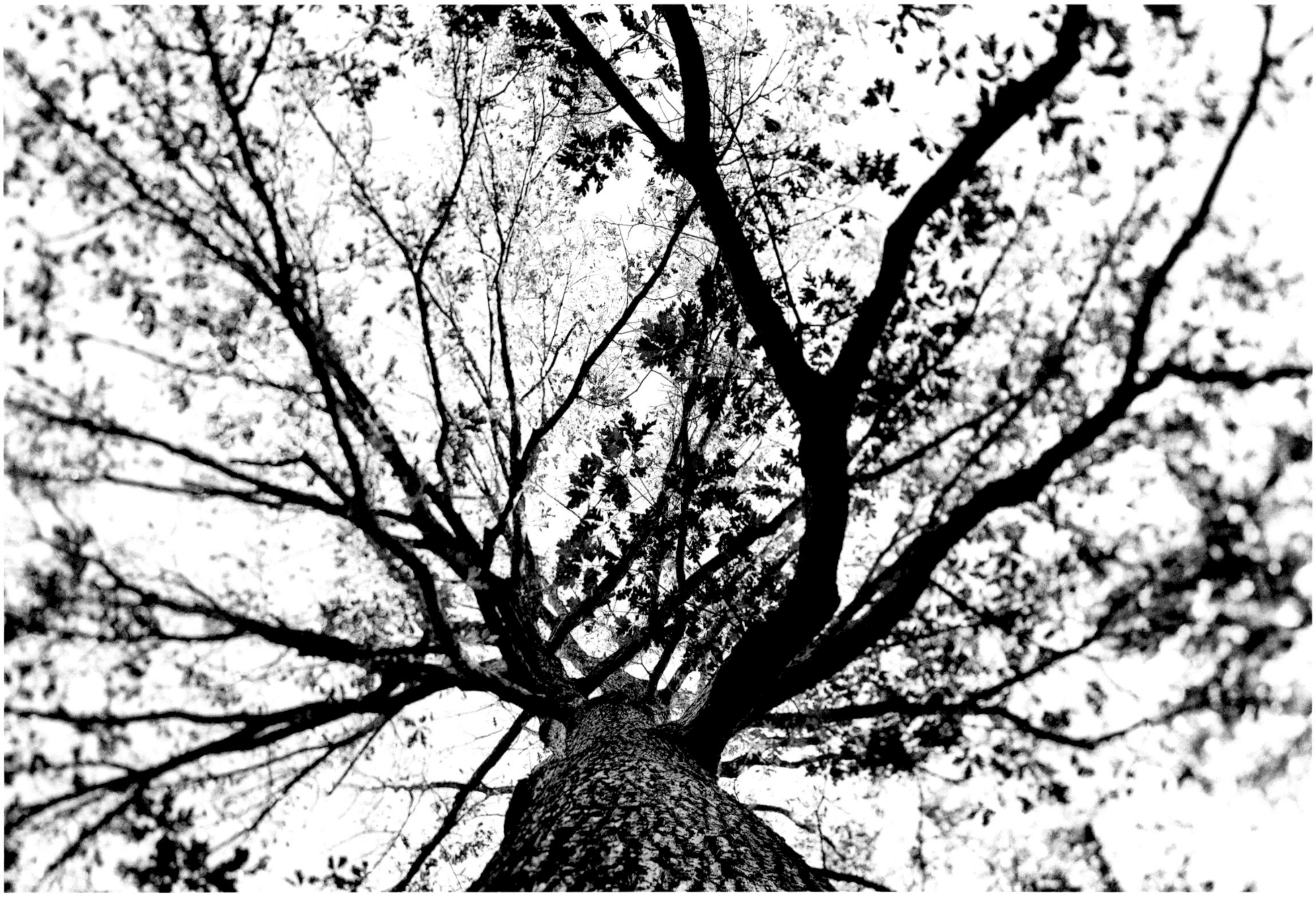

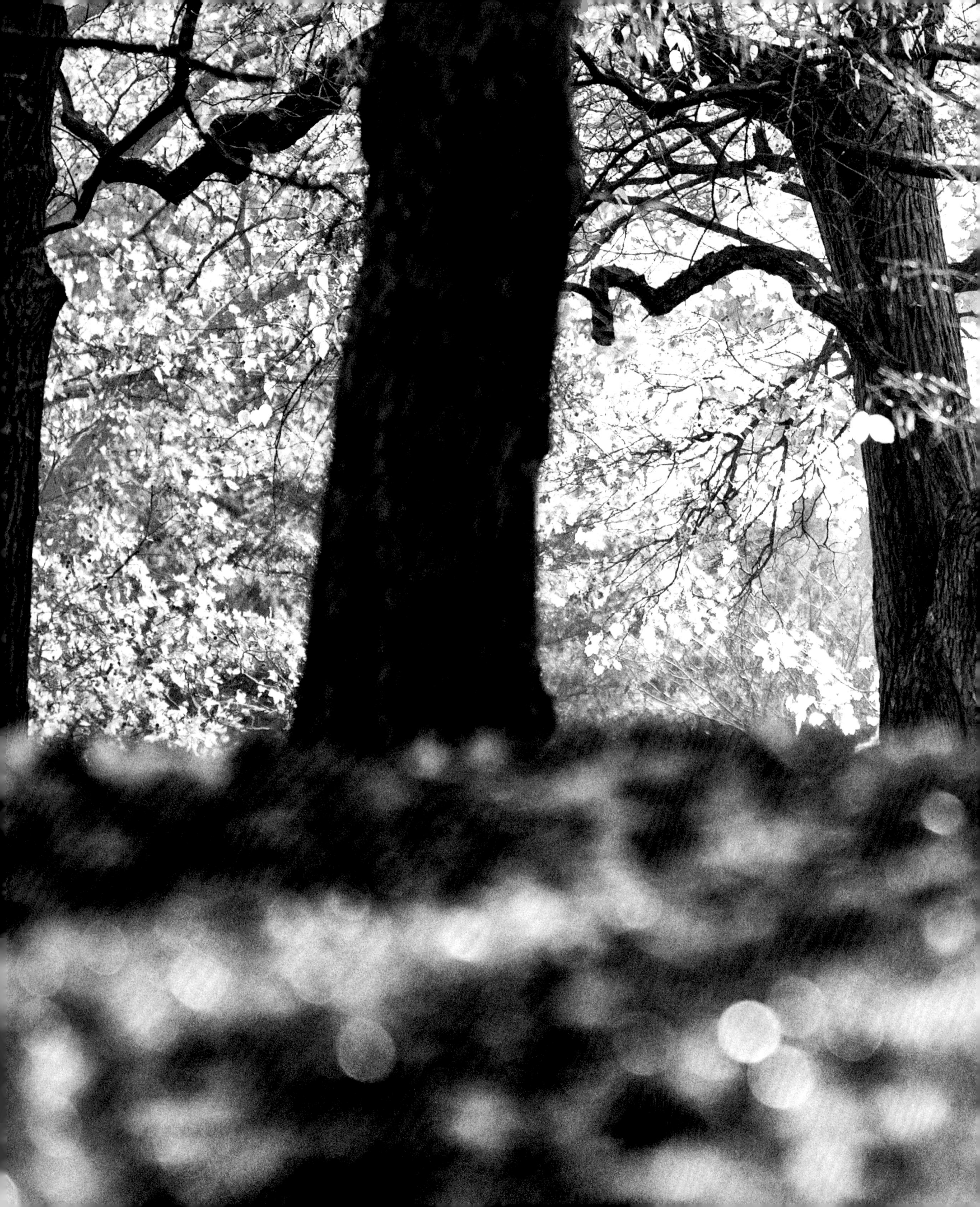

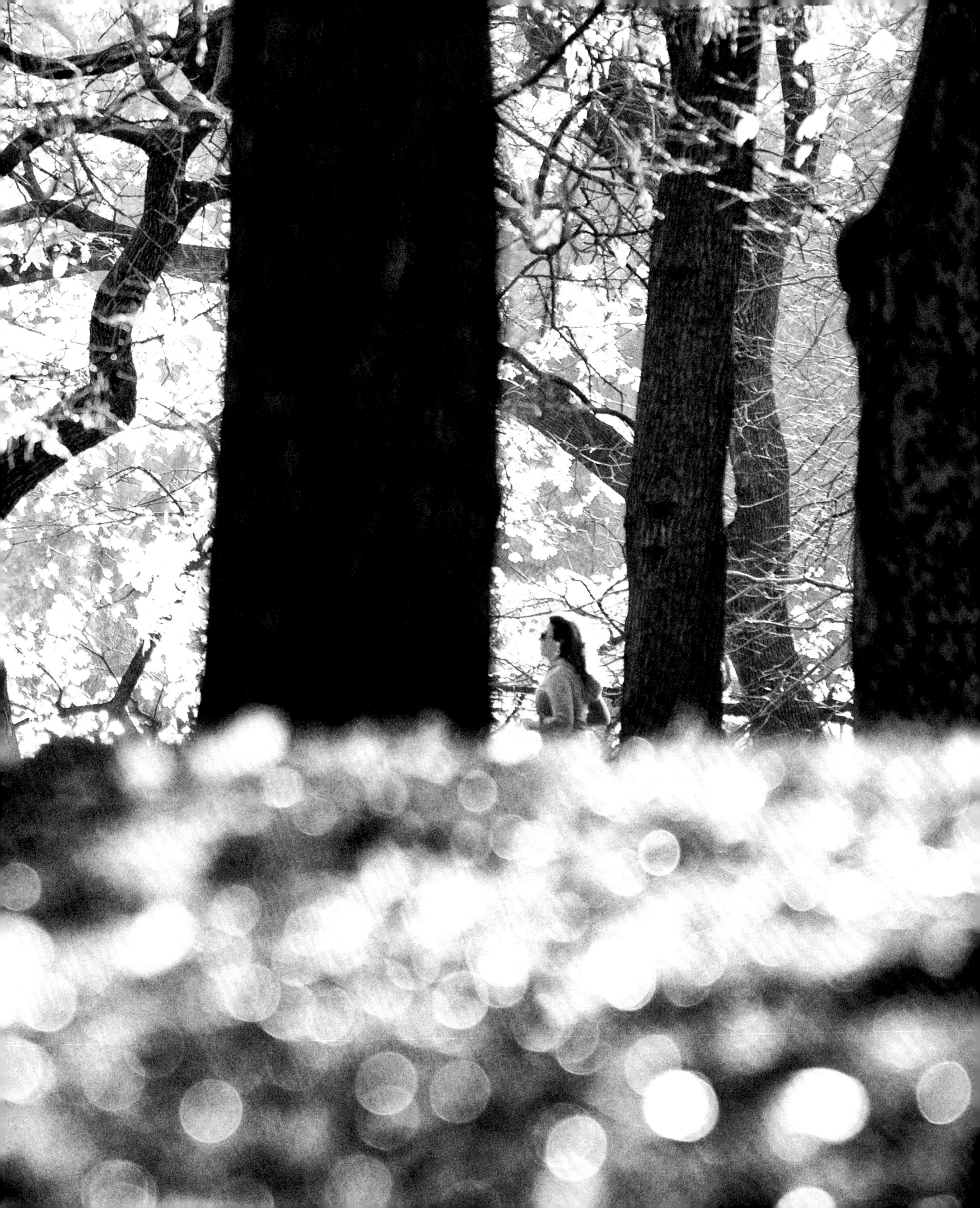

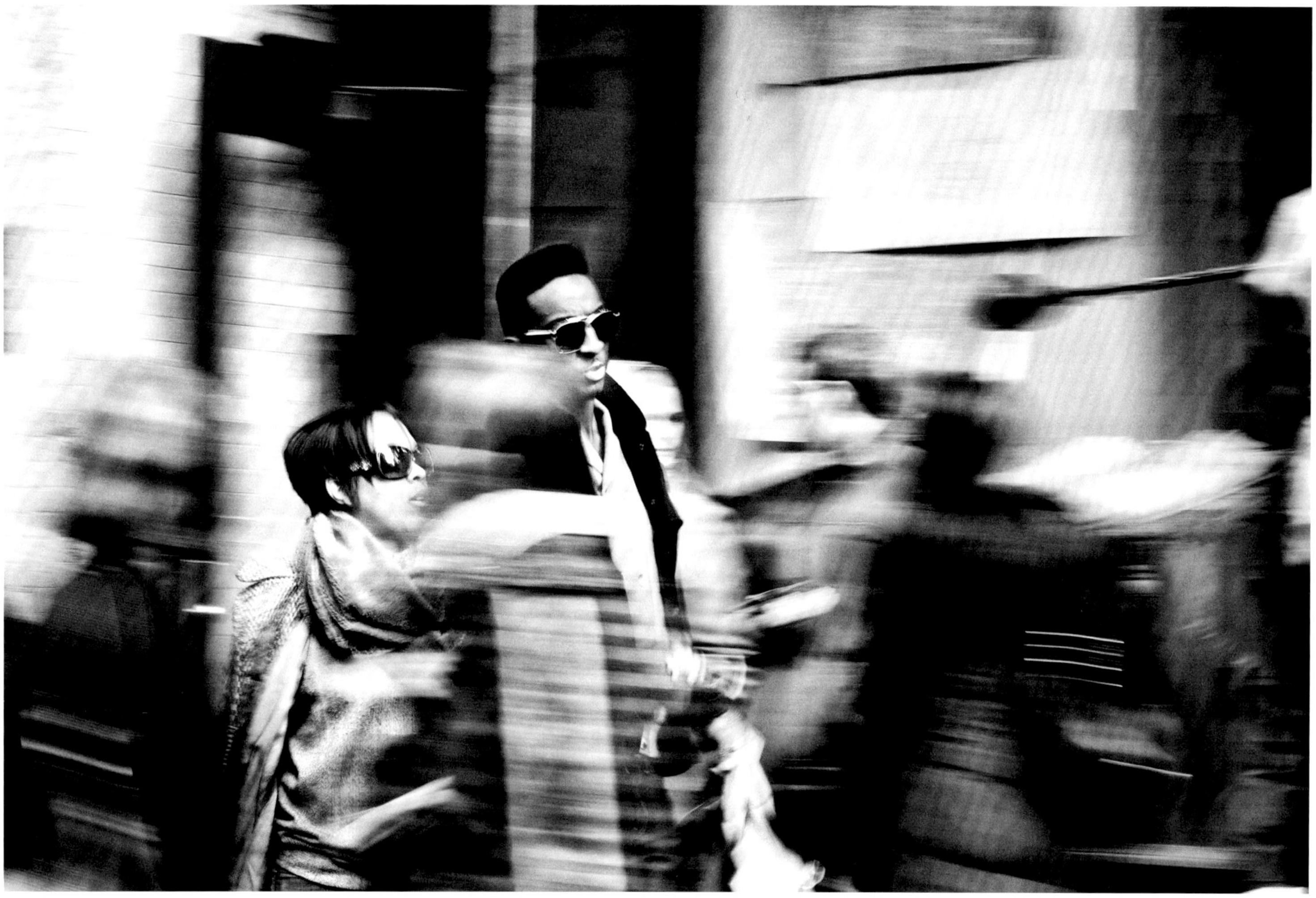

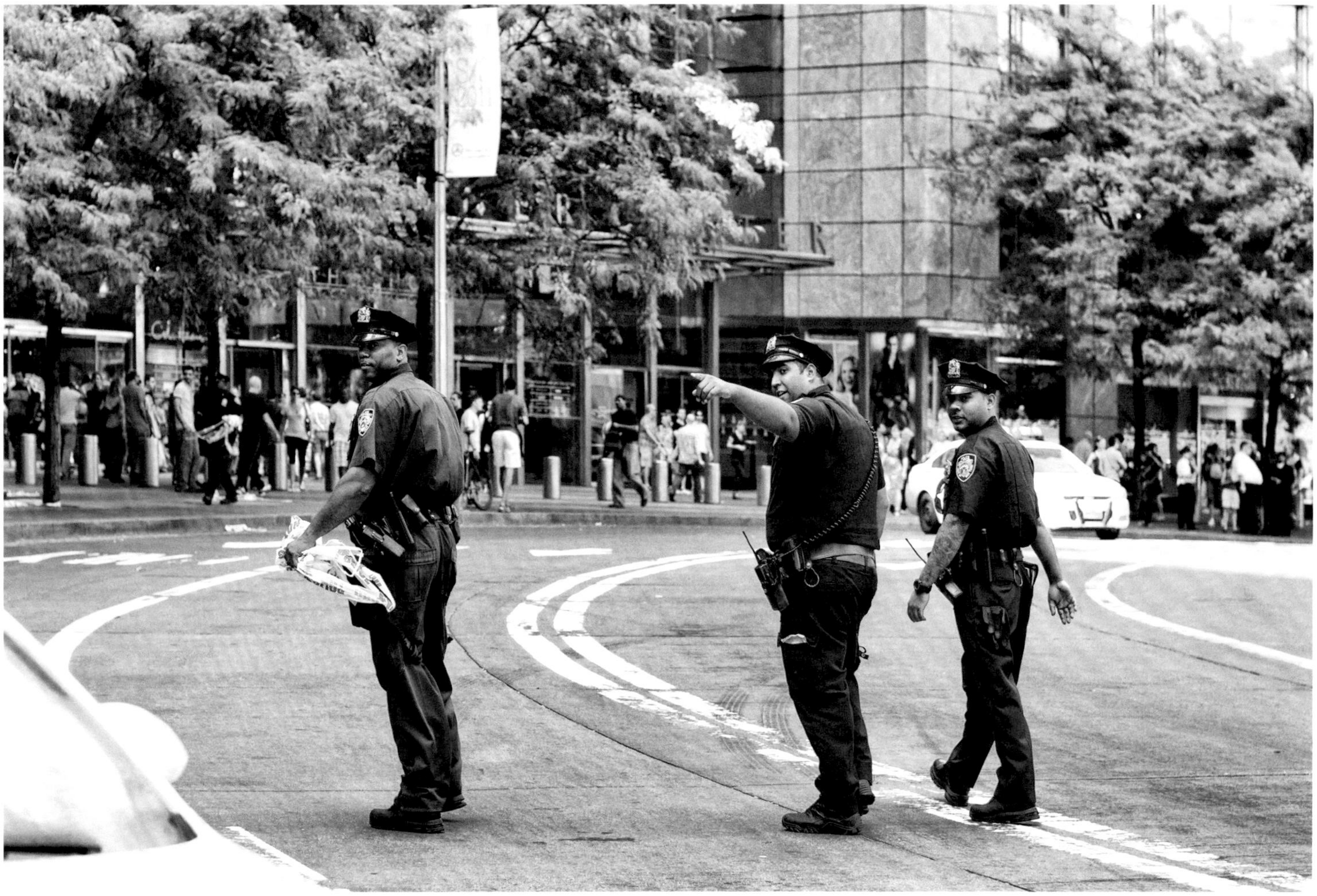

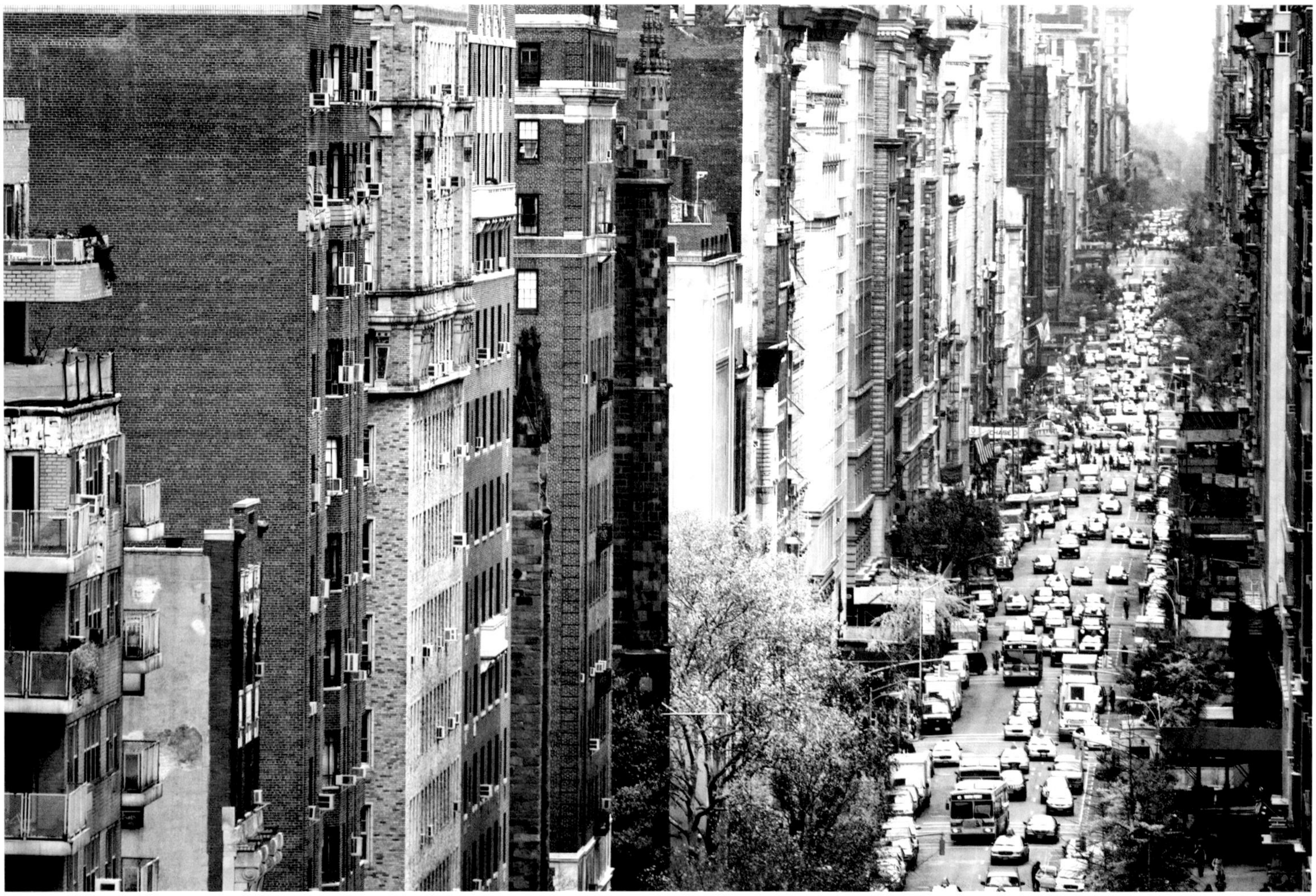

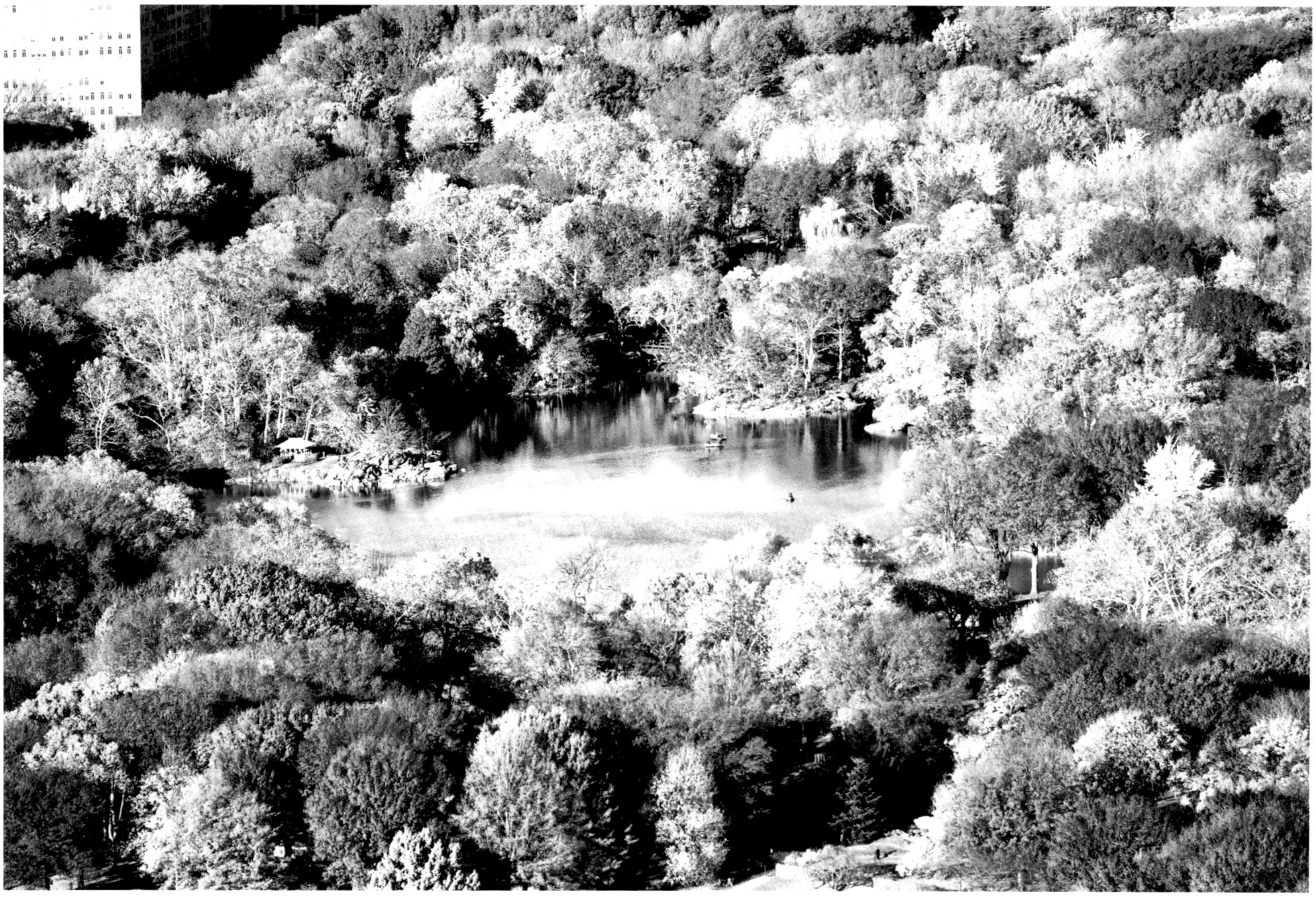

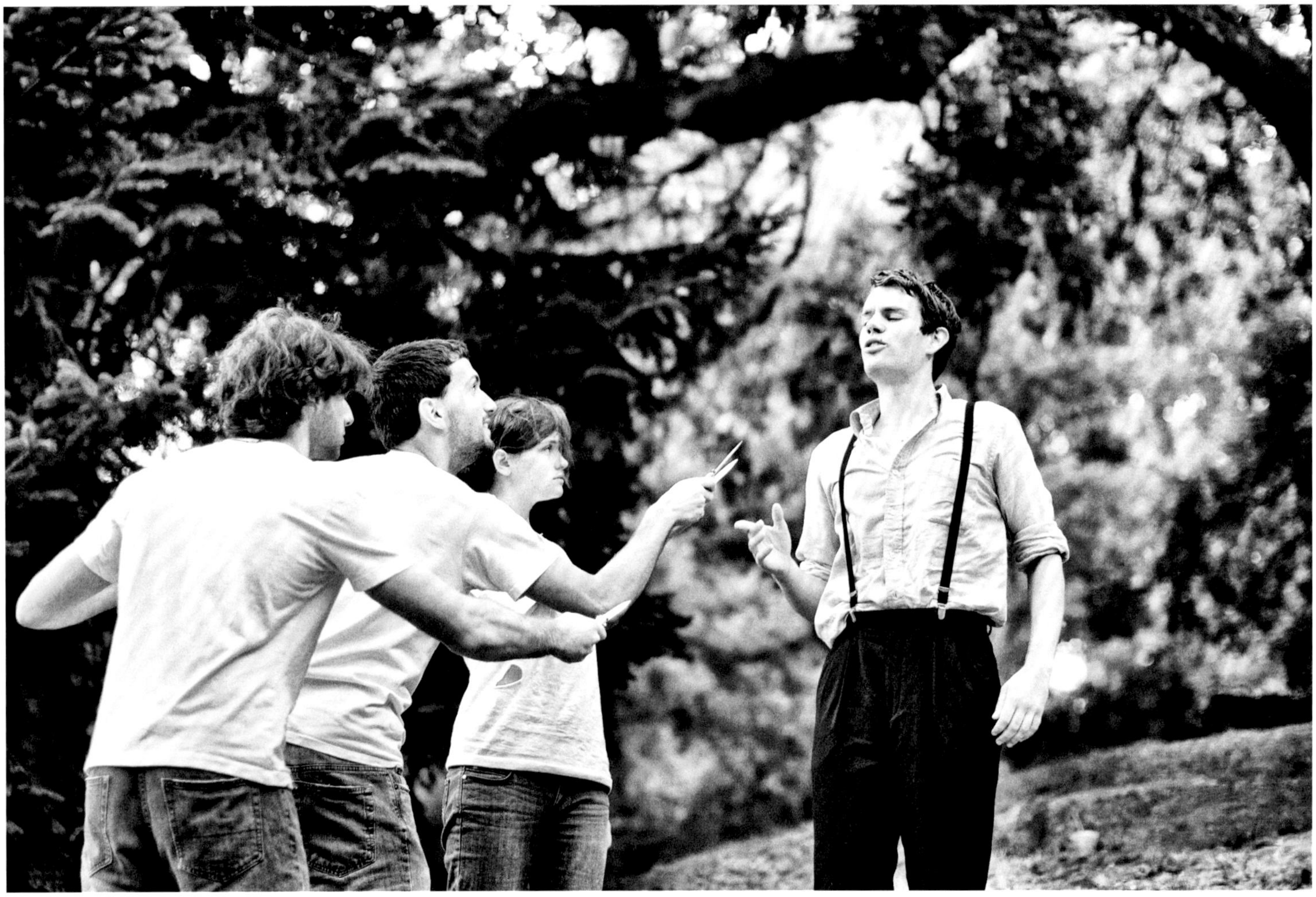

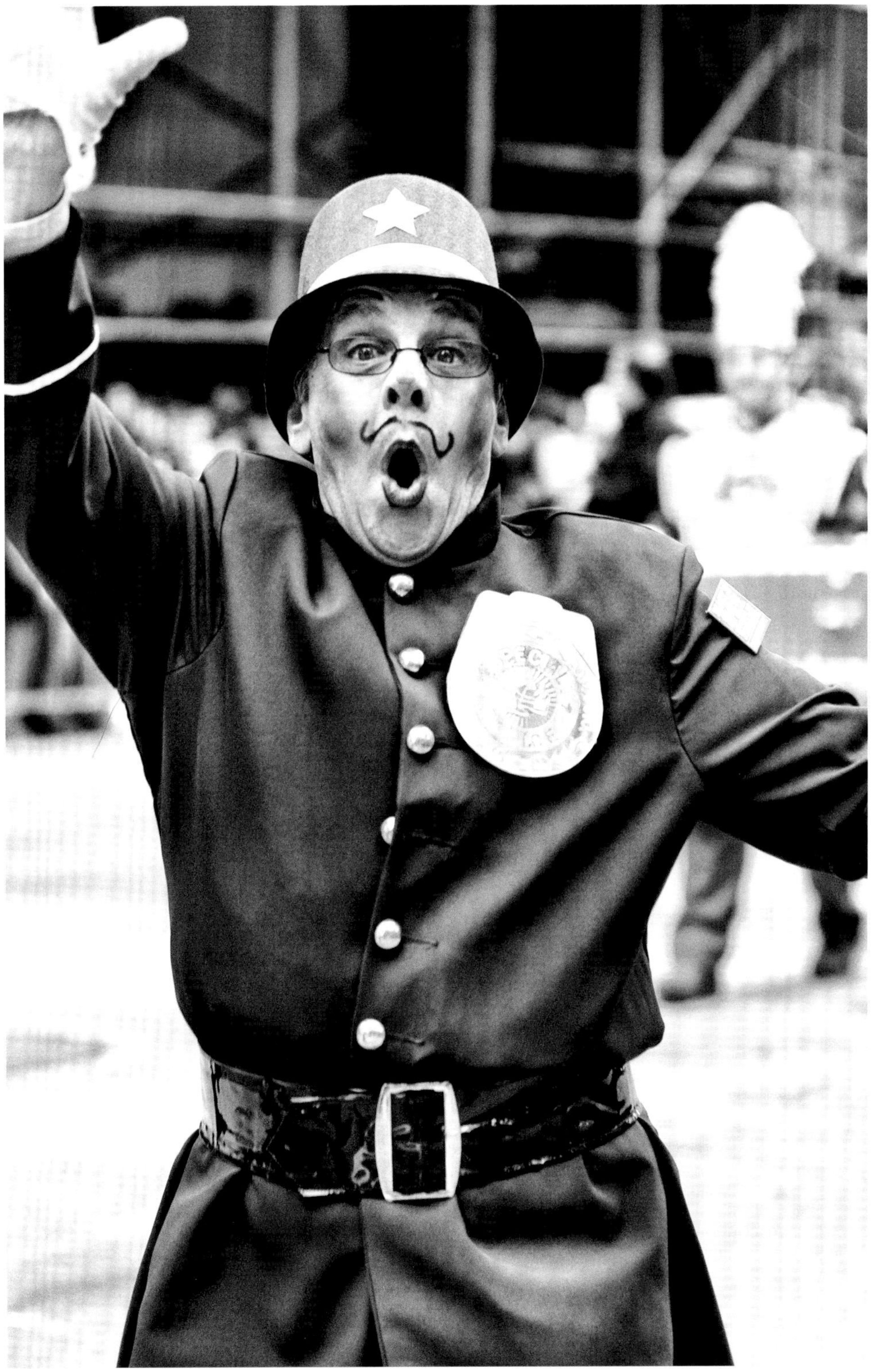

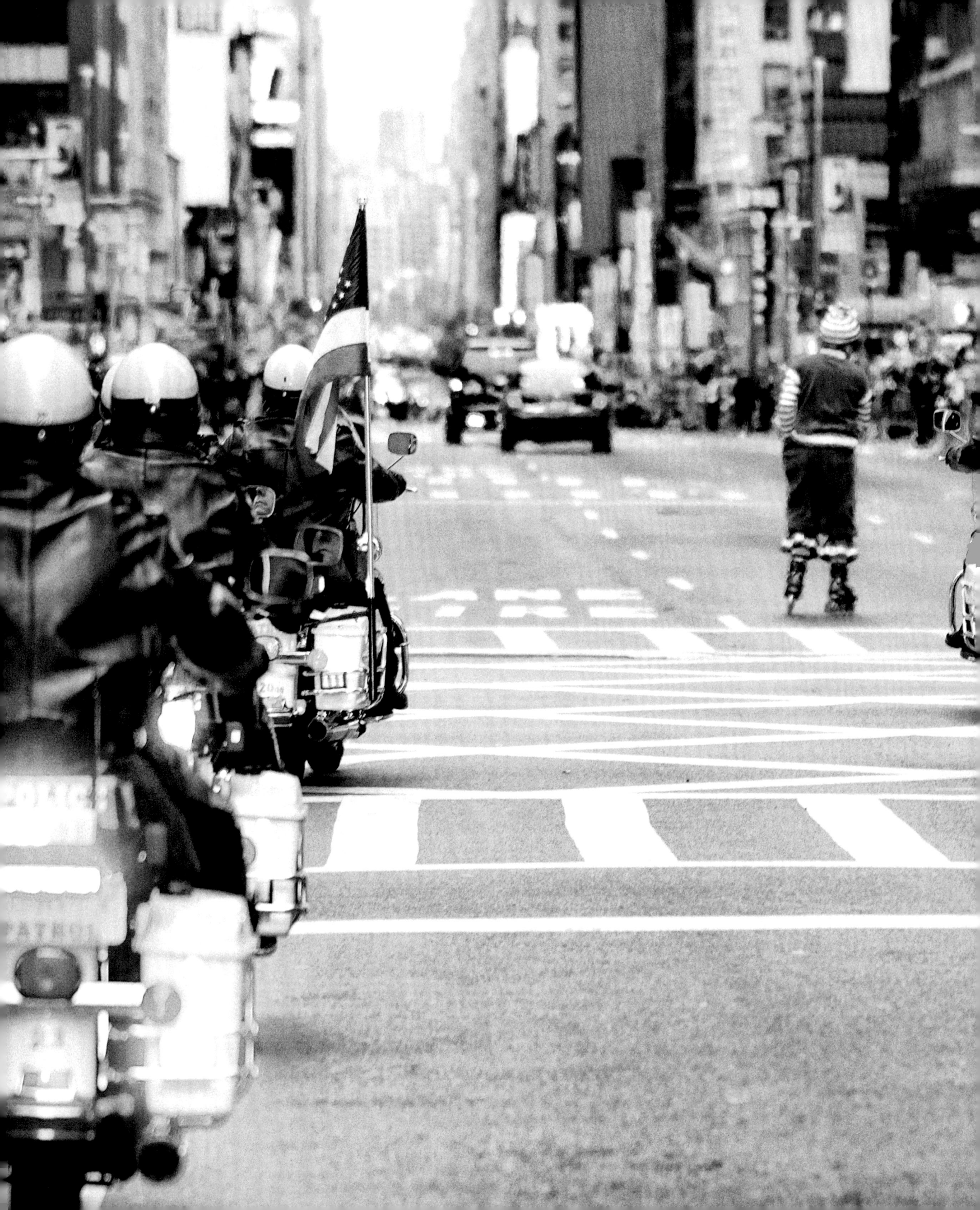

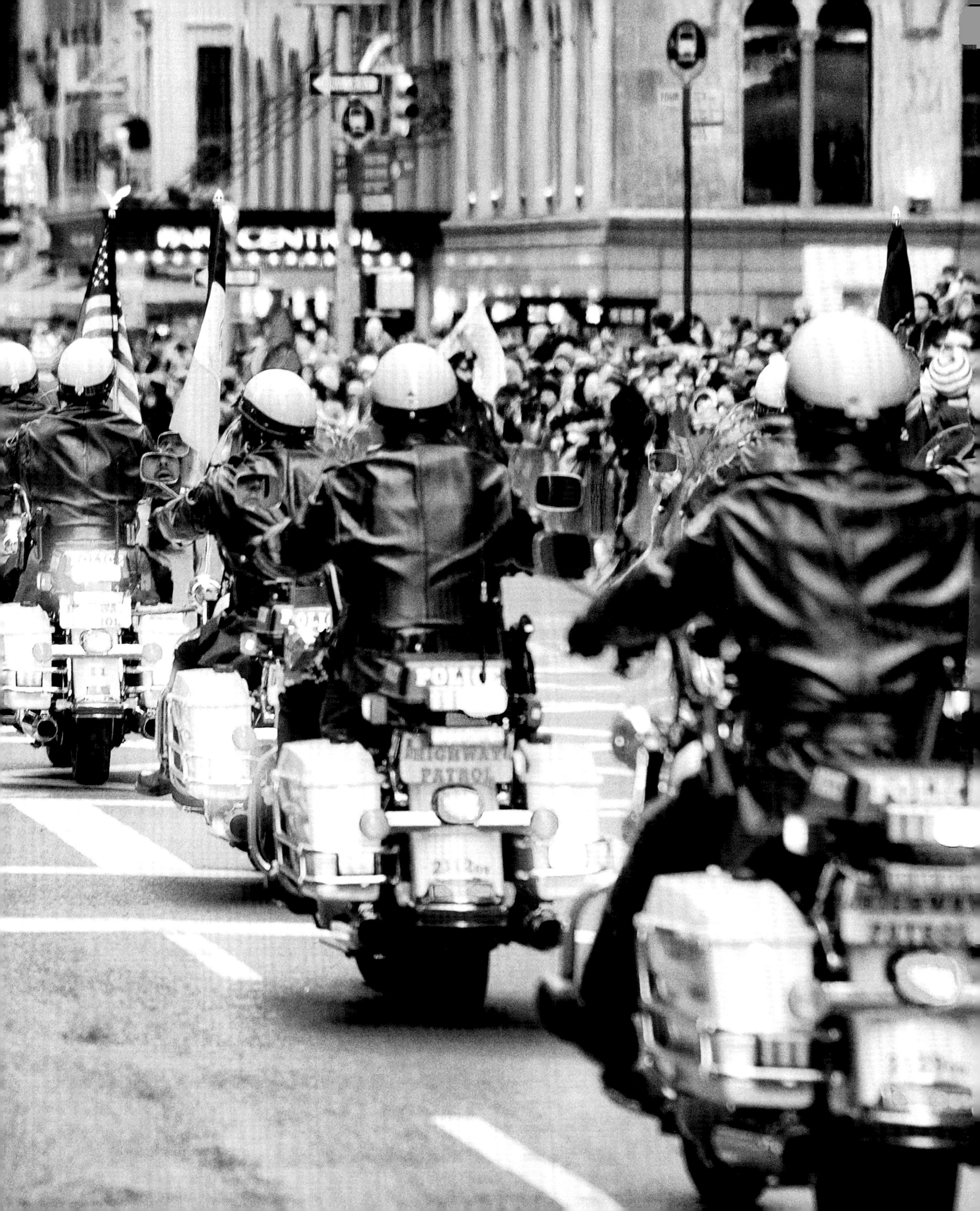
HIGHWAY
PATROL

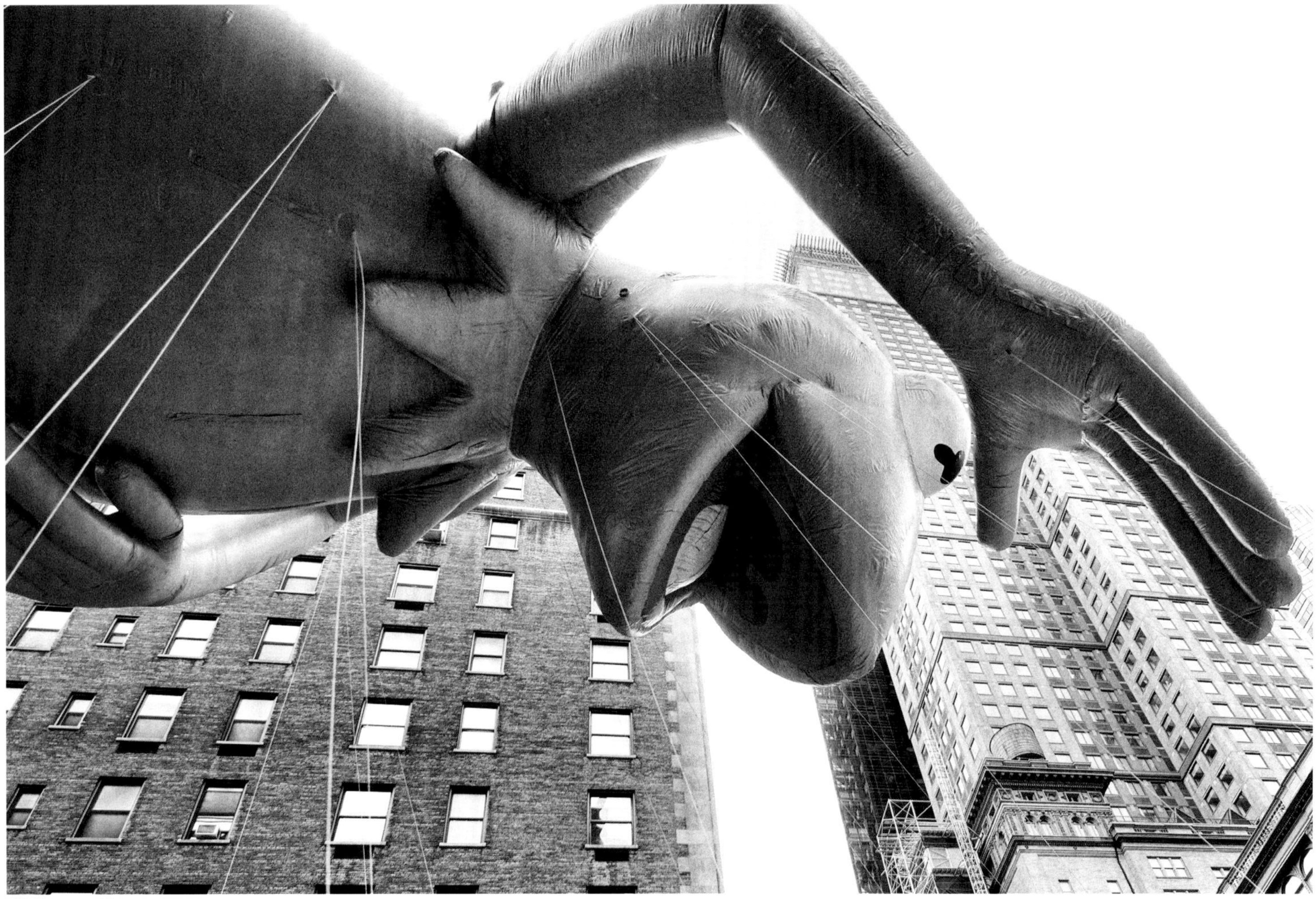

ONE WAY
BROADWAY
PARK
OFF THE MAP
PREMIERES WEDNESDAY
ANDARDS CAN STILL POSE CHOKING HA
ESPN
S COACH FISHER
HOWARD LE
Deli & Café
ONE WAY

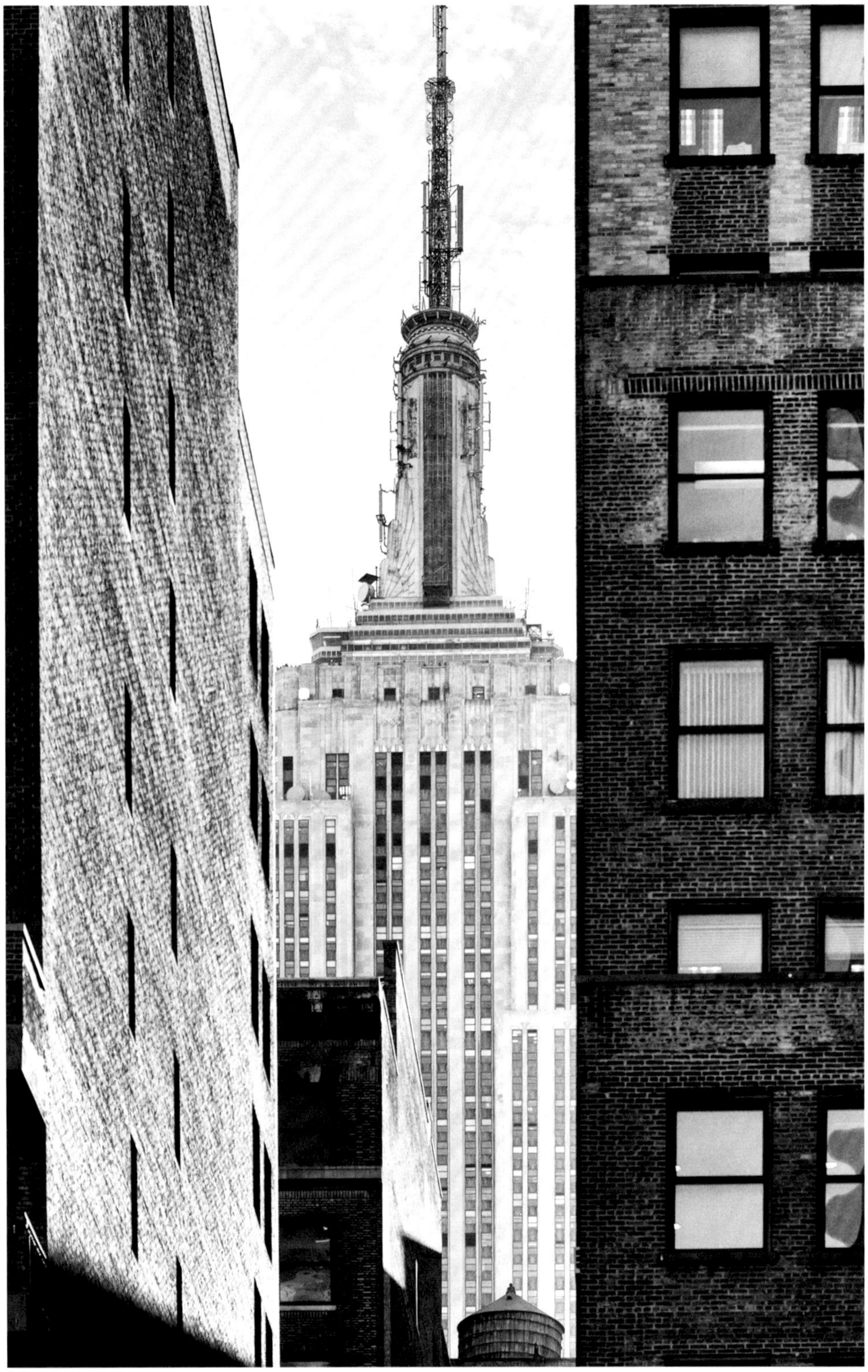

75

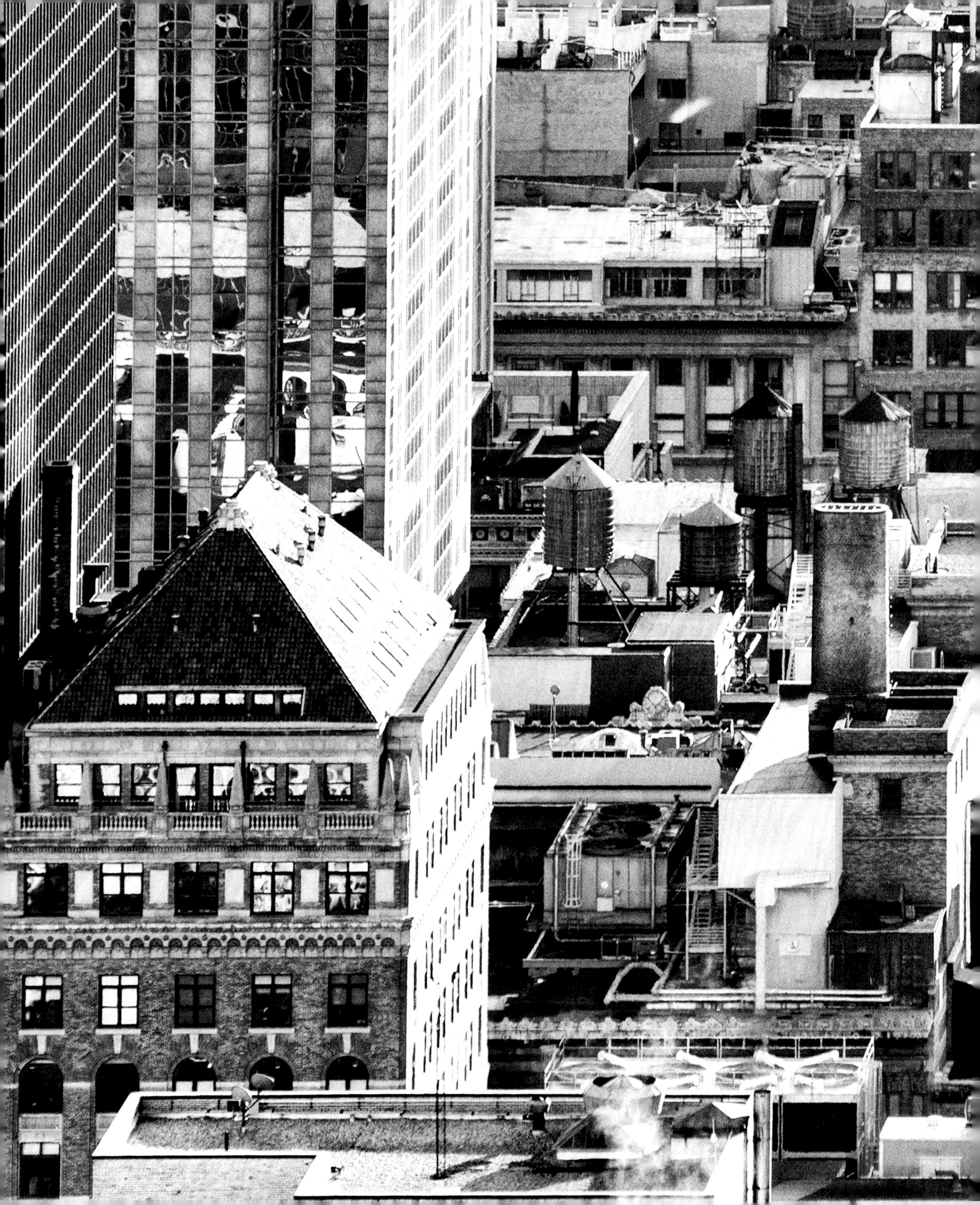

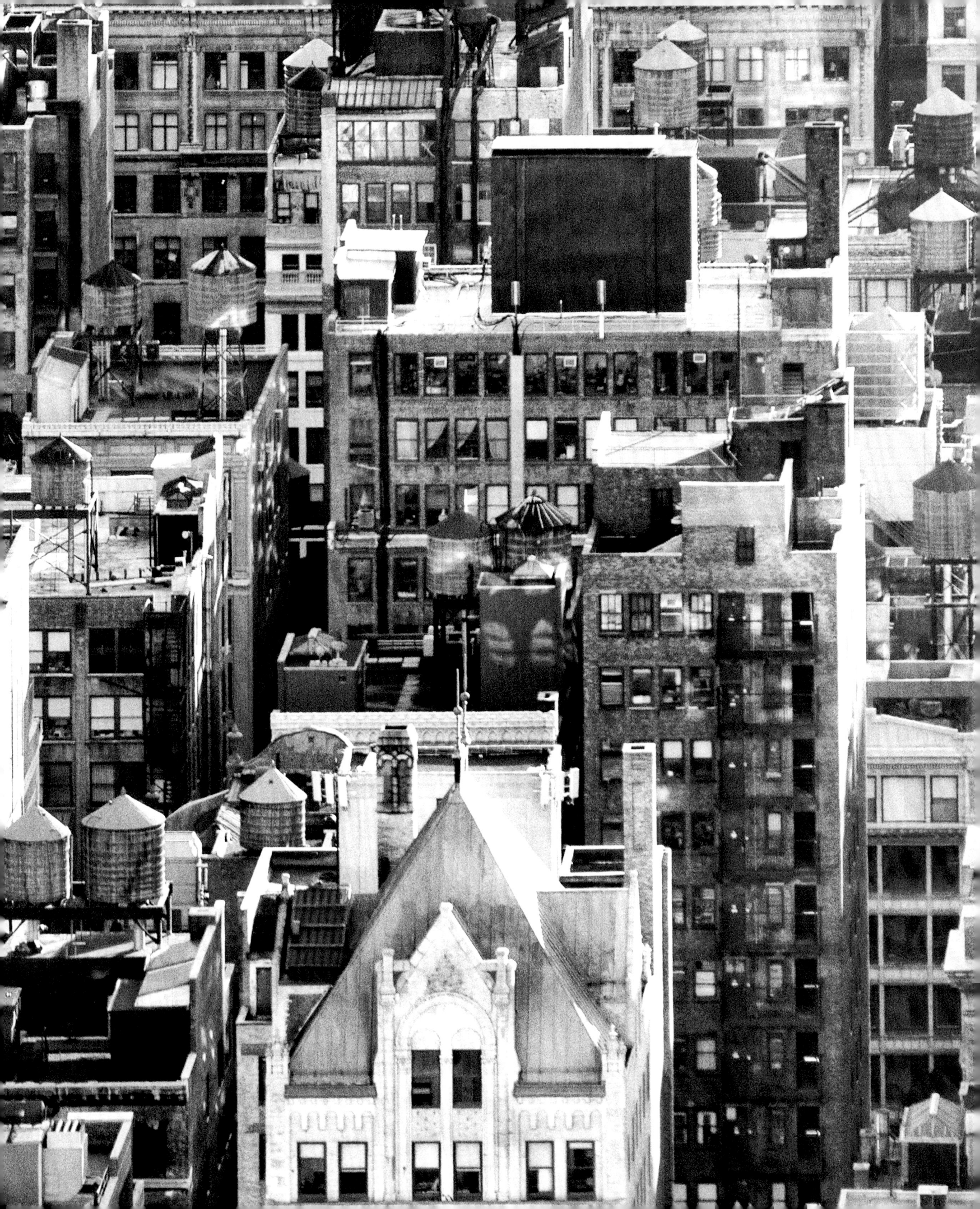

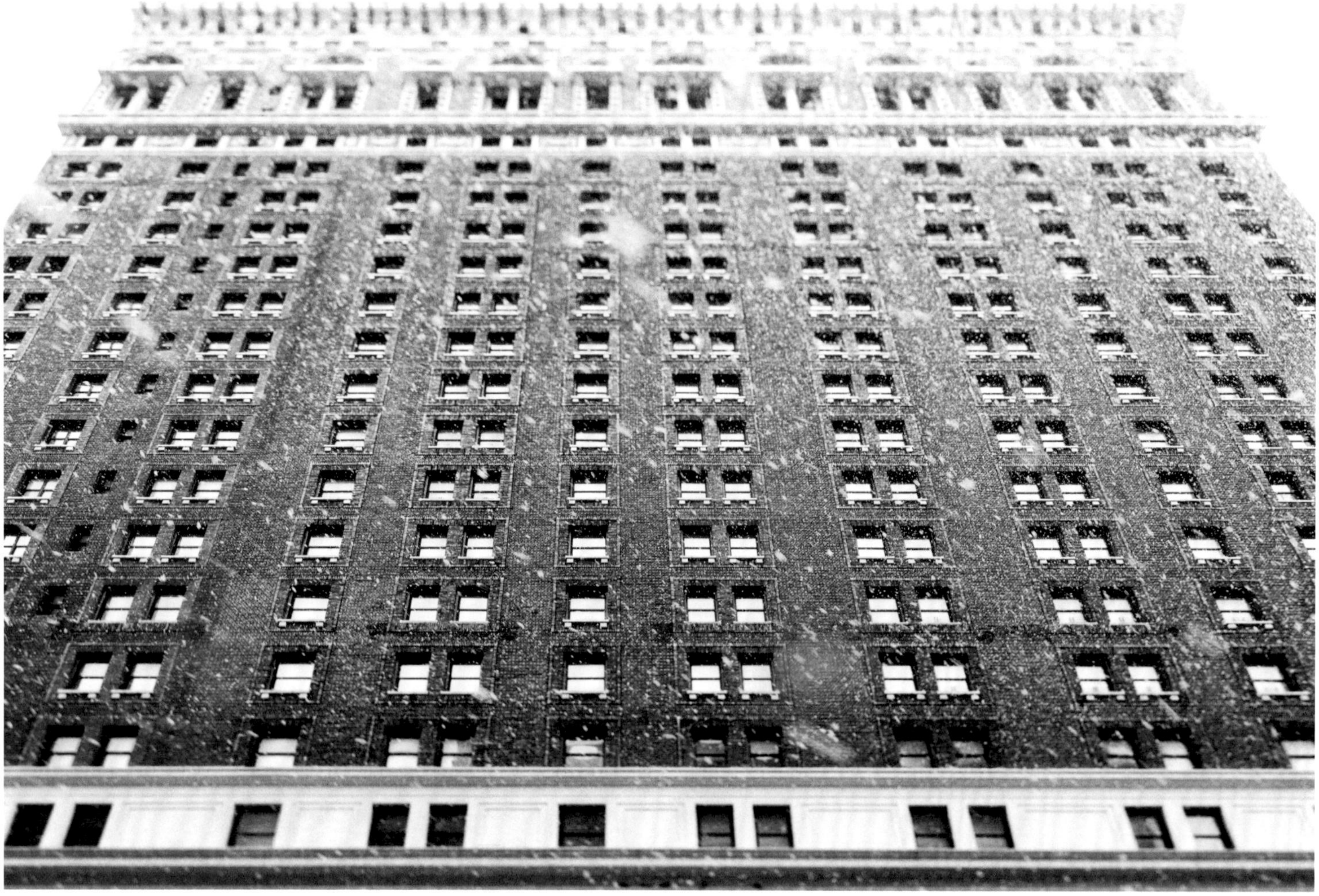

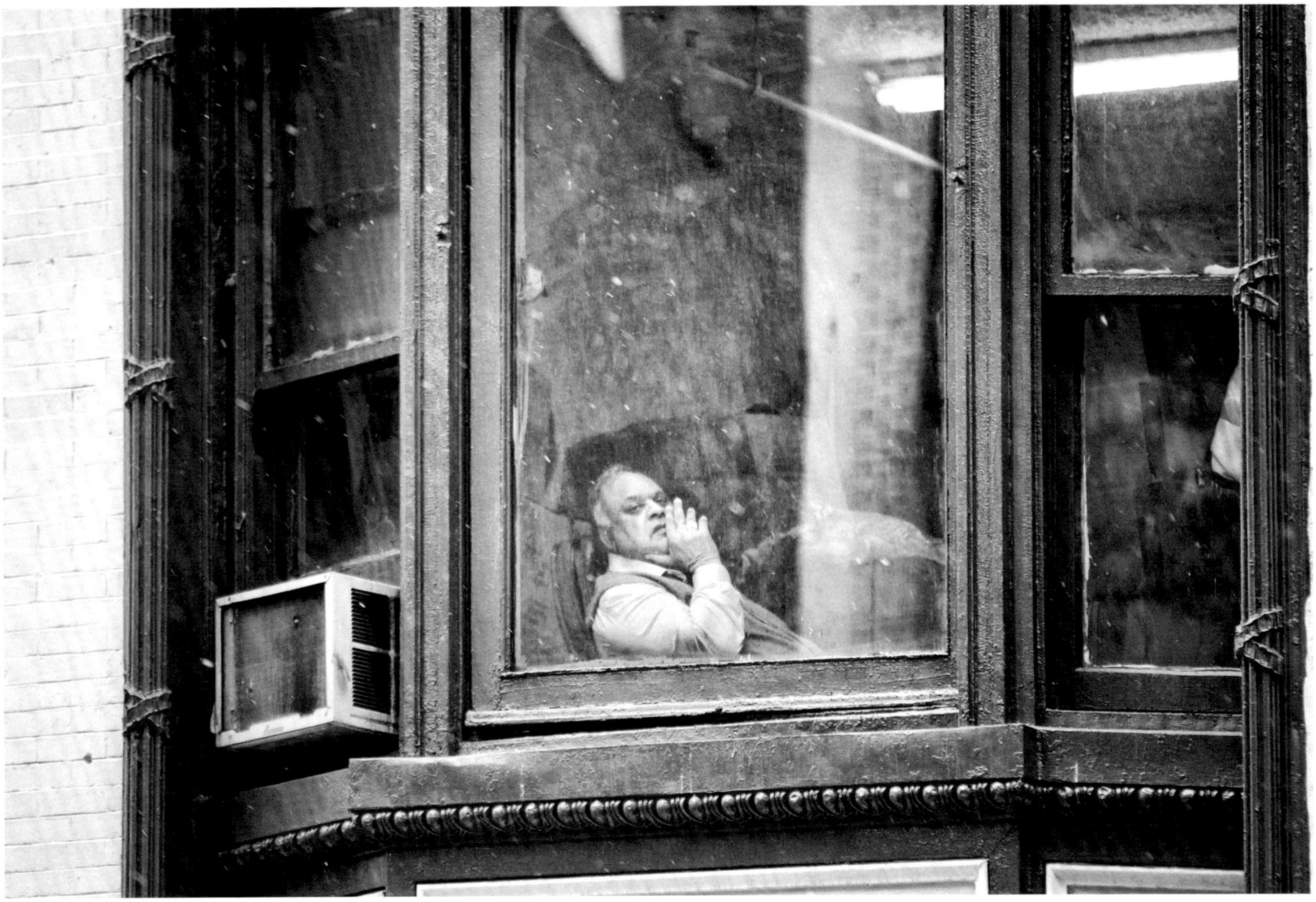

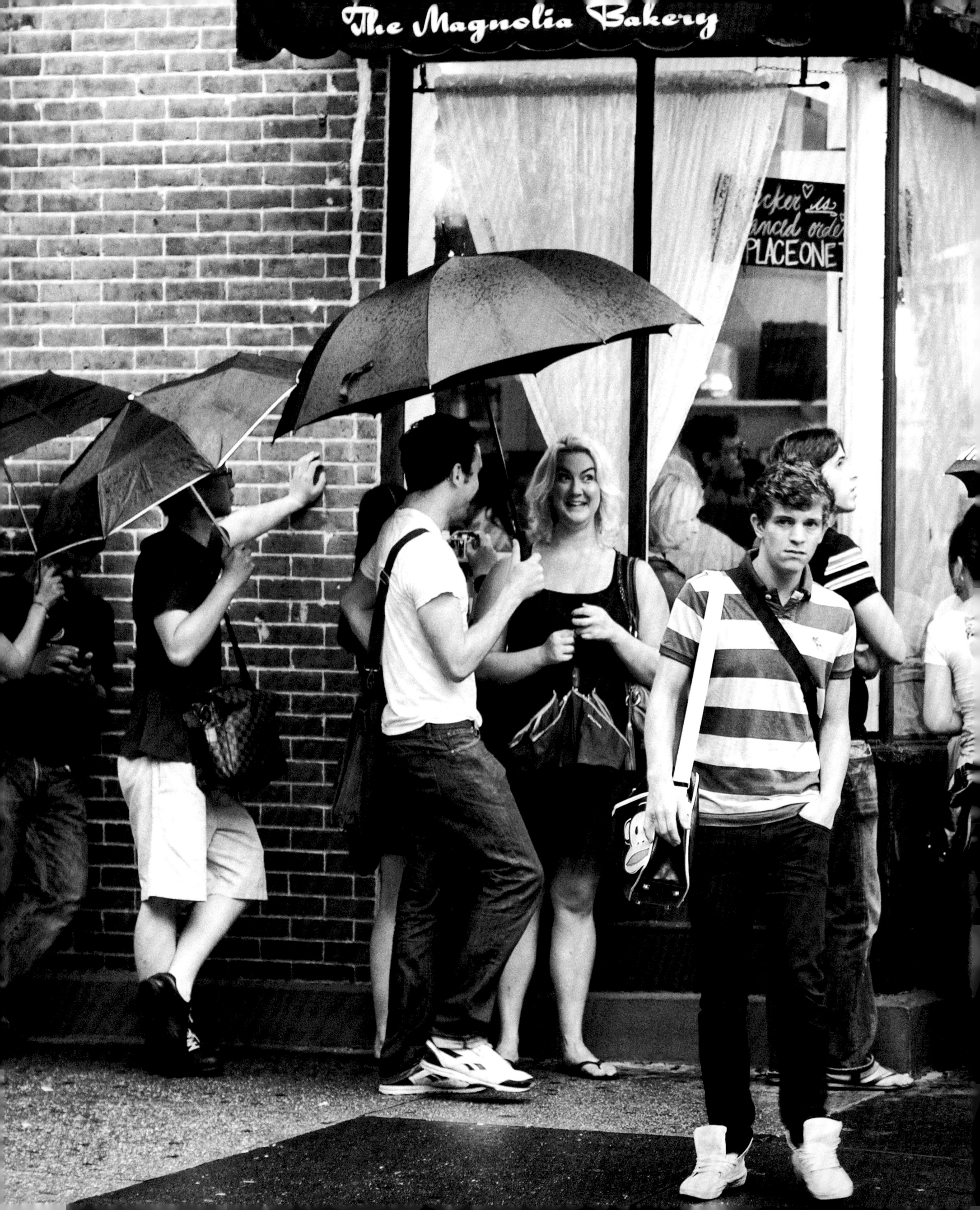
The Magnolia Bakery

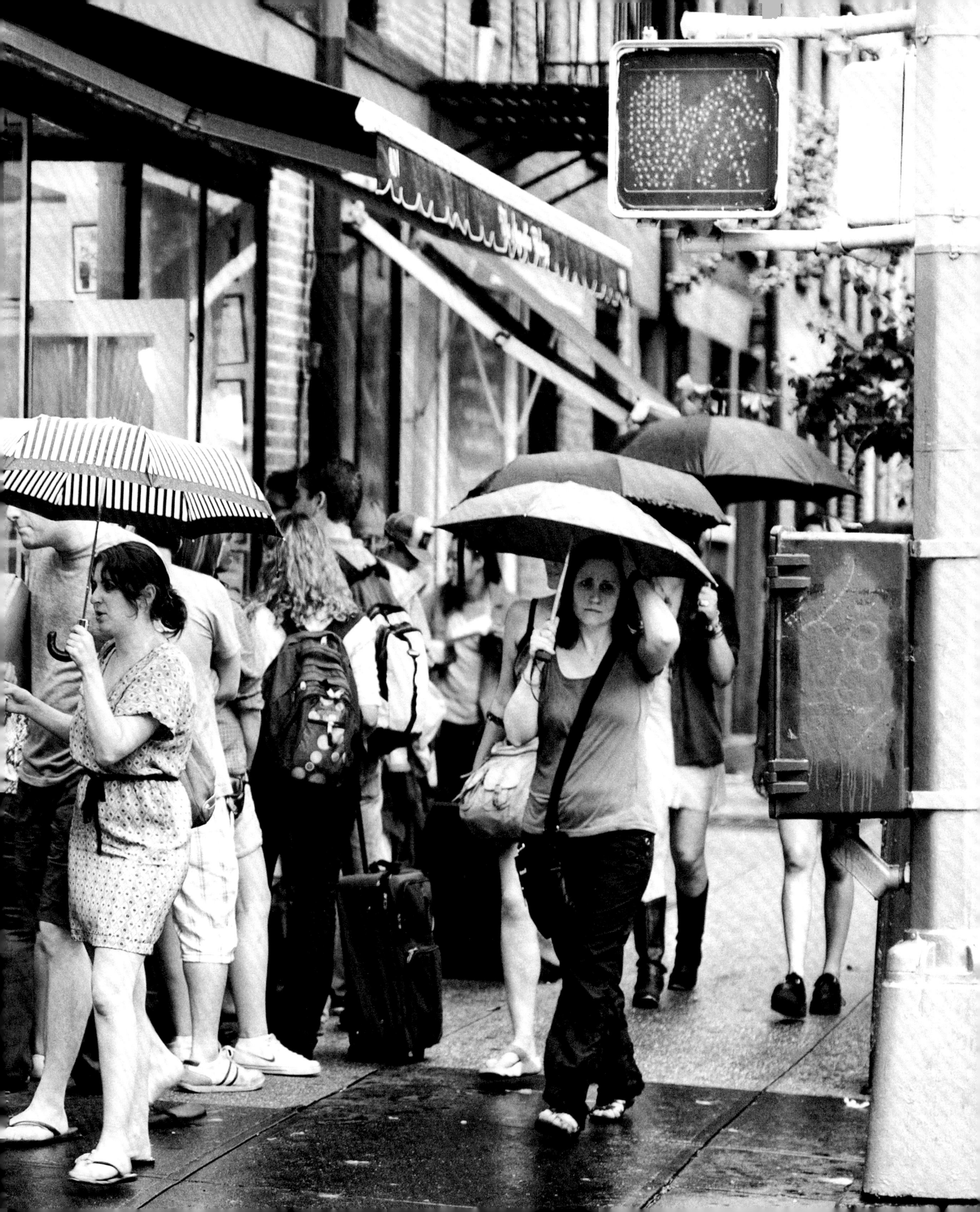

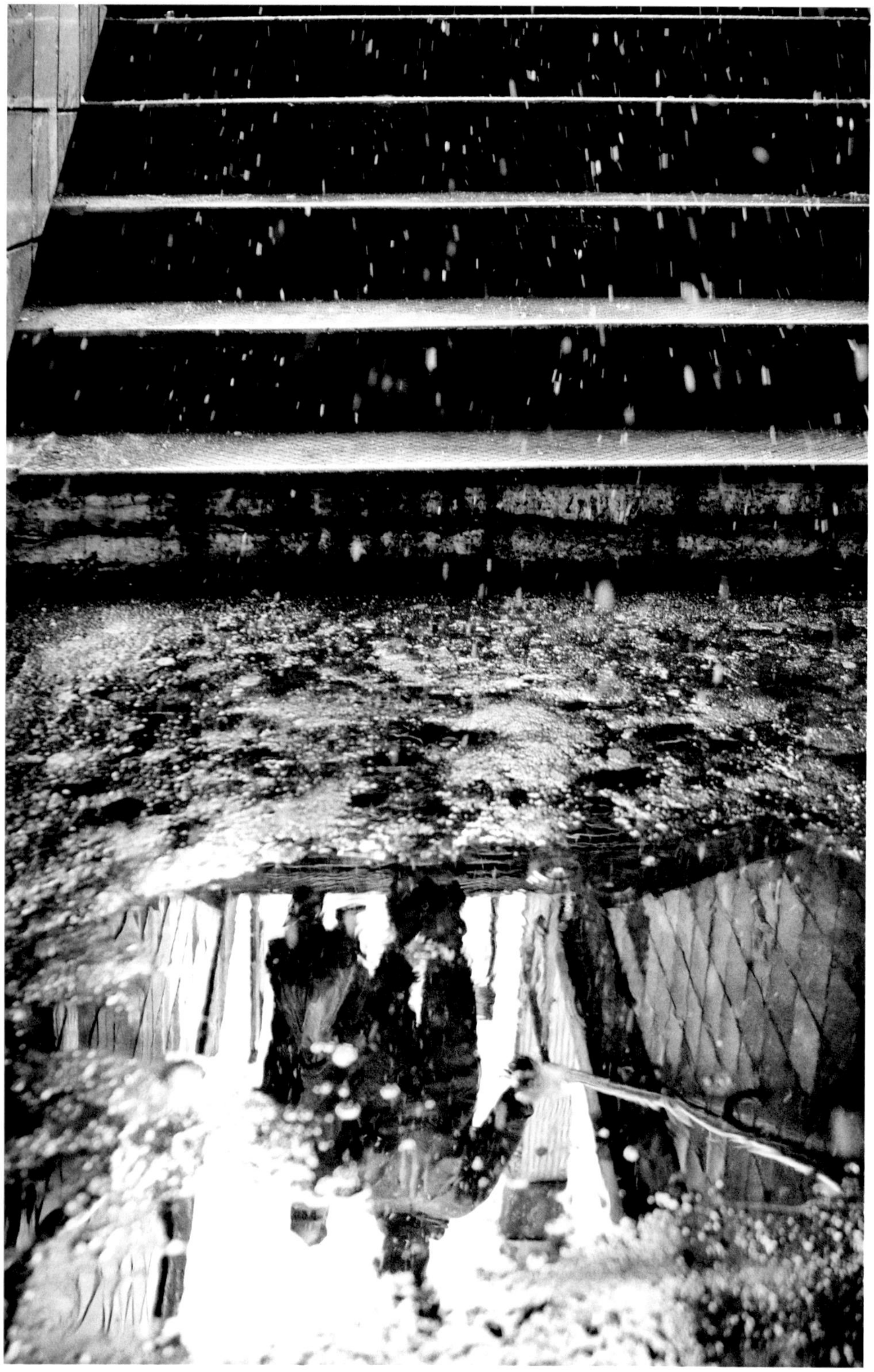

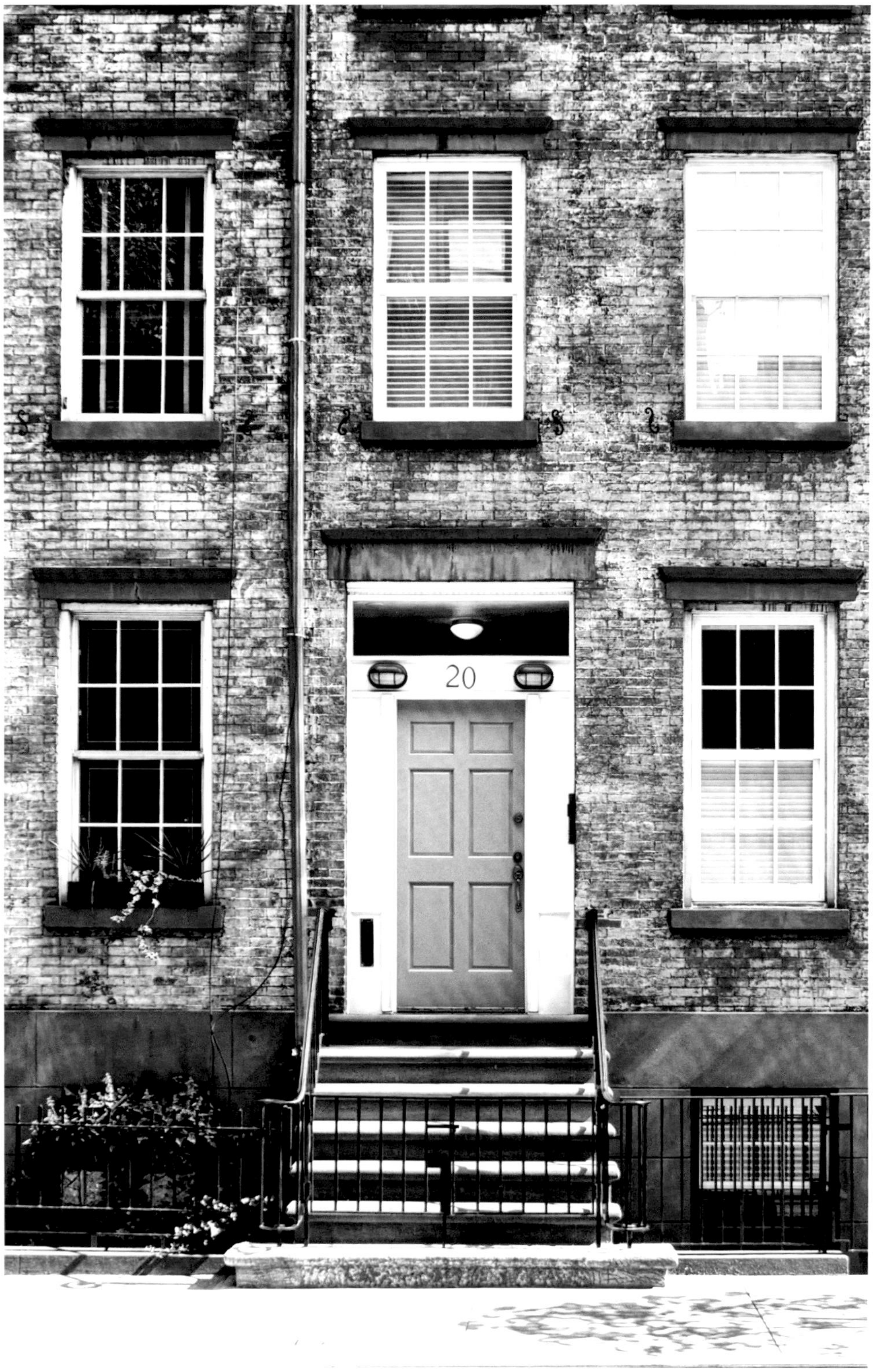
20

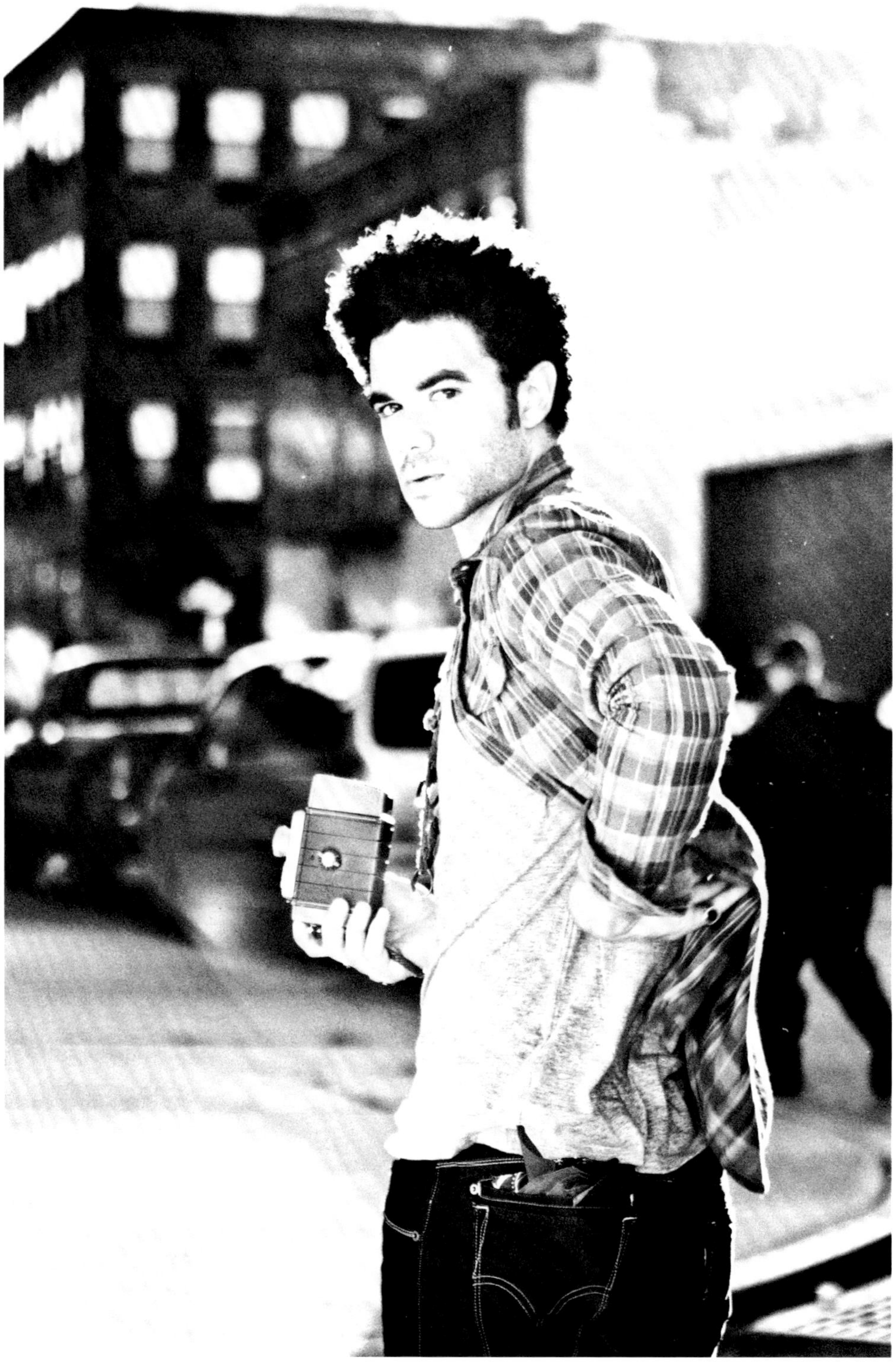

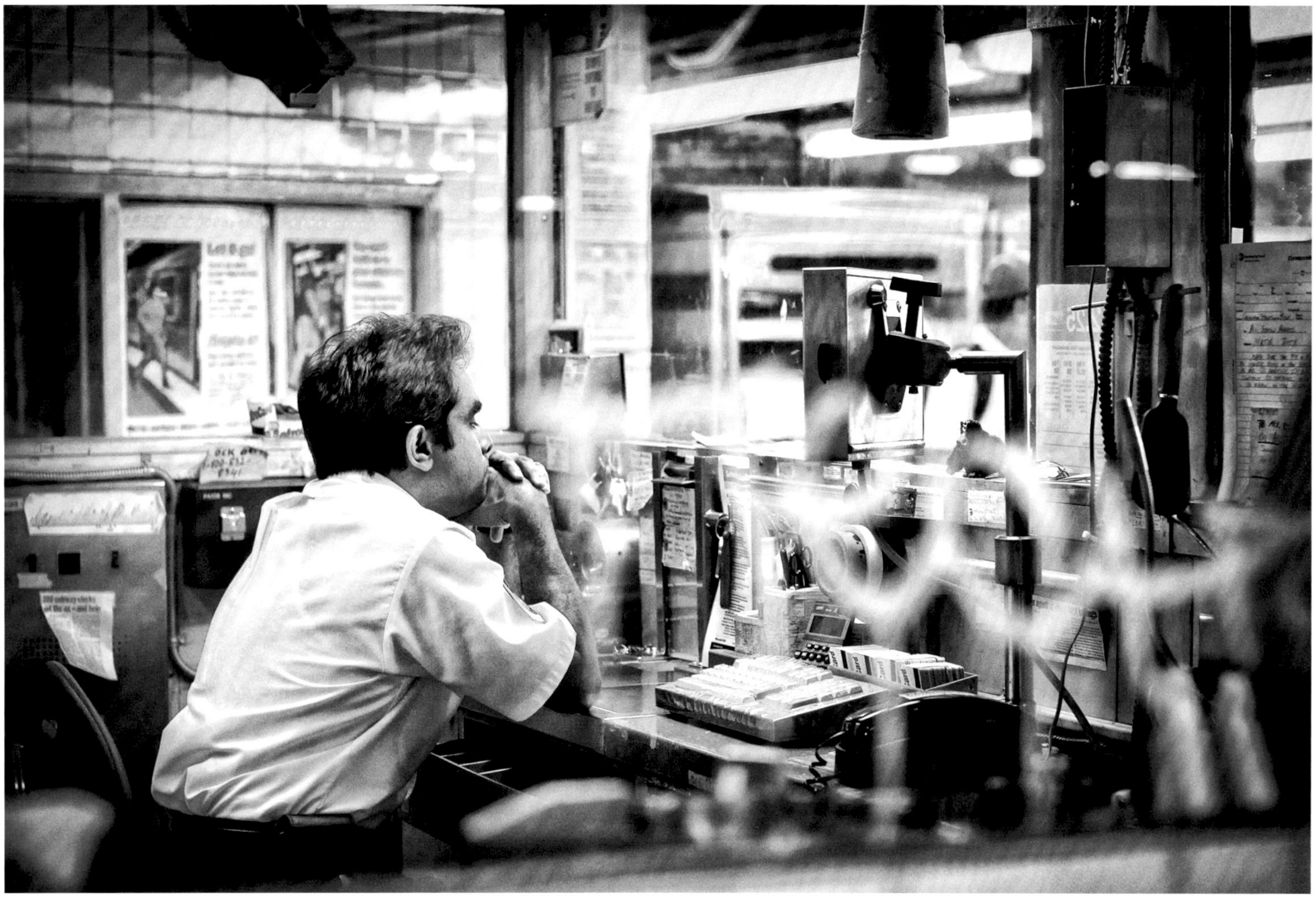

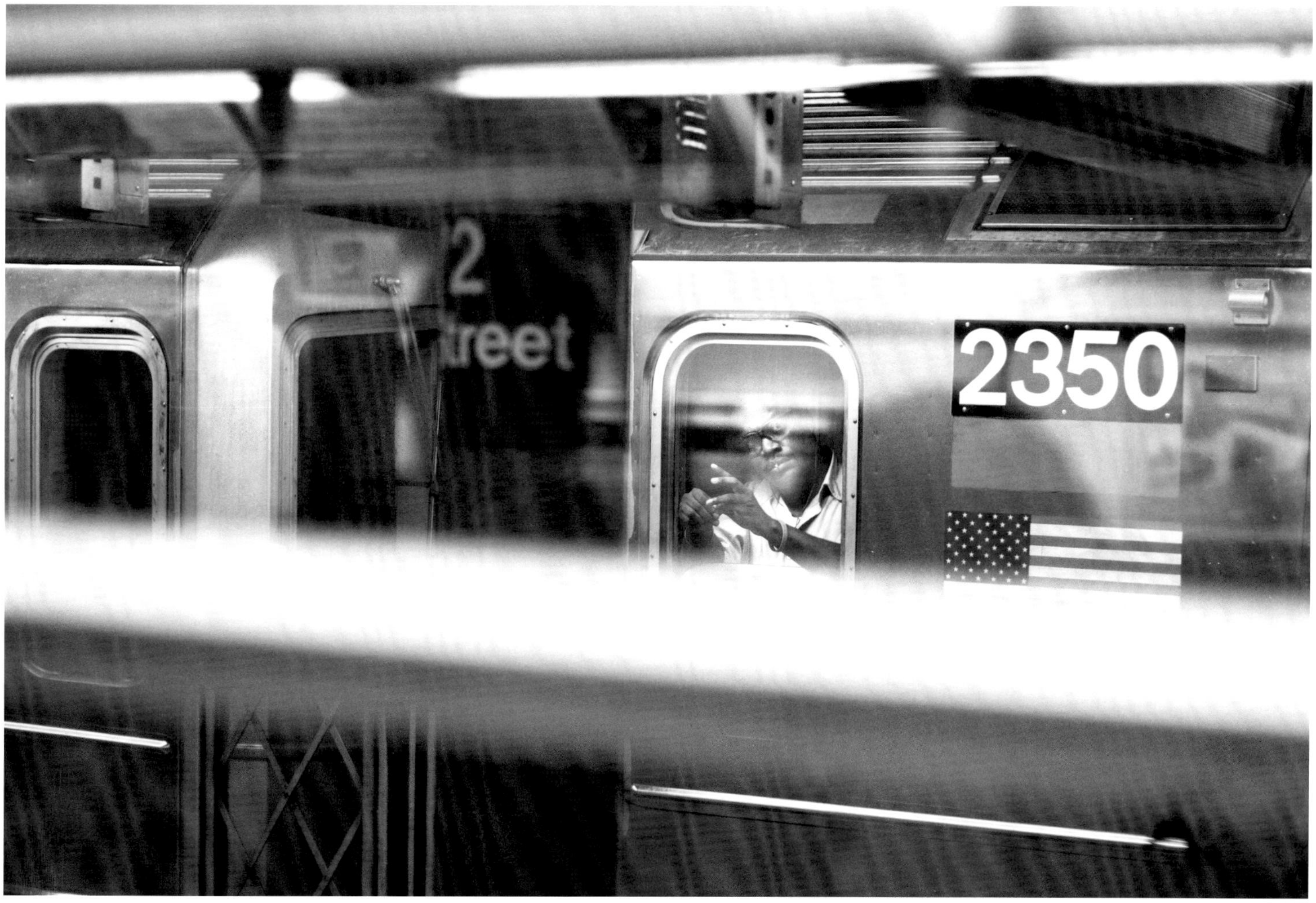
2350

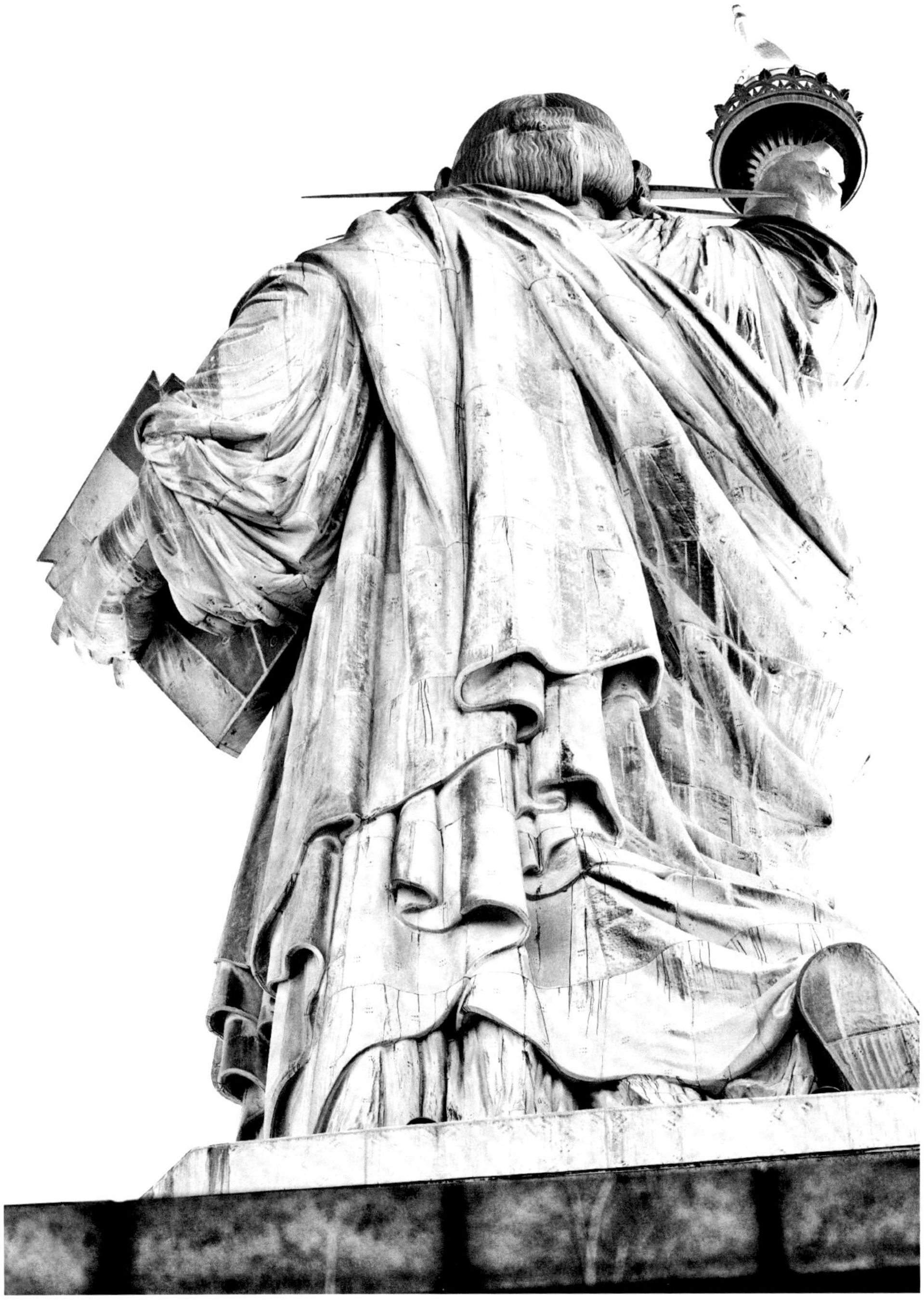

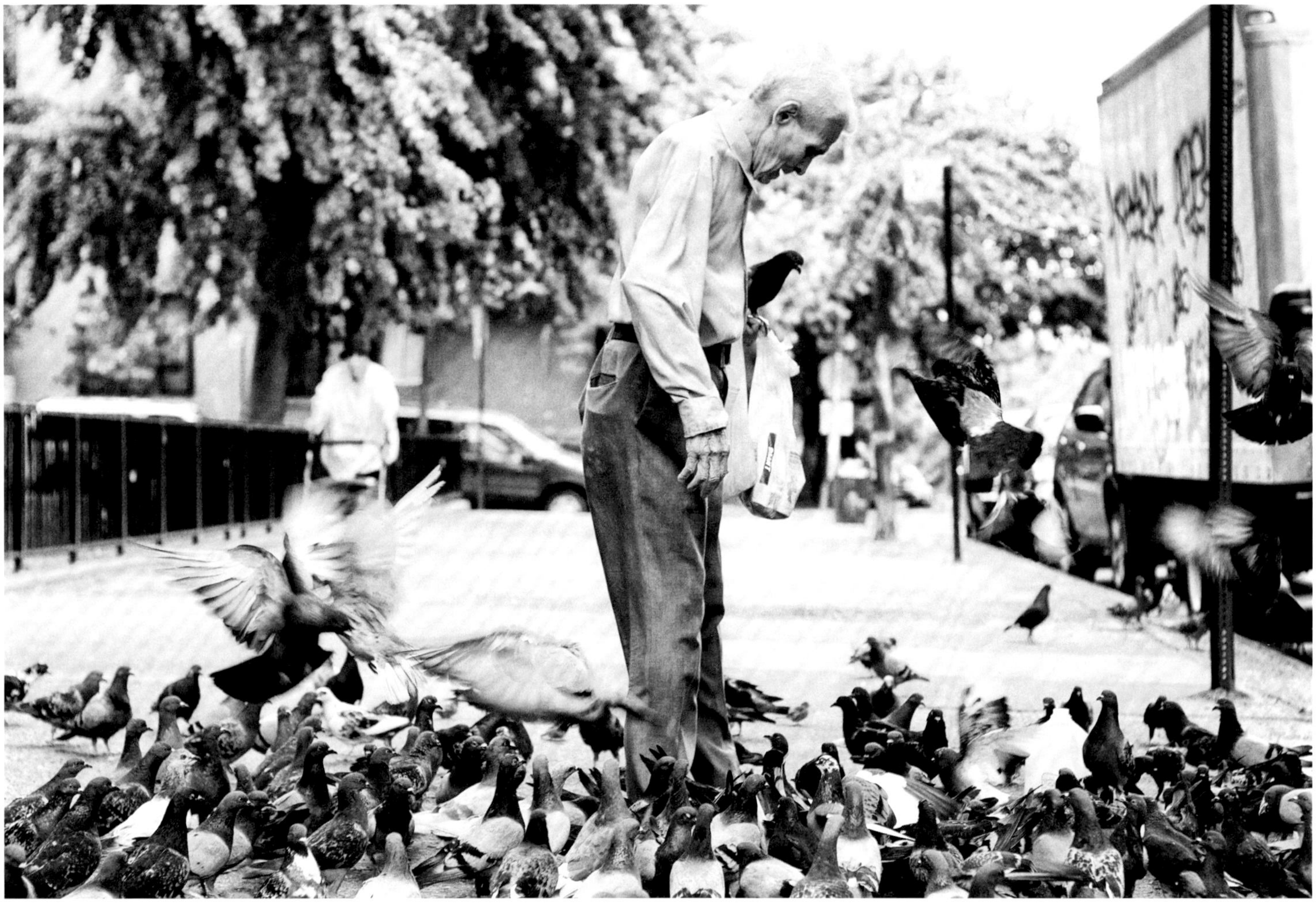

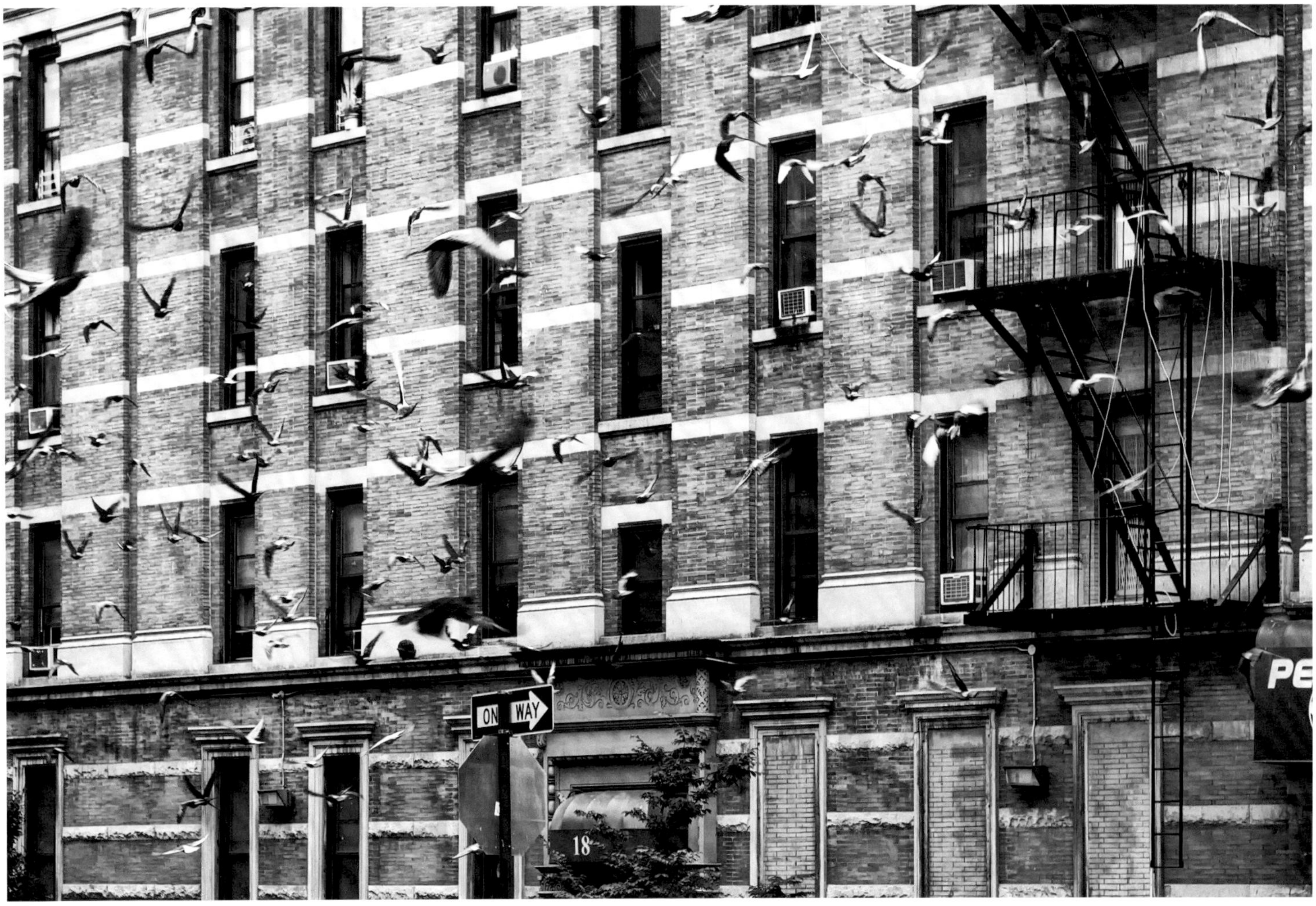
ONE WAY
18

Manhattan Q
Local, weekdays
Q Local, all times
Check lighted sig
location of next
Manhattan Lo

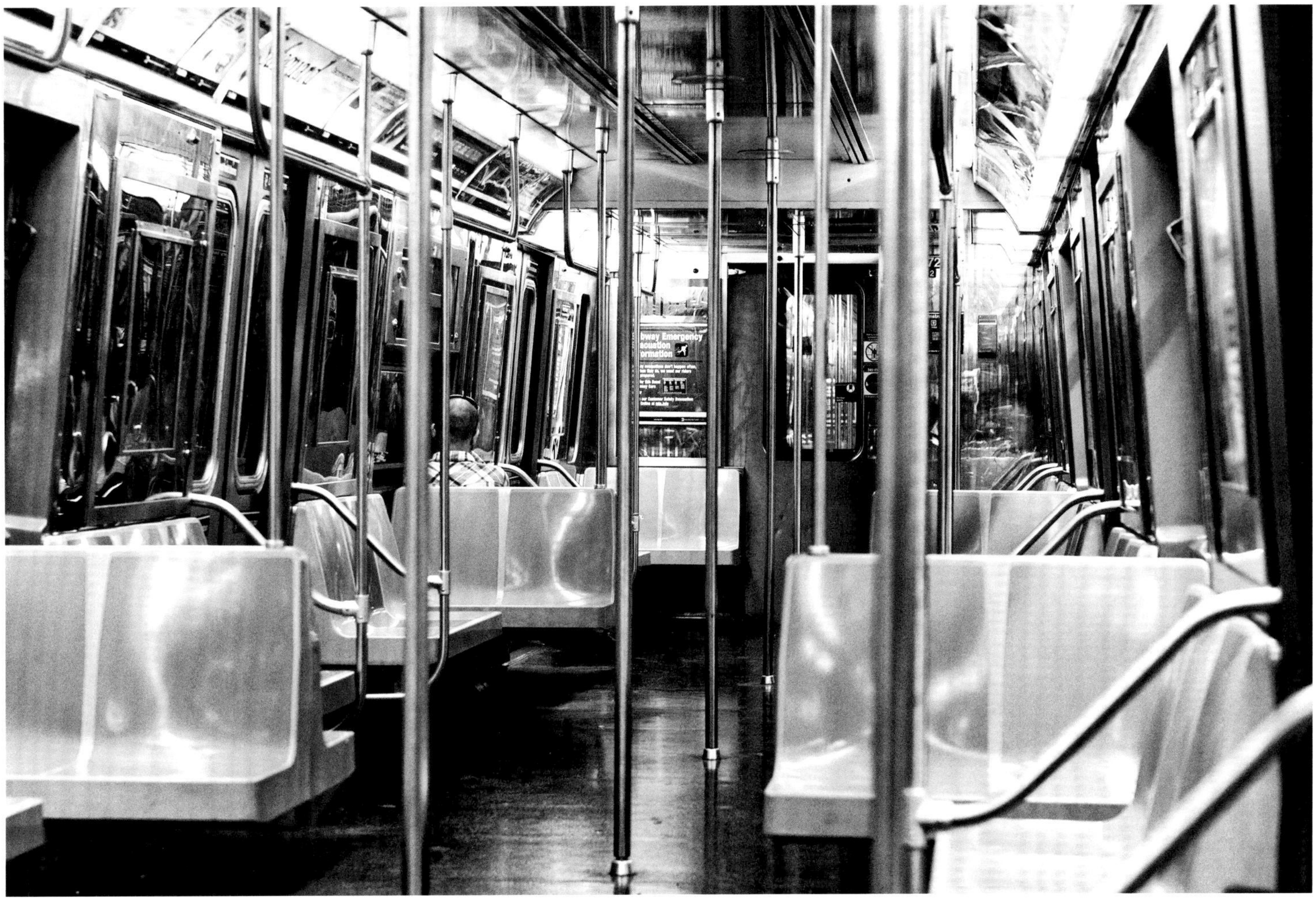

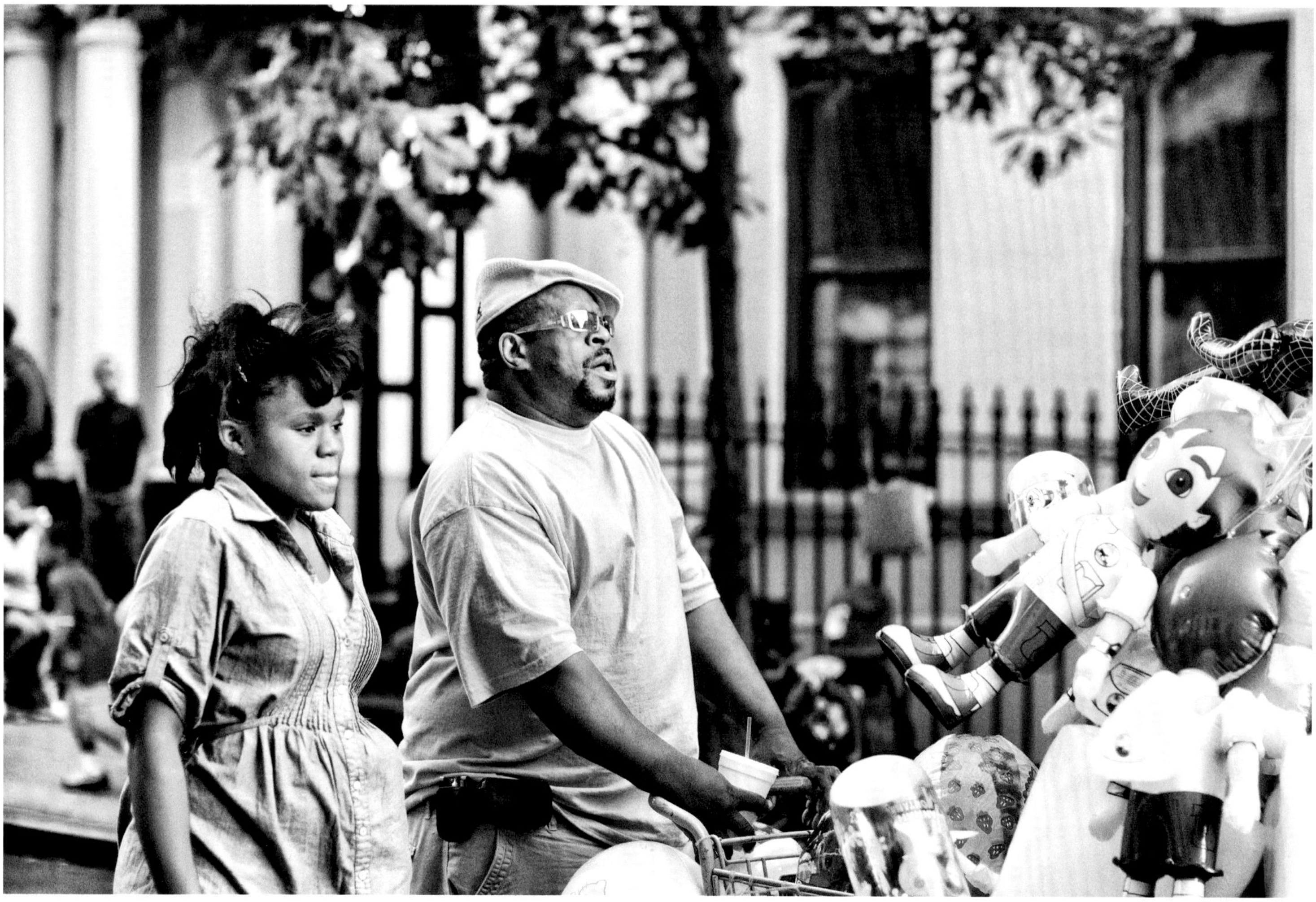

M104
GOLDEN GLOBE WINNER FOR BEST TV DRAMA AND ACTOR
MADMEN
New Season Premieres July 27
Sundays 10pm
amc
amctv.com

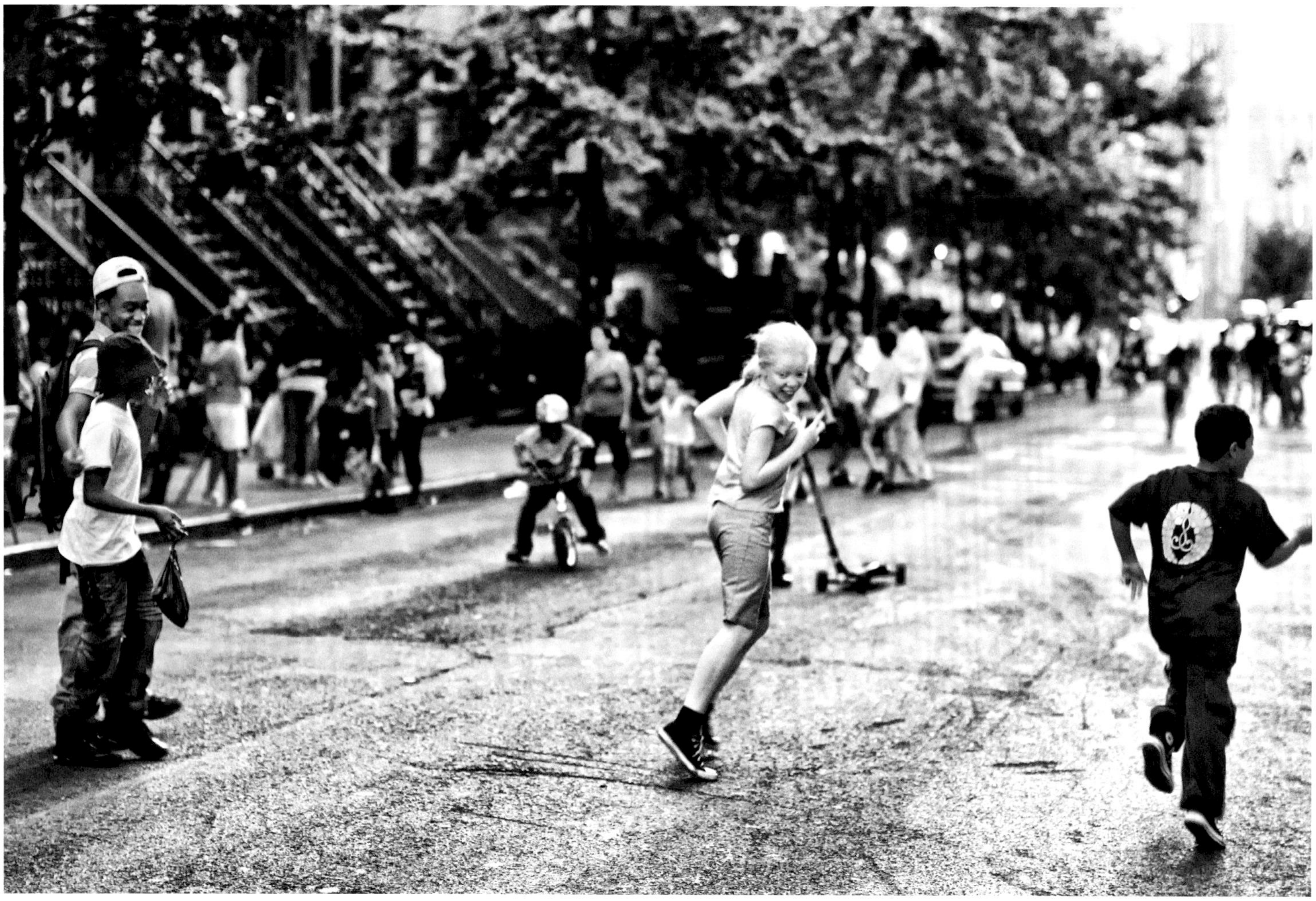

MOHAMMED SHAJAHAN
CONSTRUCTION
541 FRANKLIN AVE.
BROOKLYN NY 11238
Tel 718-638-1909
Cel 917-445-4579
IGLESIA CRISTIANA
ROCA DE HOREB, INC.
336

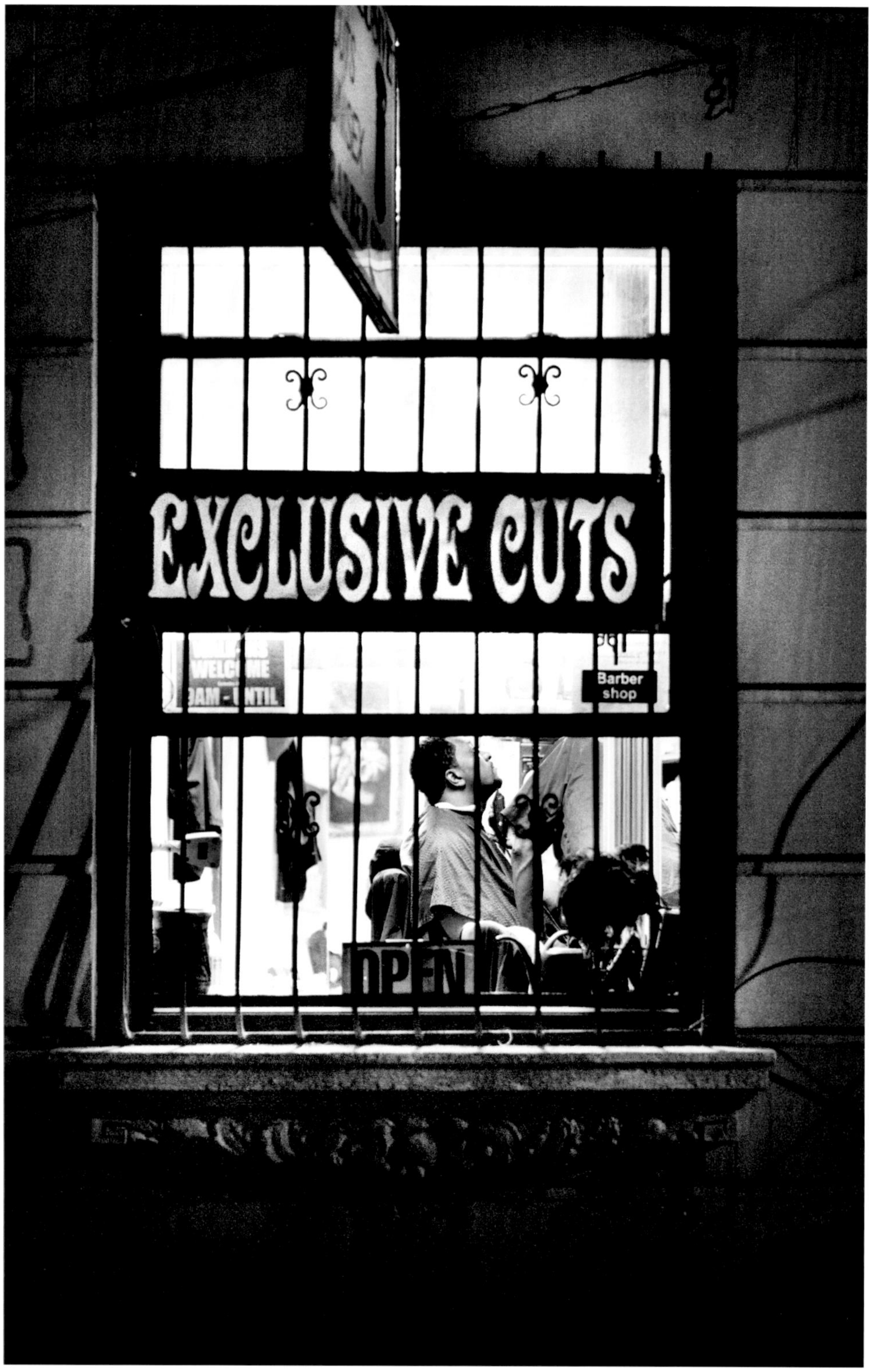
EXCLUSIVE CUTS
Barber shop
OPEN

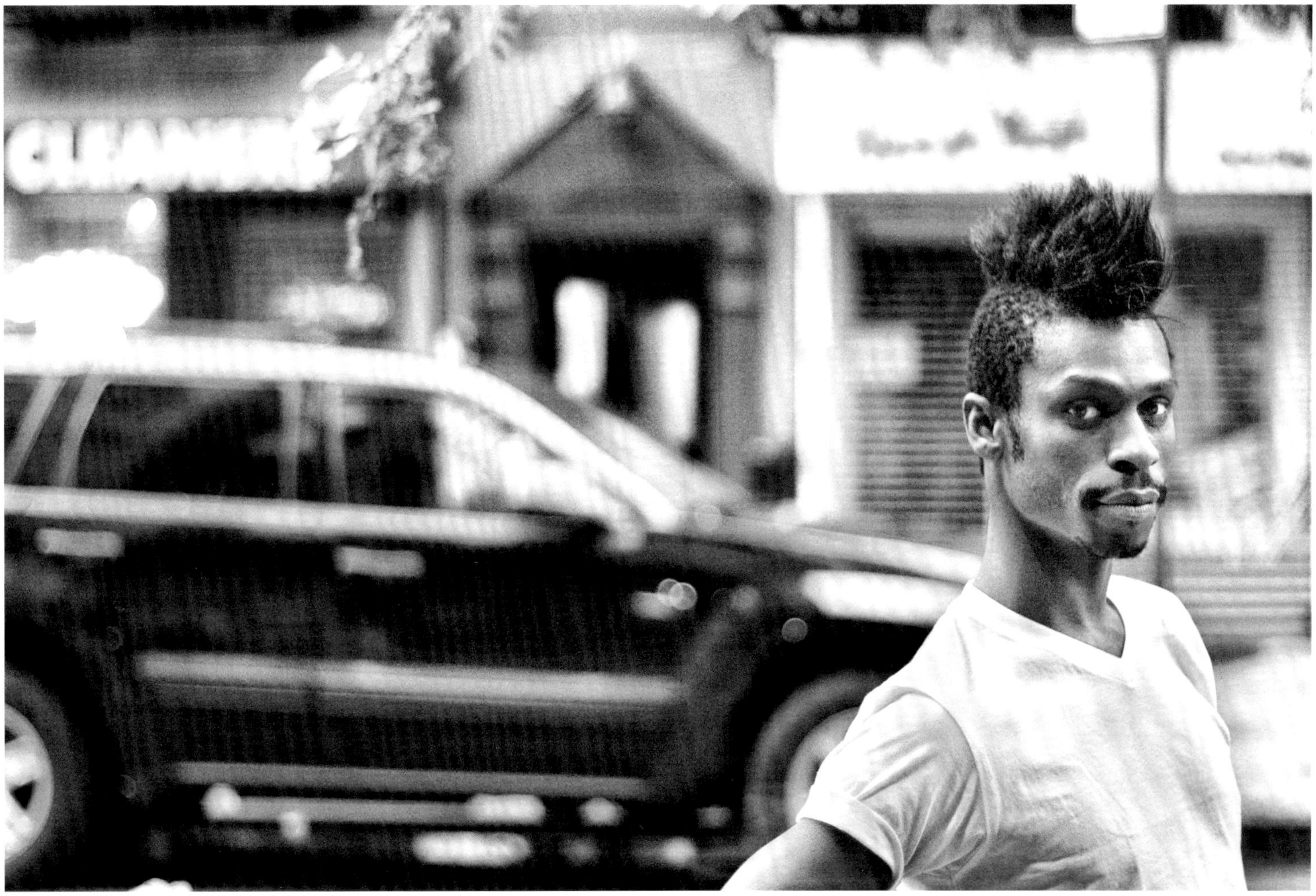

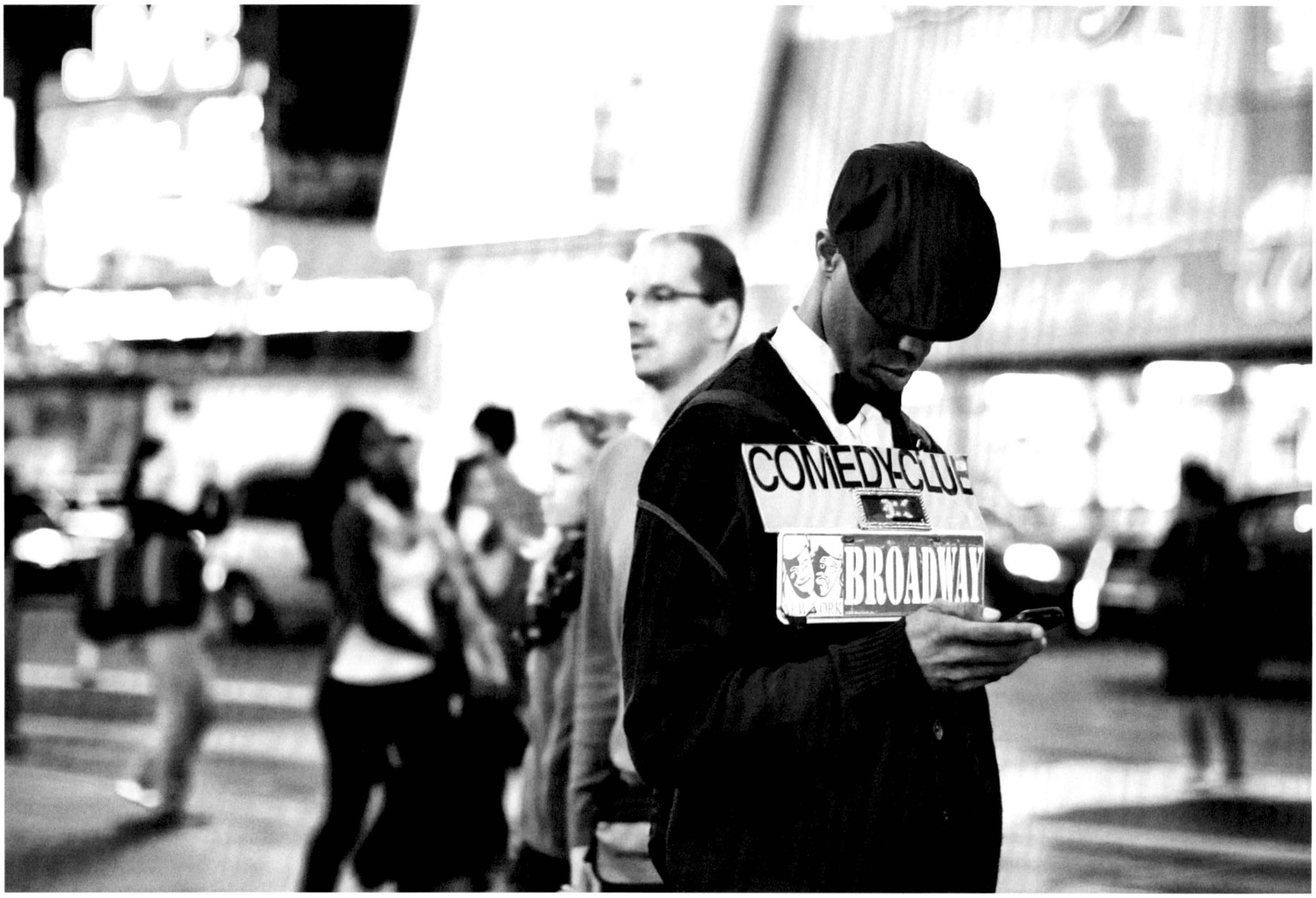
COMEDY
BROADWAY

101

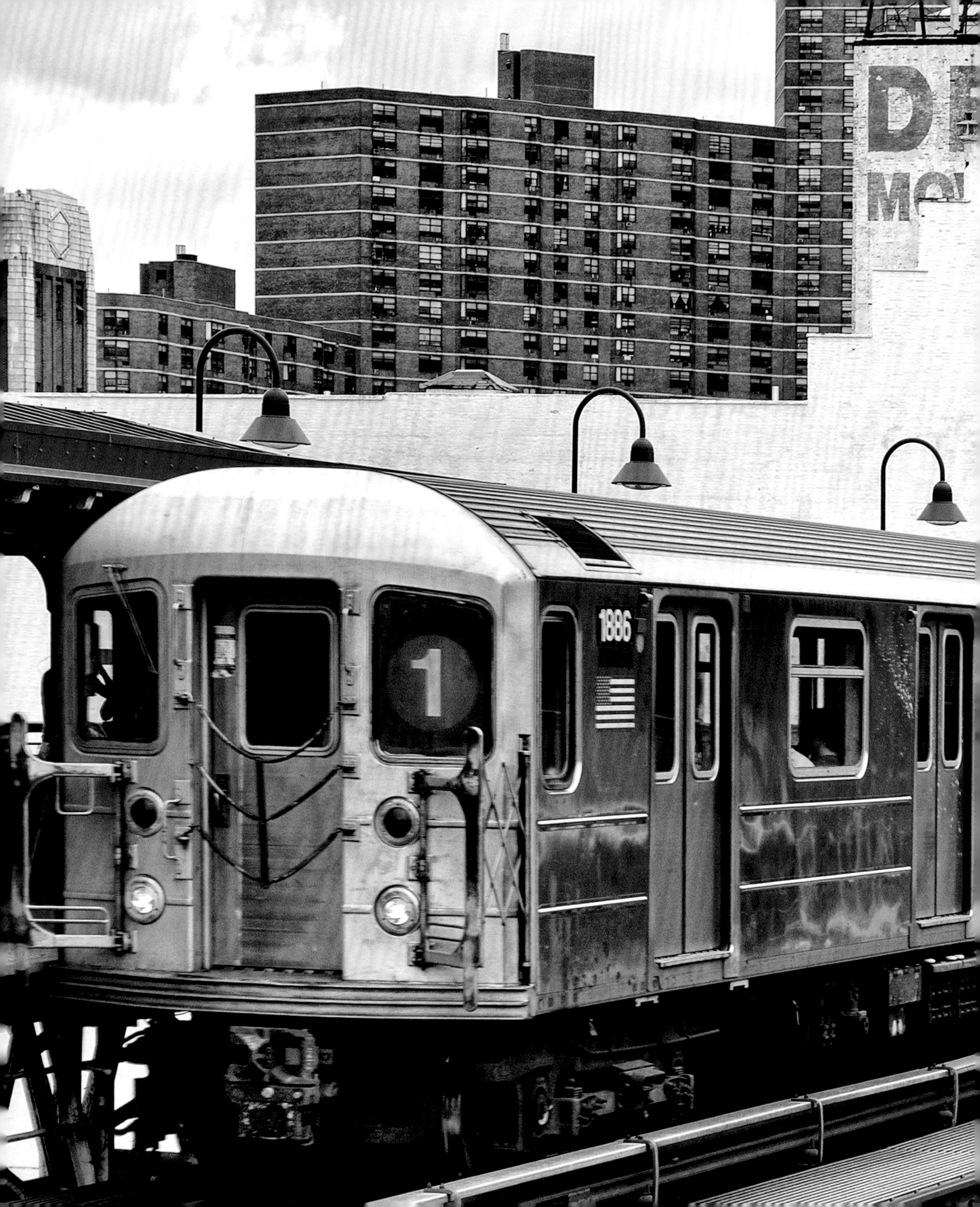
1886
1

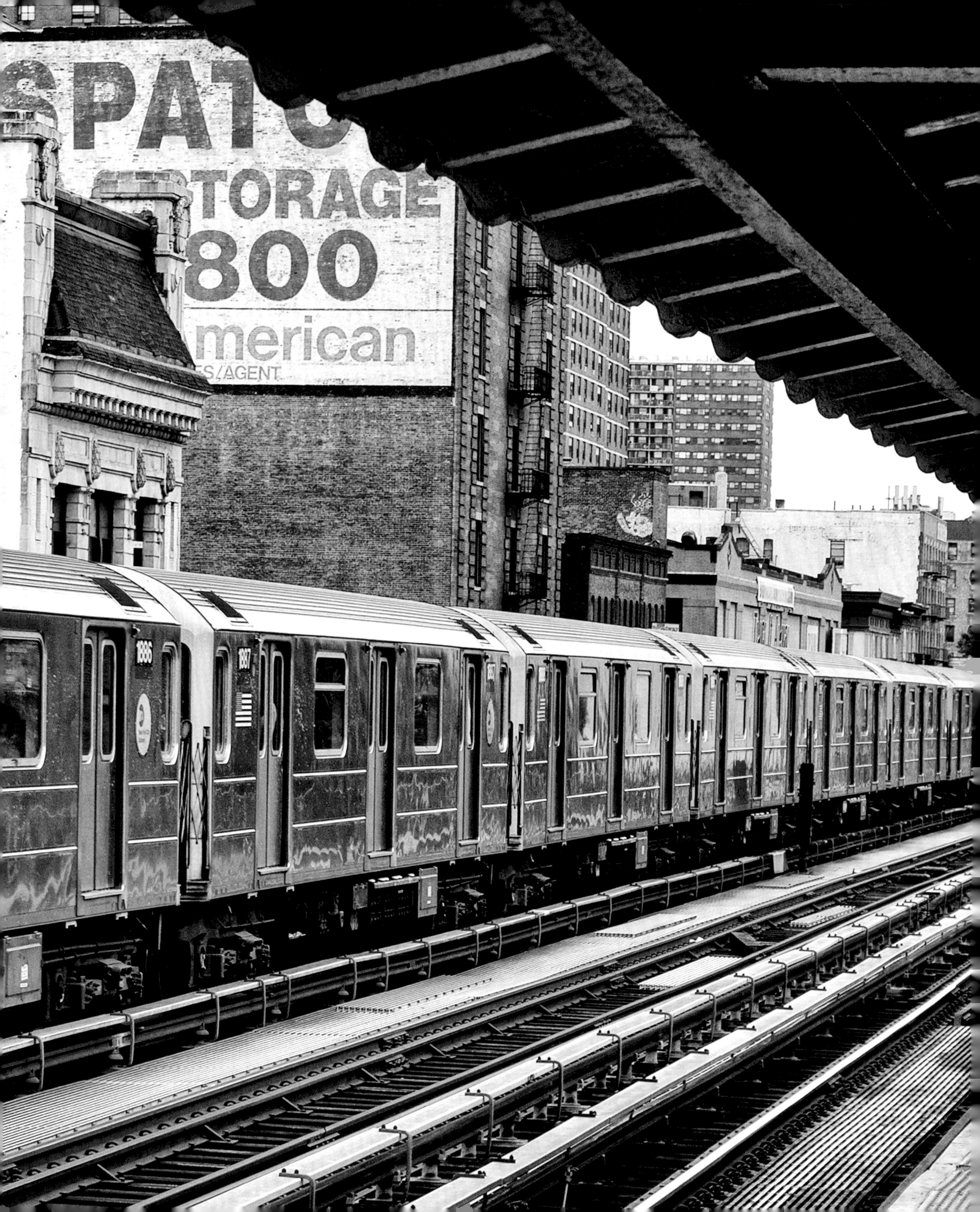
SPAT
STORAGE
800
merican
ES/AGENT
1886
1887

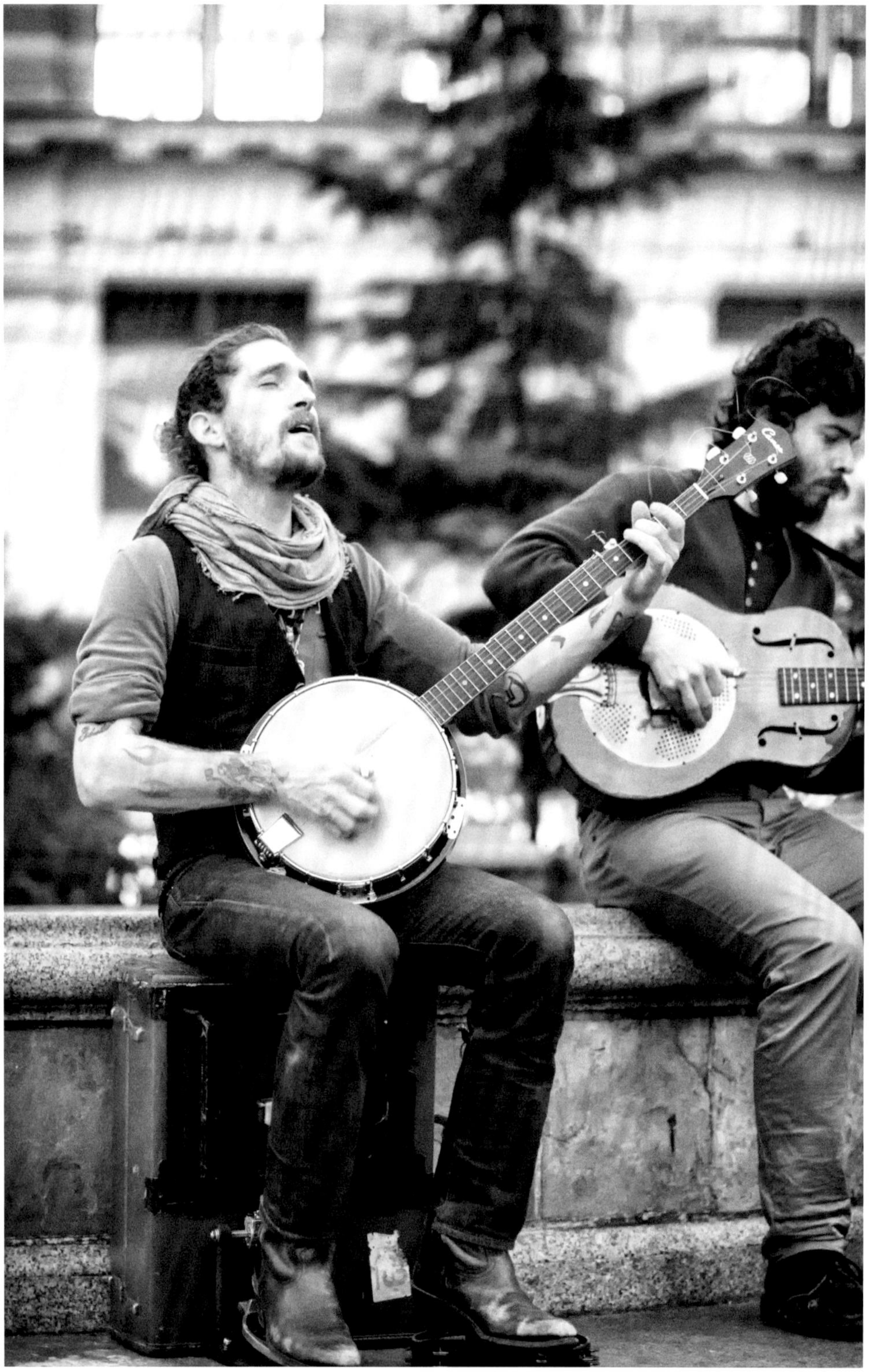

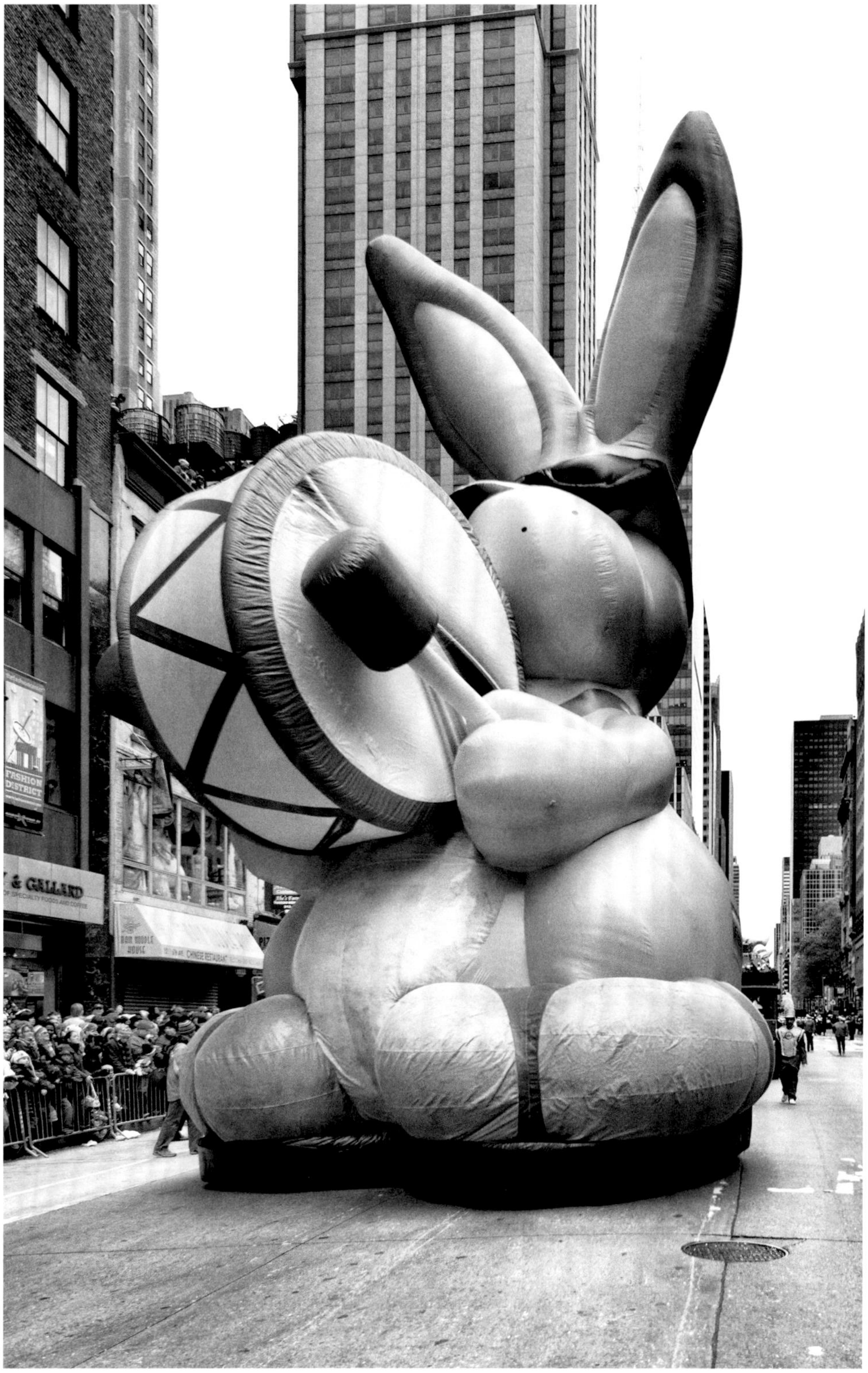
& GALLARD
FASHION DISTRICT

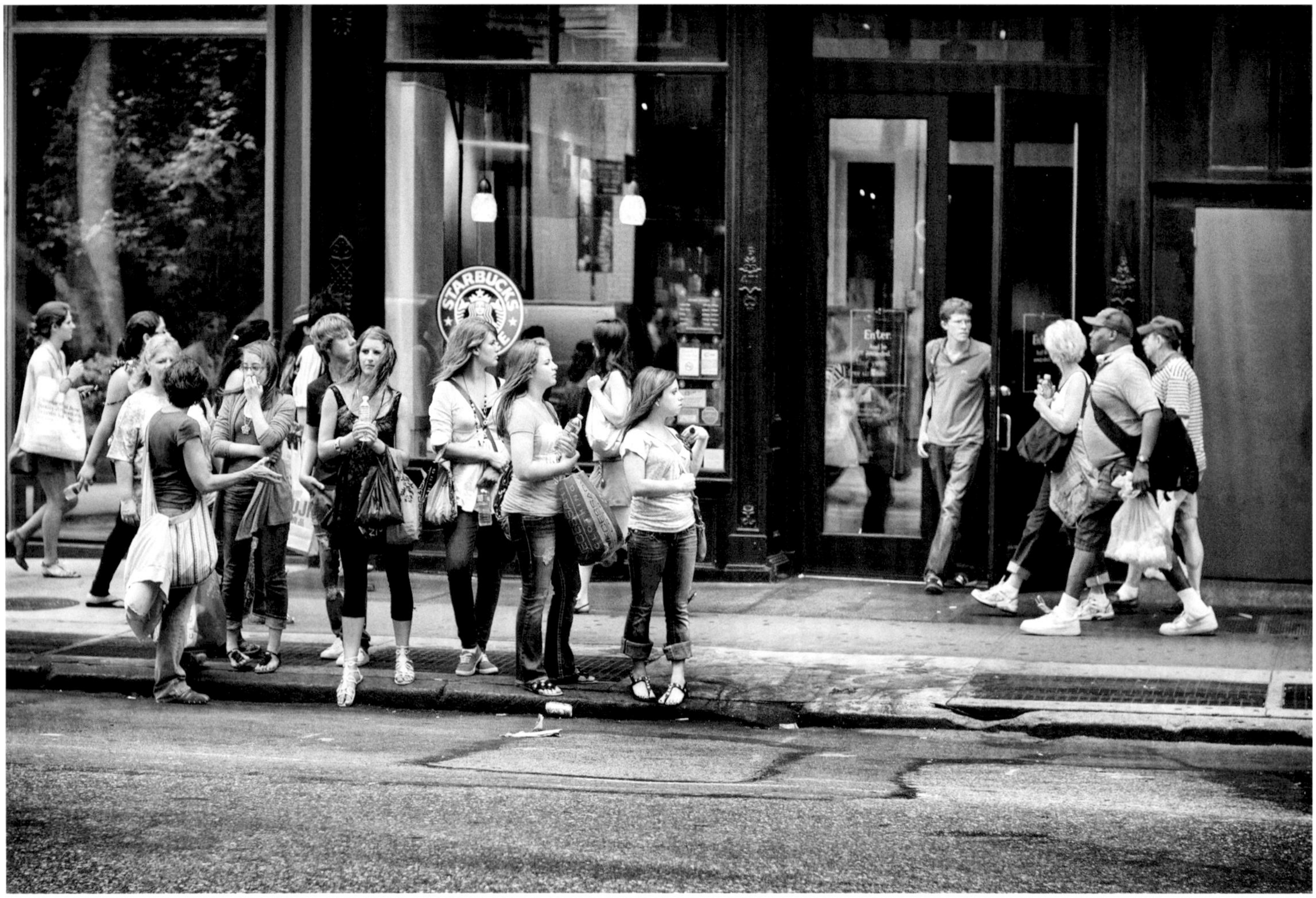
STARBUCKS
Enter

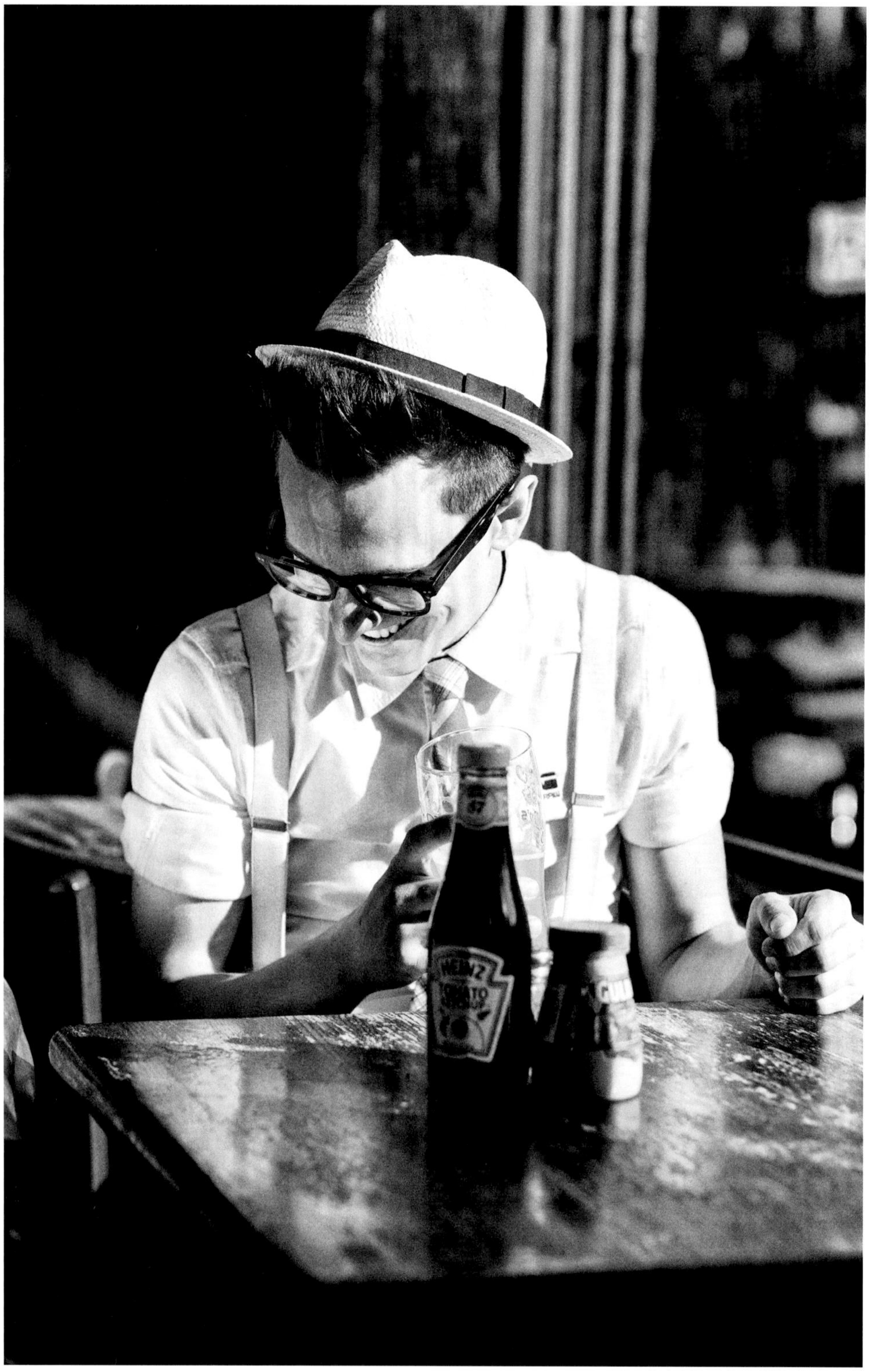
HEINZ

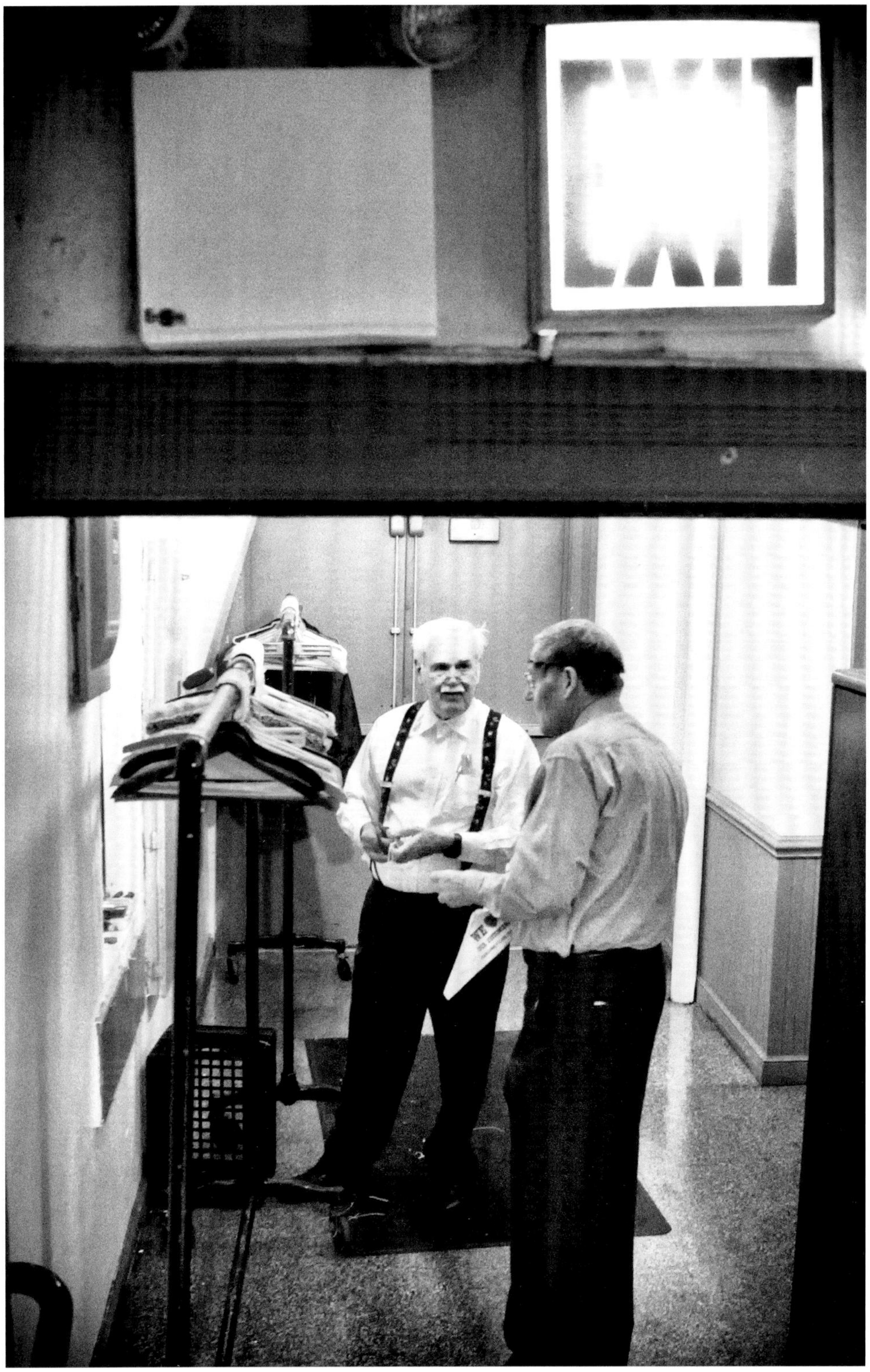
EXIT

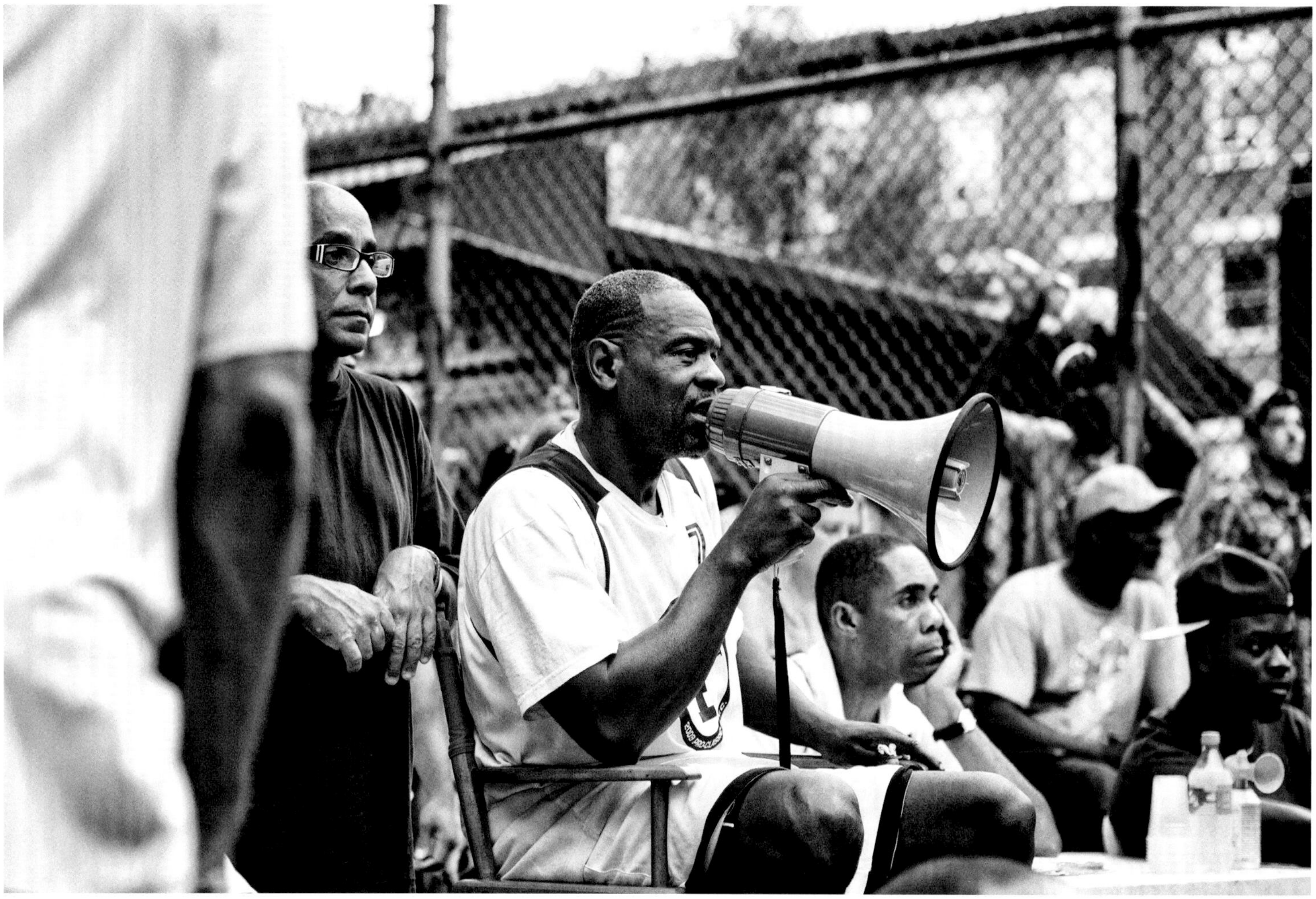

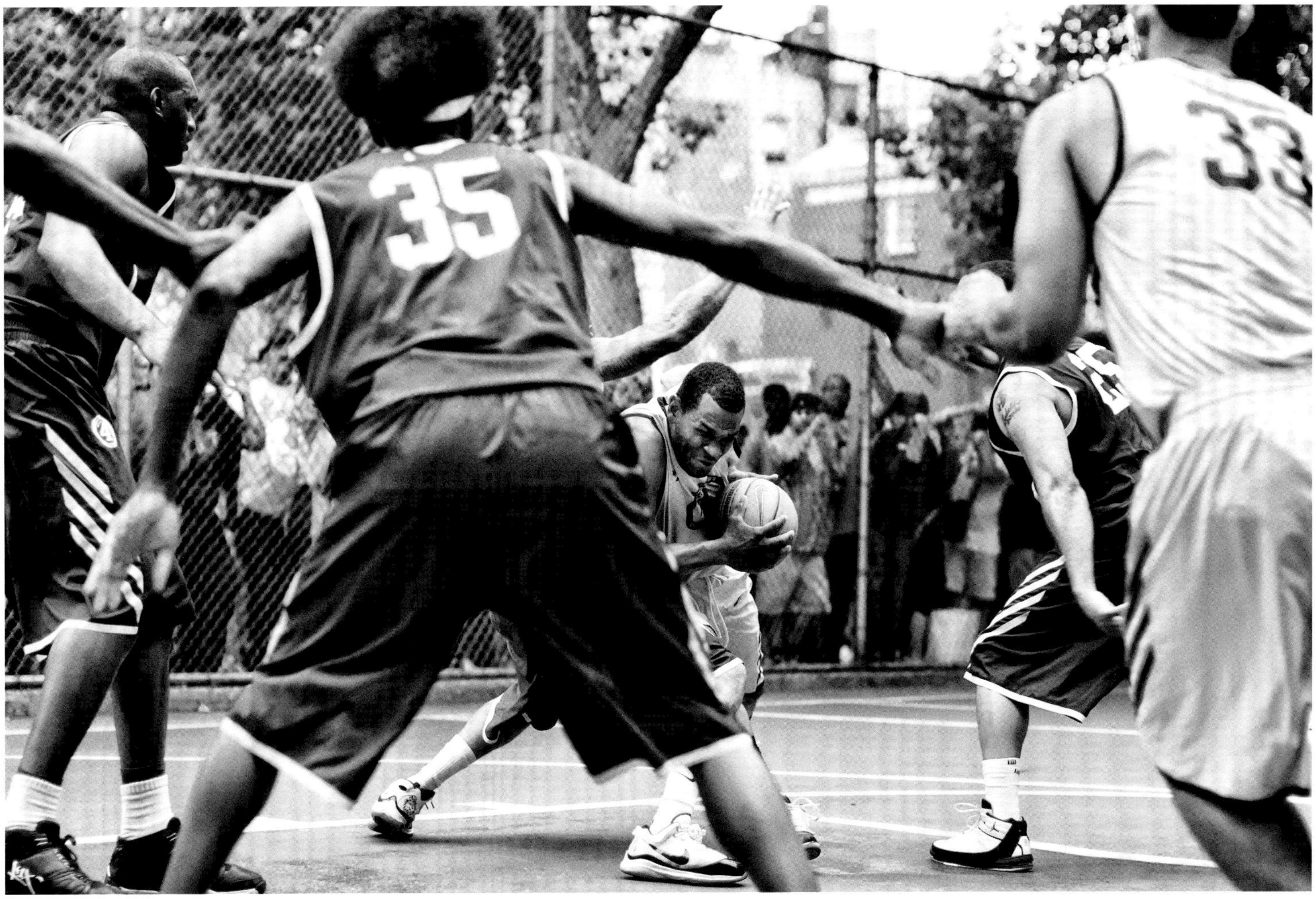
35
33

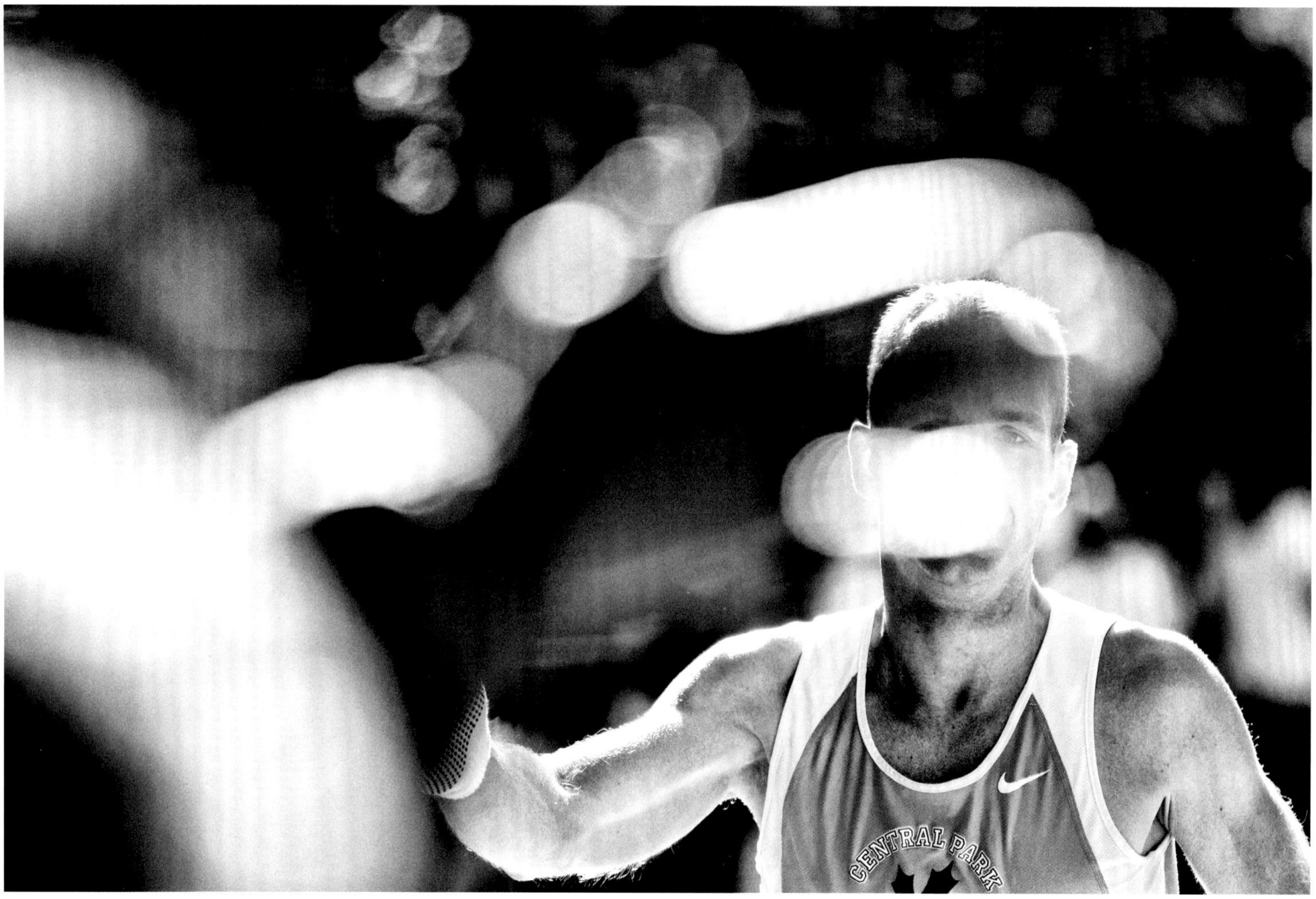
CENTRAL PARK

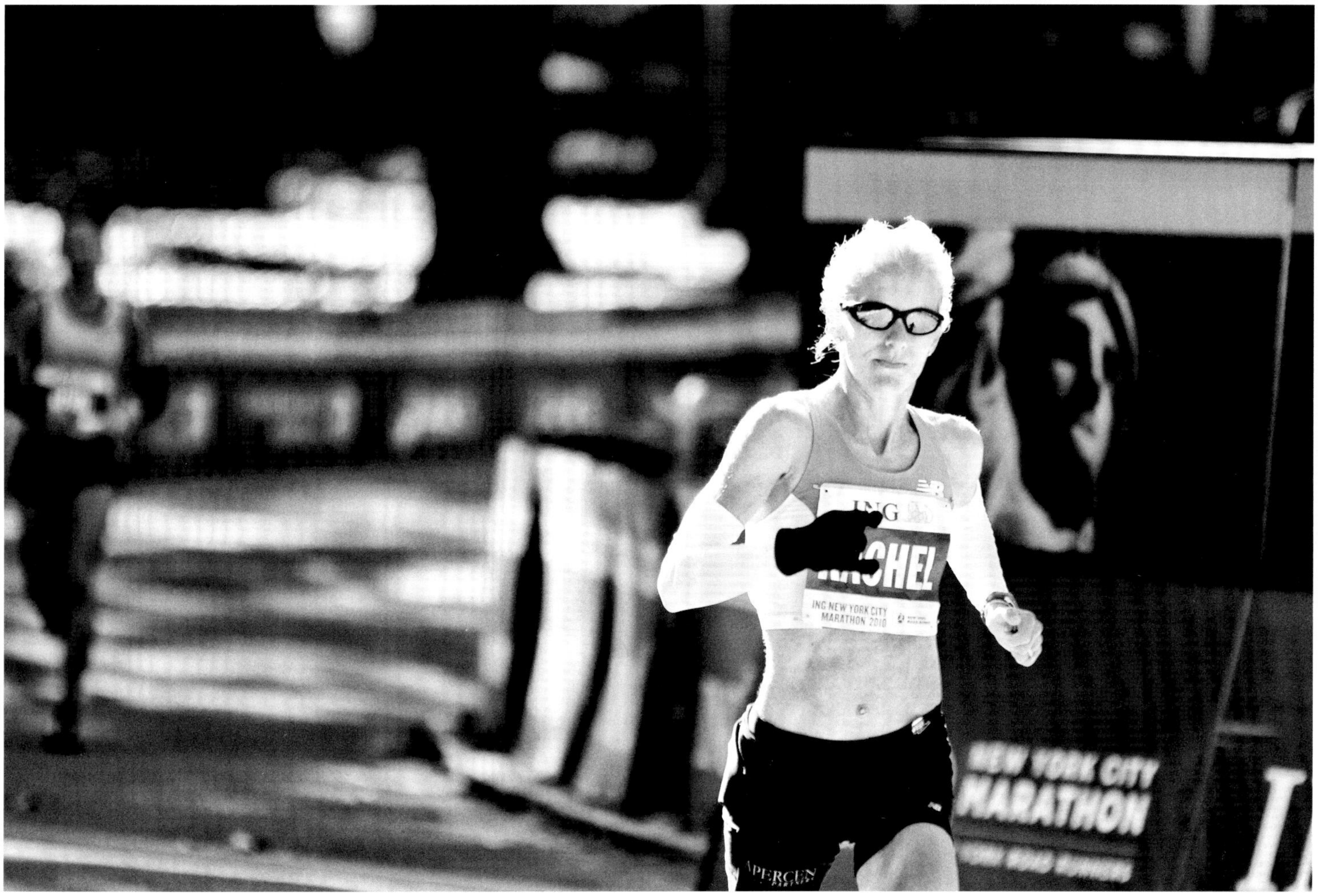
ING
ING NEW YORK CITY
MARATHON 2010
NEW YORK CITY
MARATHON

BLIND PERSONS CROSSING
TURNING VEHICLES
TURNING VEHICLES
WEBUY
CASH LOANS
PAWNBROKERS
DIAMONDS - JEWELRY - GOLD - WATCHES
MUSIC - ELECTRONICS - COMPUTERS
125 Street Subway Station
BLIND PERSONS CROSSING AHEAD

NO PARKING
NO PARKING
NO PARKING
NO PARKING
NO PARKING
NO PARKING
NO PARKING
NO PARKING
NO PARKING
NO PARKING
OPEN

Magid
HANDBAGS
EVENING
RESORT
COCKTAIL
STRAW
BAG CO.
INC.
Magid
HANDBAGS

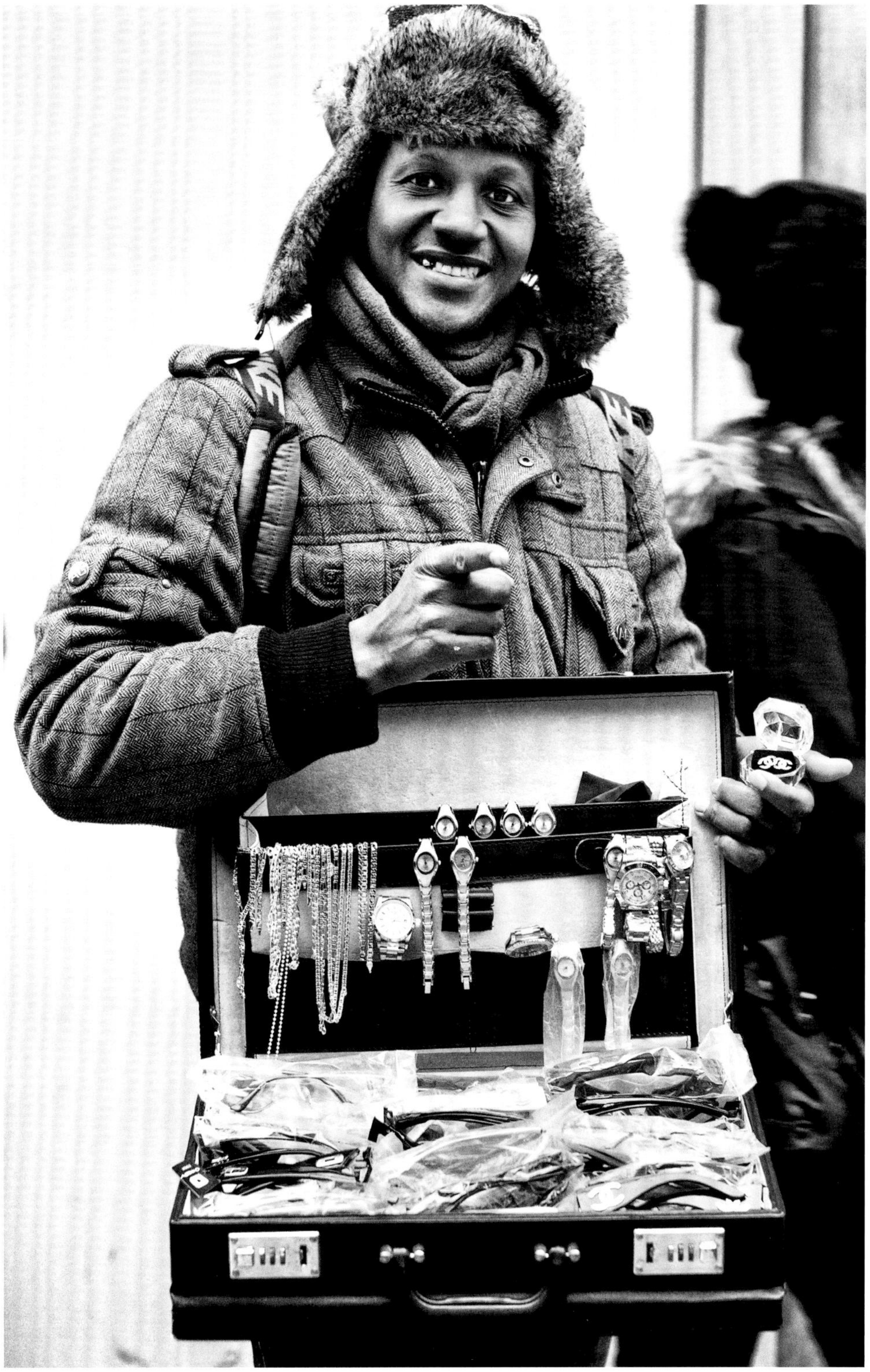

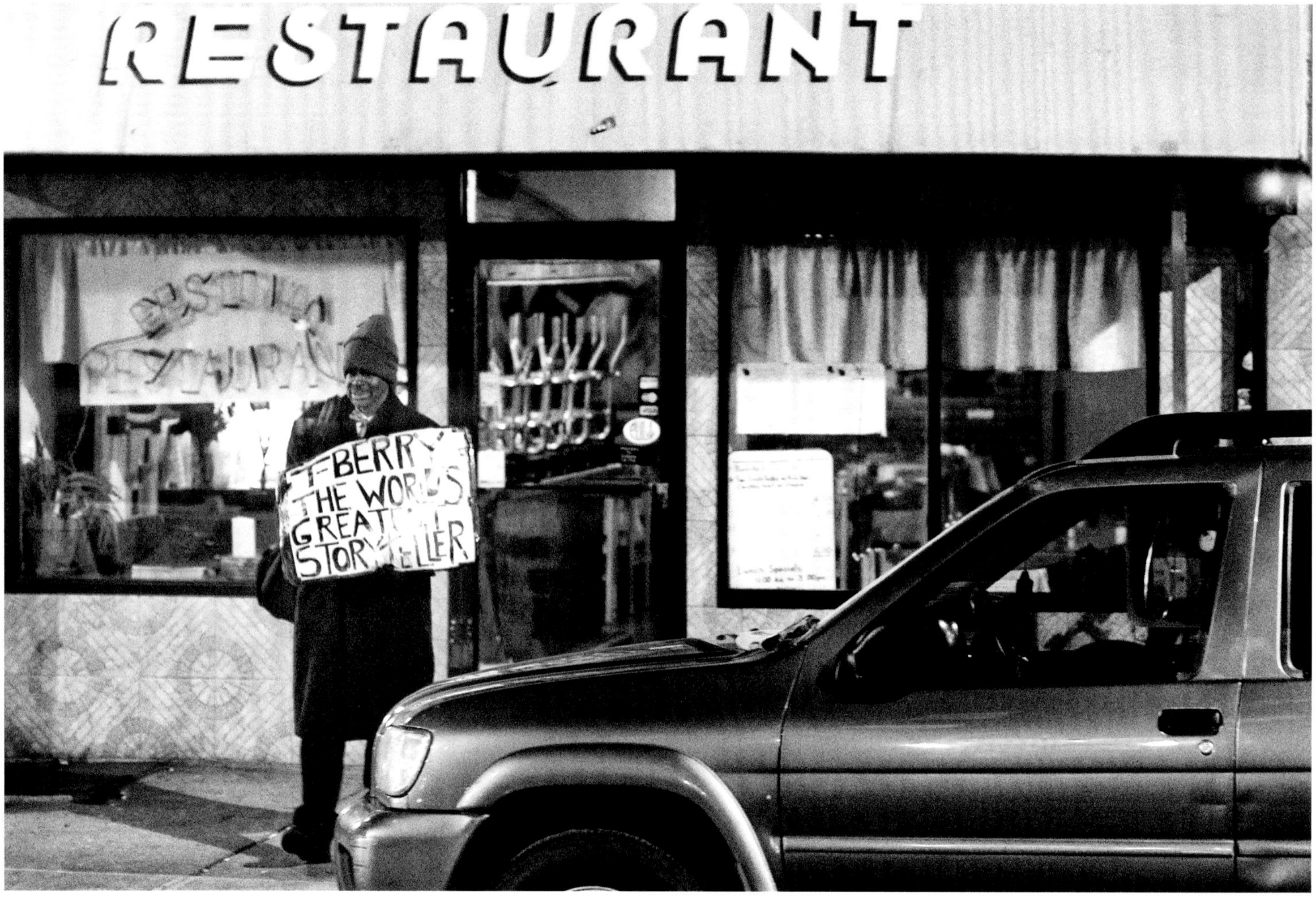
RESTAURANT

The New York Times

"All the News That's Fit to Print"

VOL. CLX .. No. 55,229 © 2010 The New York Times NEW YORK, FRIDAY, NOVEMBER 19, 2010

Obama Lines Up Reinforcements for Arms Treaty Fight
Former Secretaries of State Henry A. Kissinger, right, and James A. Baker III, second from left, joined President Obama, Vice...
DOUG MILLS/THE NEW YORK TIMES

Financier Sued By New York In Fraud Case

Rattner and U.S. Settle — He Fights Cuomo

By LOUISE STORY and PETER LATTMAN

Steven L. Rattner, the financier who oversaw the federal rescue of the auto industry, was formally accused by New York's attorney general, Andrew M. Cuomo, on Thursday of engaging in a kickback scheme involving the state's pension system.

On the same day that Mr. Rattner was being celebrated on Wall Street for his role in turning around General Motors, he found himself embroiled in a bitter public battle with Mr. Cuomo, he settled similar charges with the Securities and Exchange Commission and he escalated a separate legal fight against his former investment firm. [Page B1.]

Even as a resurgent G.M. went public again in a huge stock sale on Thursday, Mr. Cuomo sought to banish Mr. Rattner for life from the securities business in New York.

CENSURE U... BY ETHICS... IN RAN...

VOTE BY HOU...

Facing a For... for Unpaid ... Hidden ...

By DAVID KOC...

WASHINGTON — ... ethics committee ... recommended th... tive Charles B. R... ly censured for ... duct, the most s... ment the House c... member short of e...

The 9-to-1 vote ... emotional day an... that the panel's ch... Lofgren, Democra... called "wrenching... Mr. Rangel strugg... himself as he ple... from the panel.

"I don't know h... I have to live," s... 80, his eyes water...

Late Edi...

Today, mostly sunn... high 48. Tonight, m... breezy, low 41. To... sunny, milder, gusty... Weather map appea...

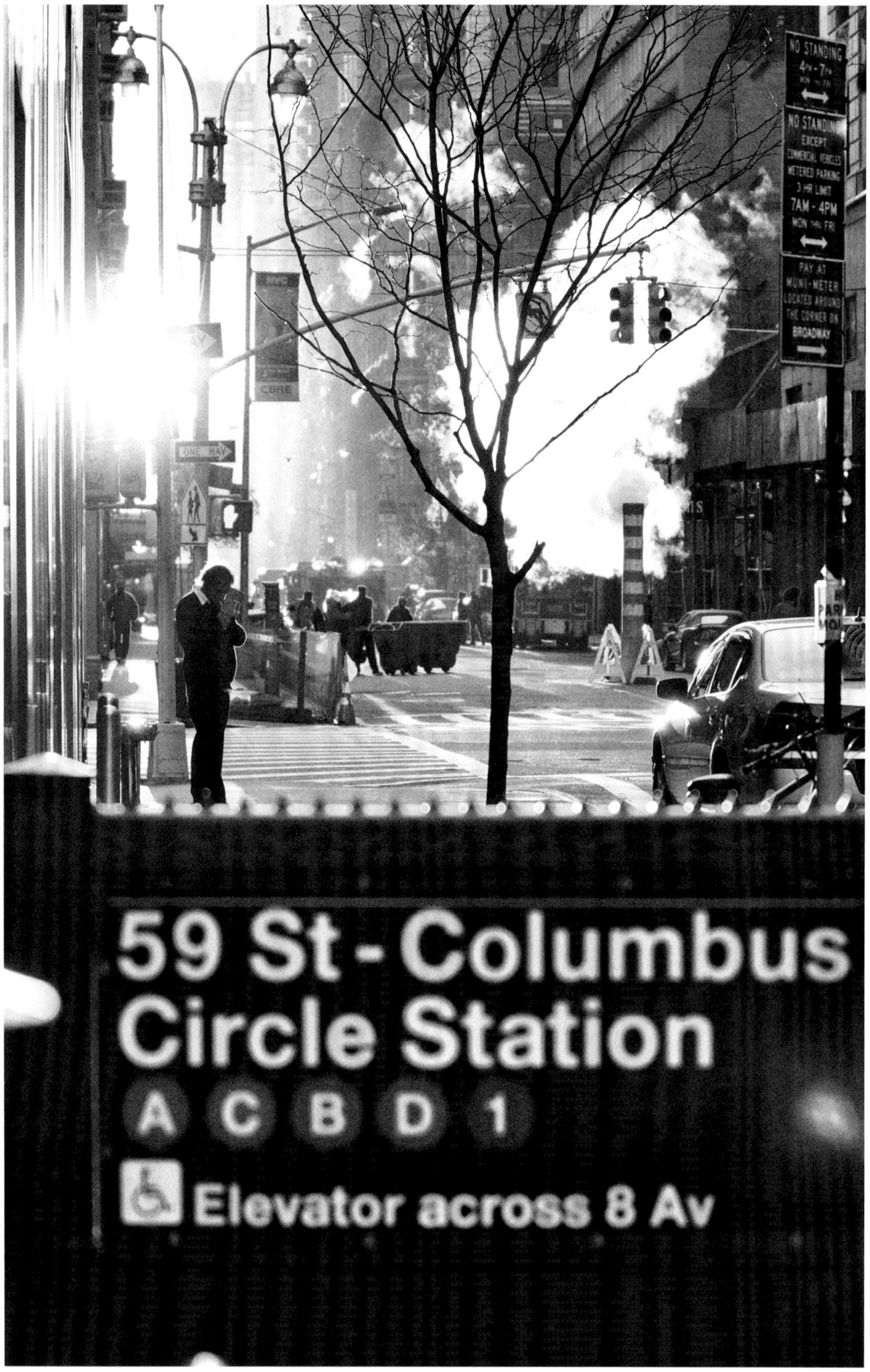
59 St - Columbus
Circle Station
A C B D 1
Elevator across 8 Av

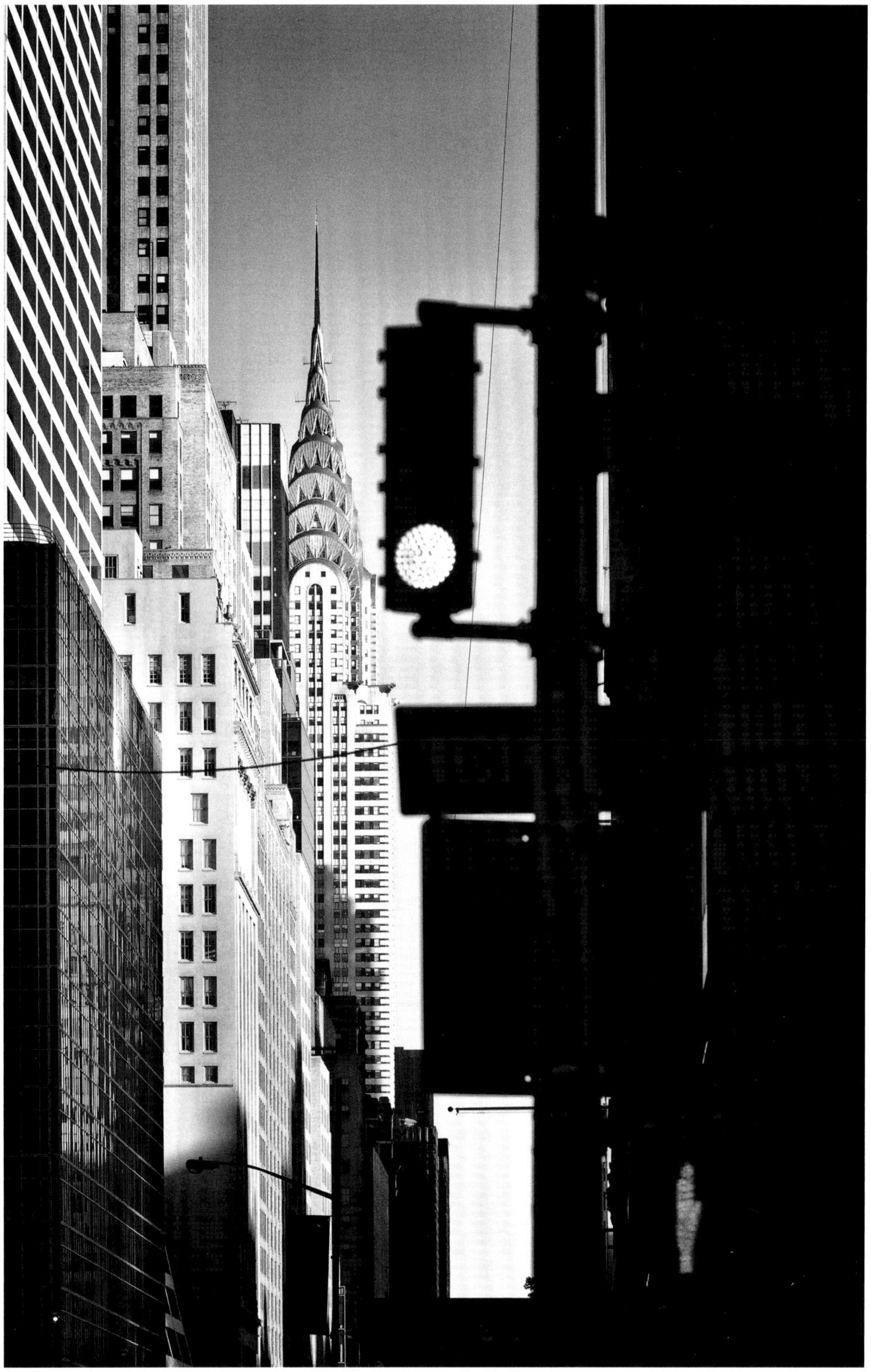

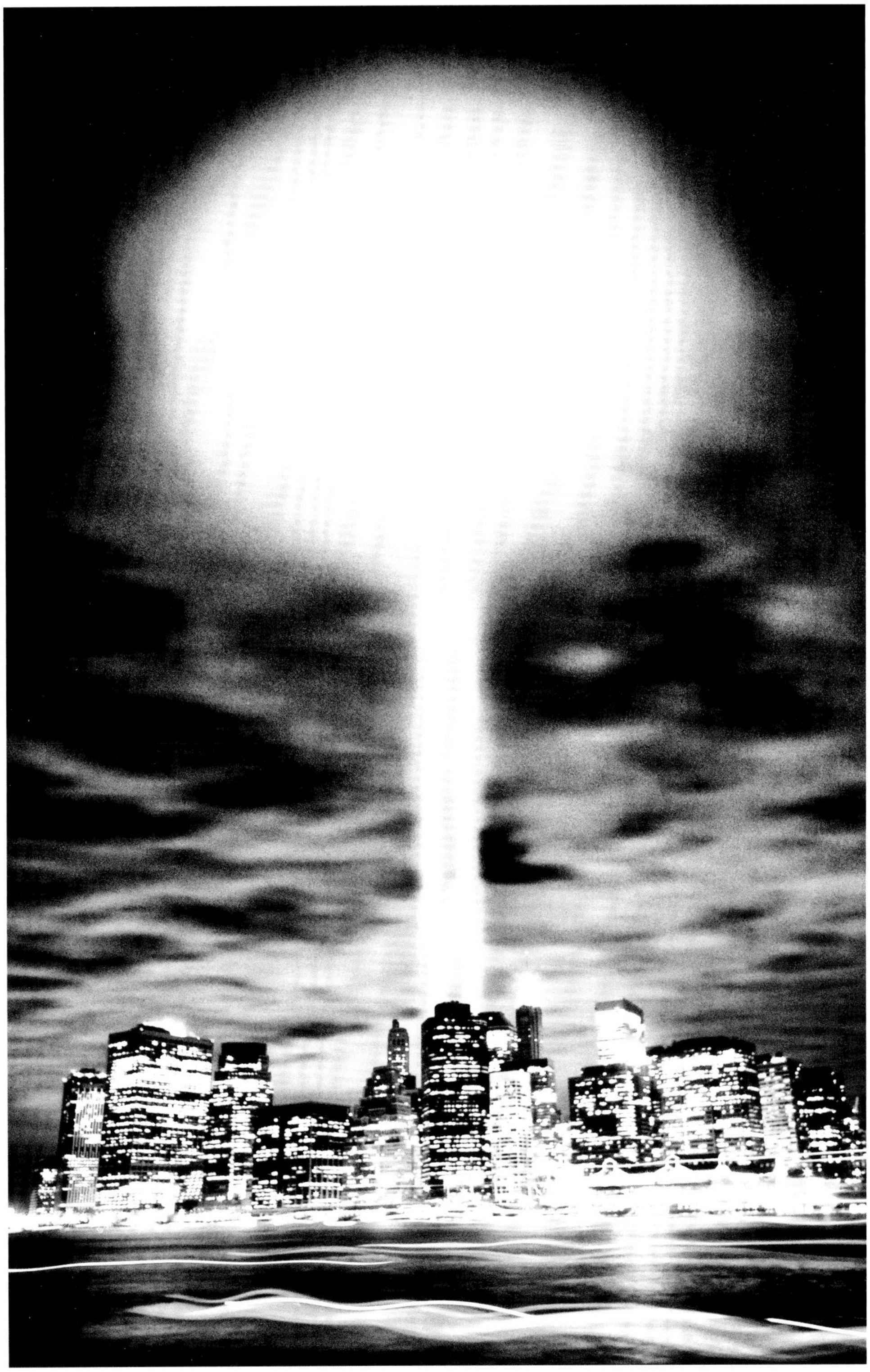

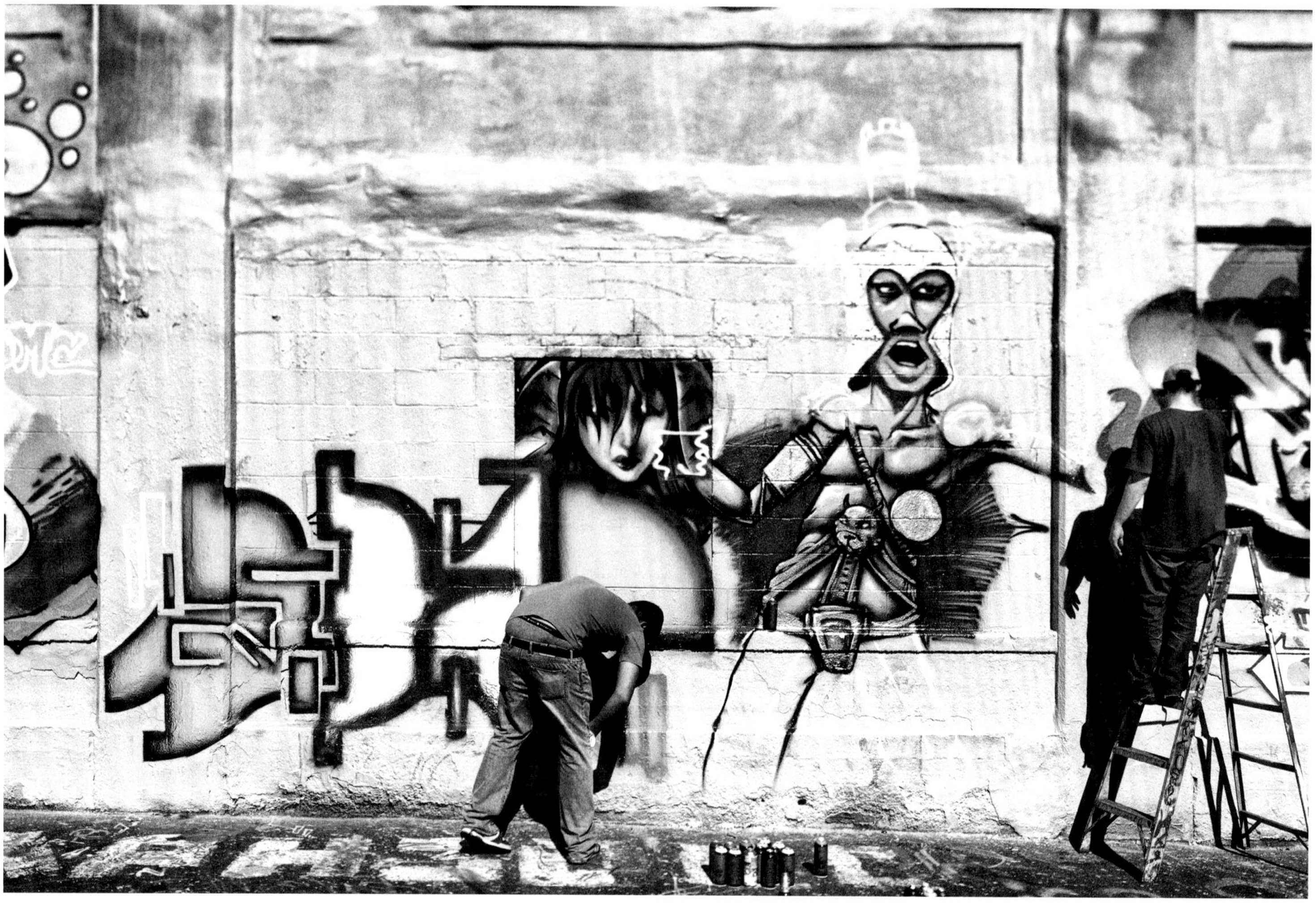

125

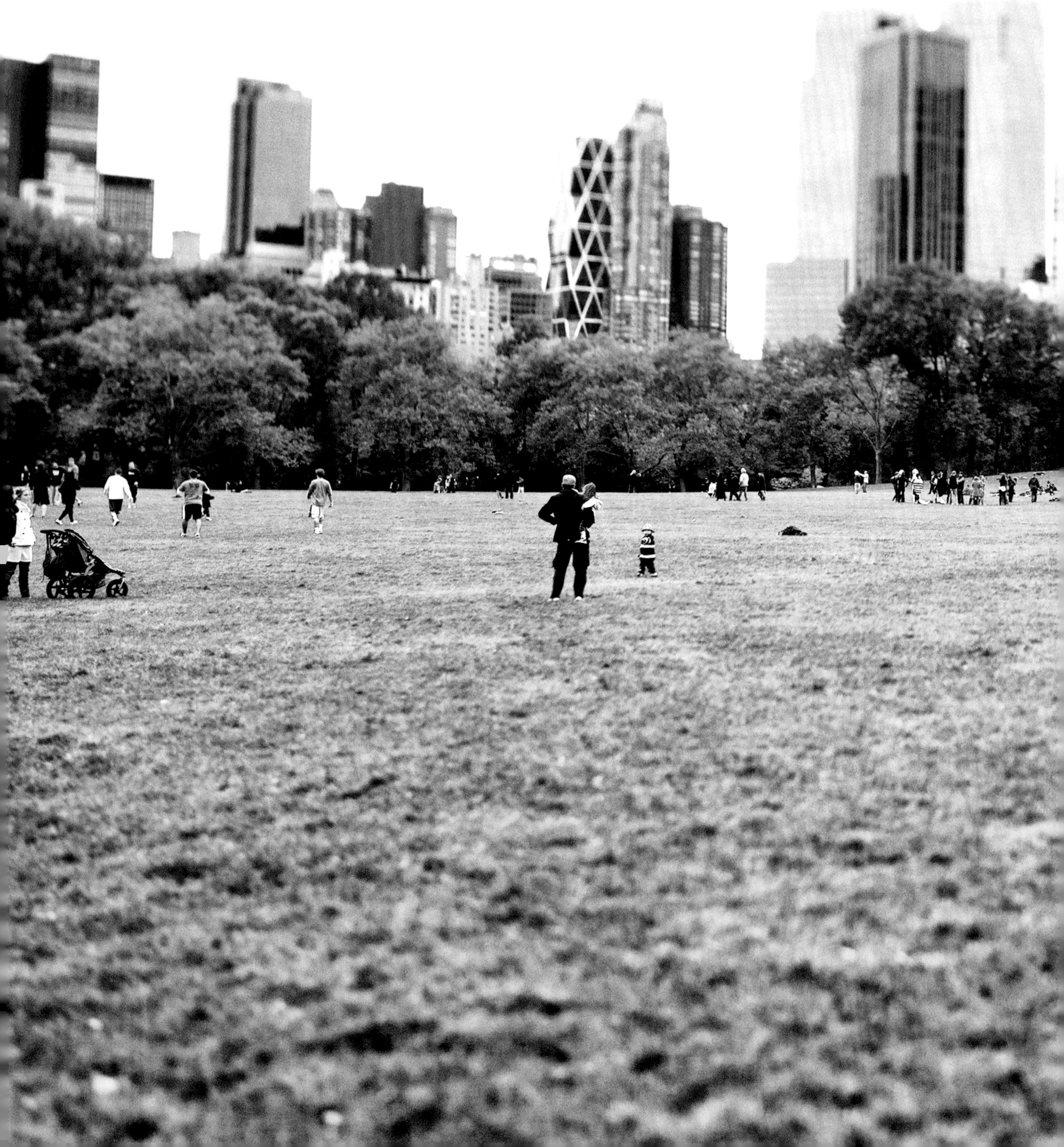

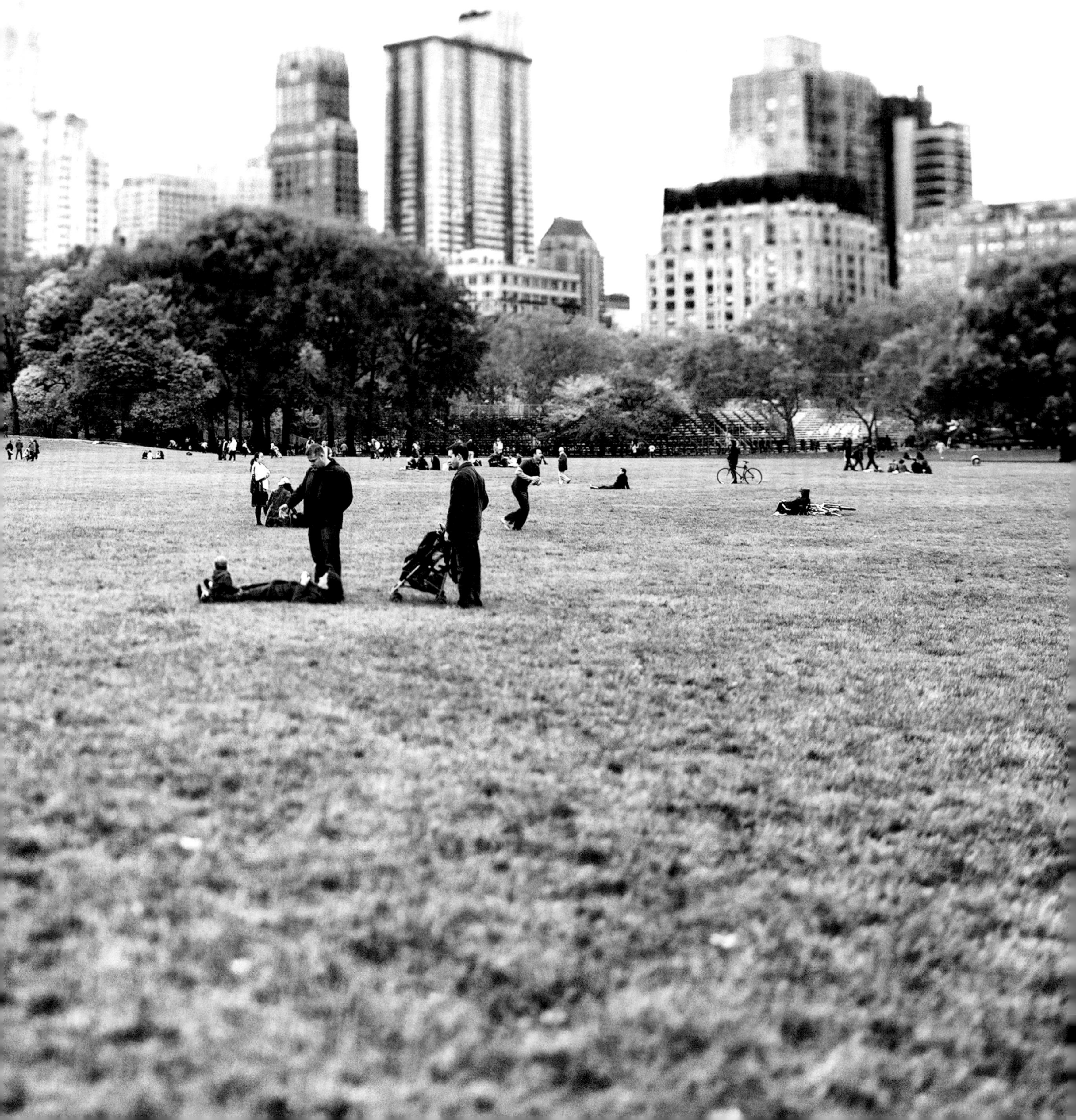

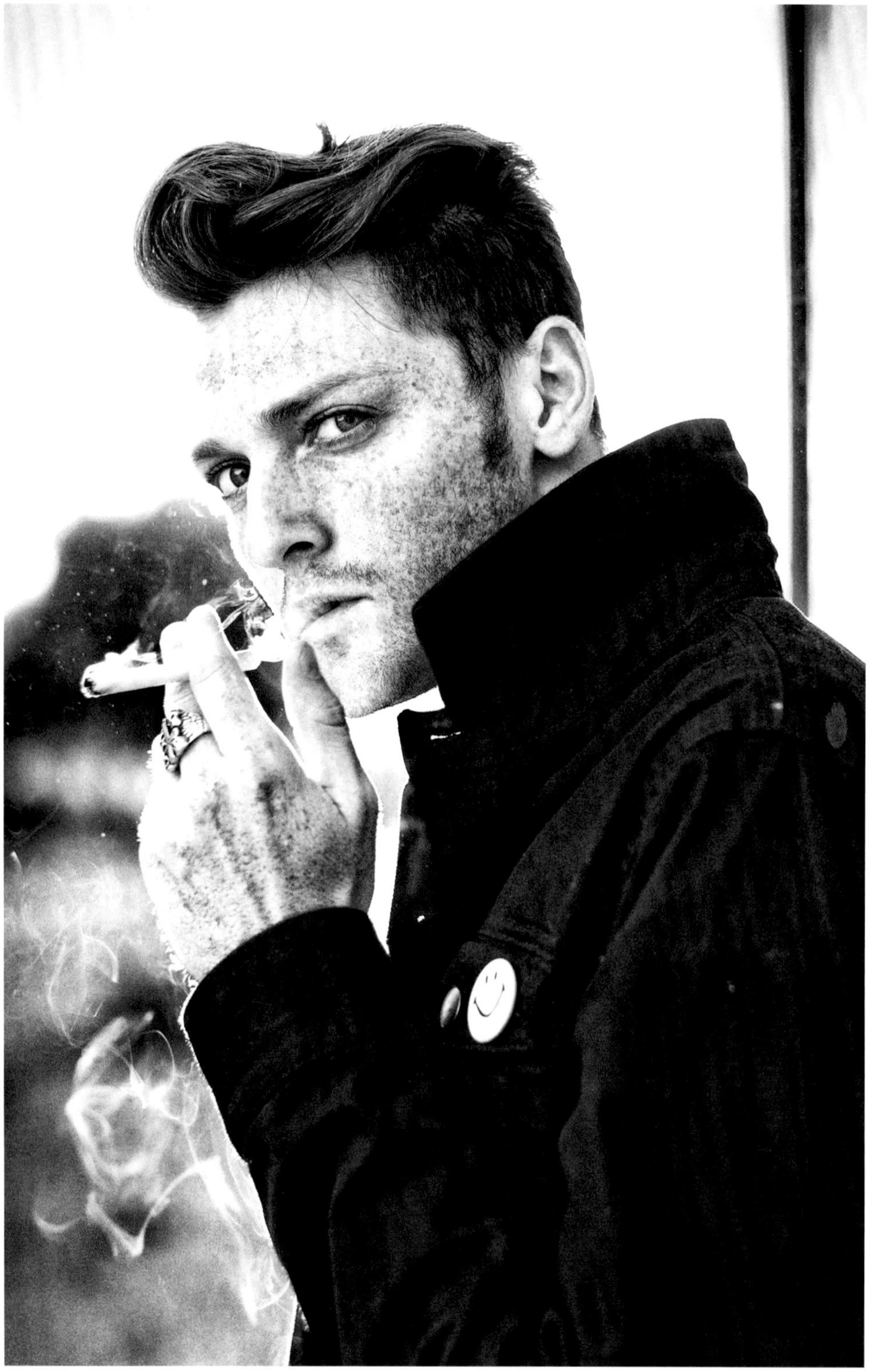

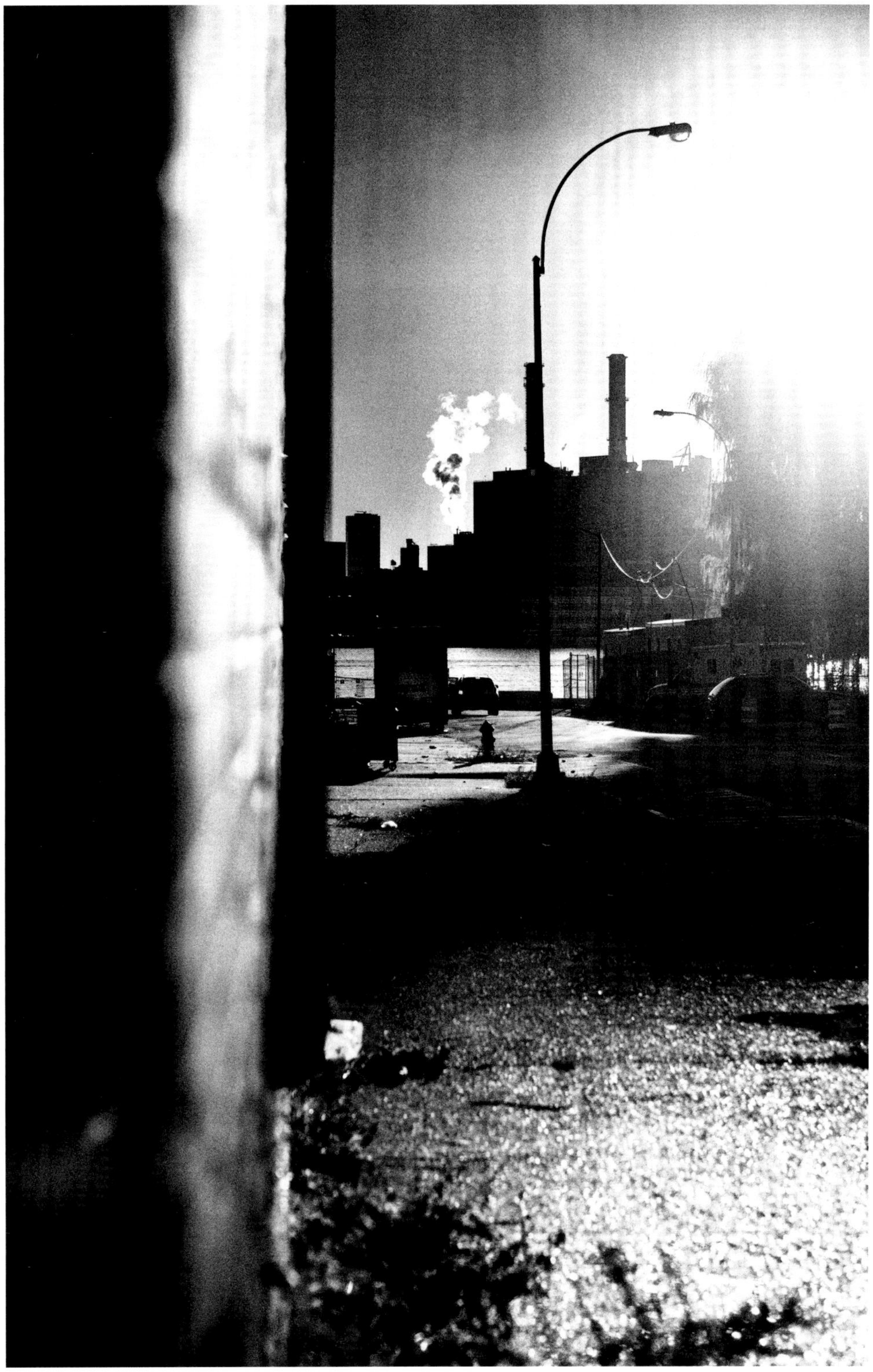

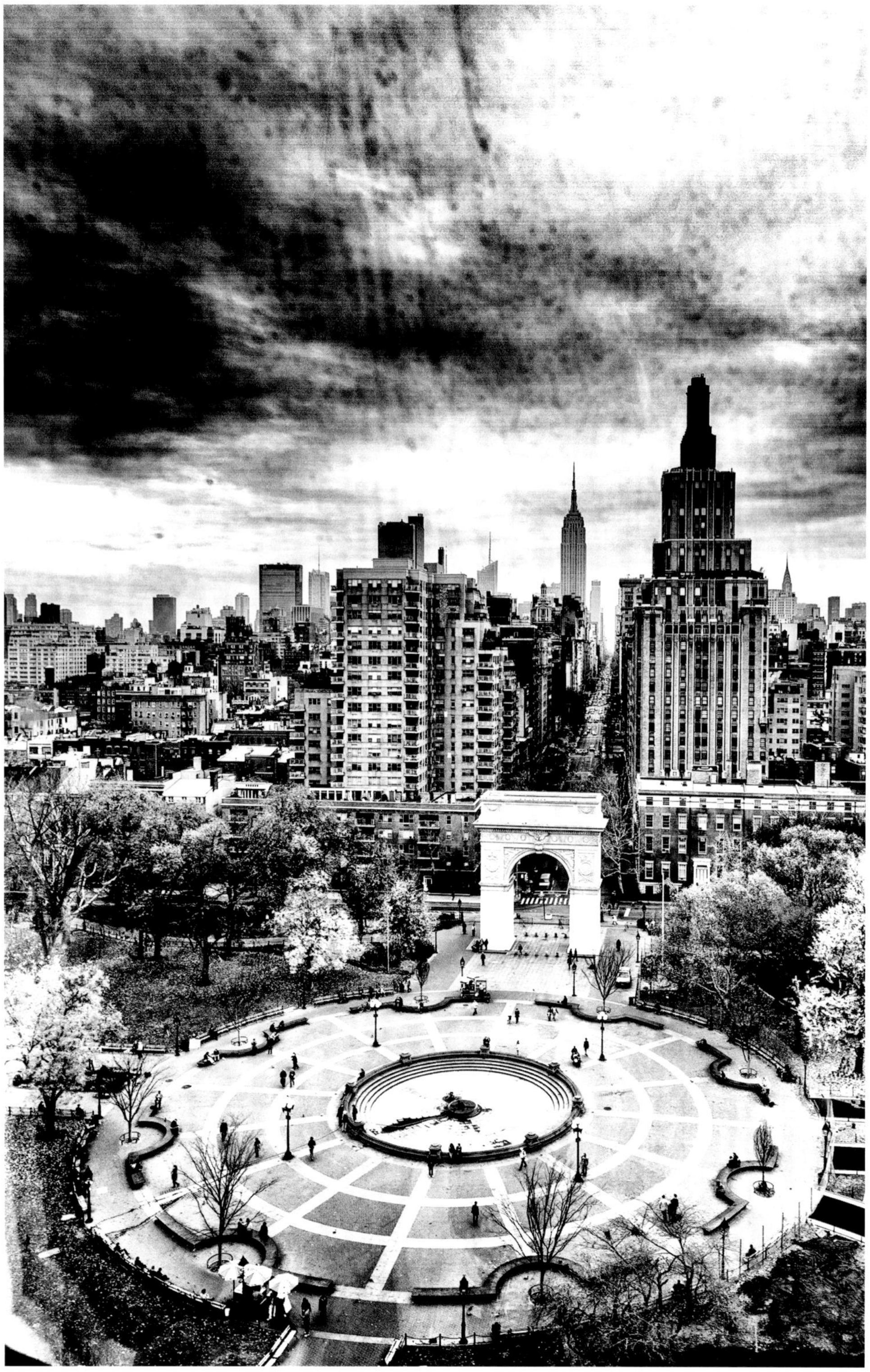

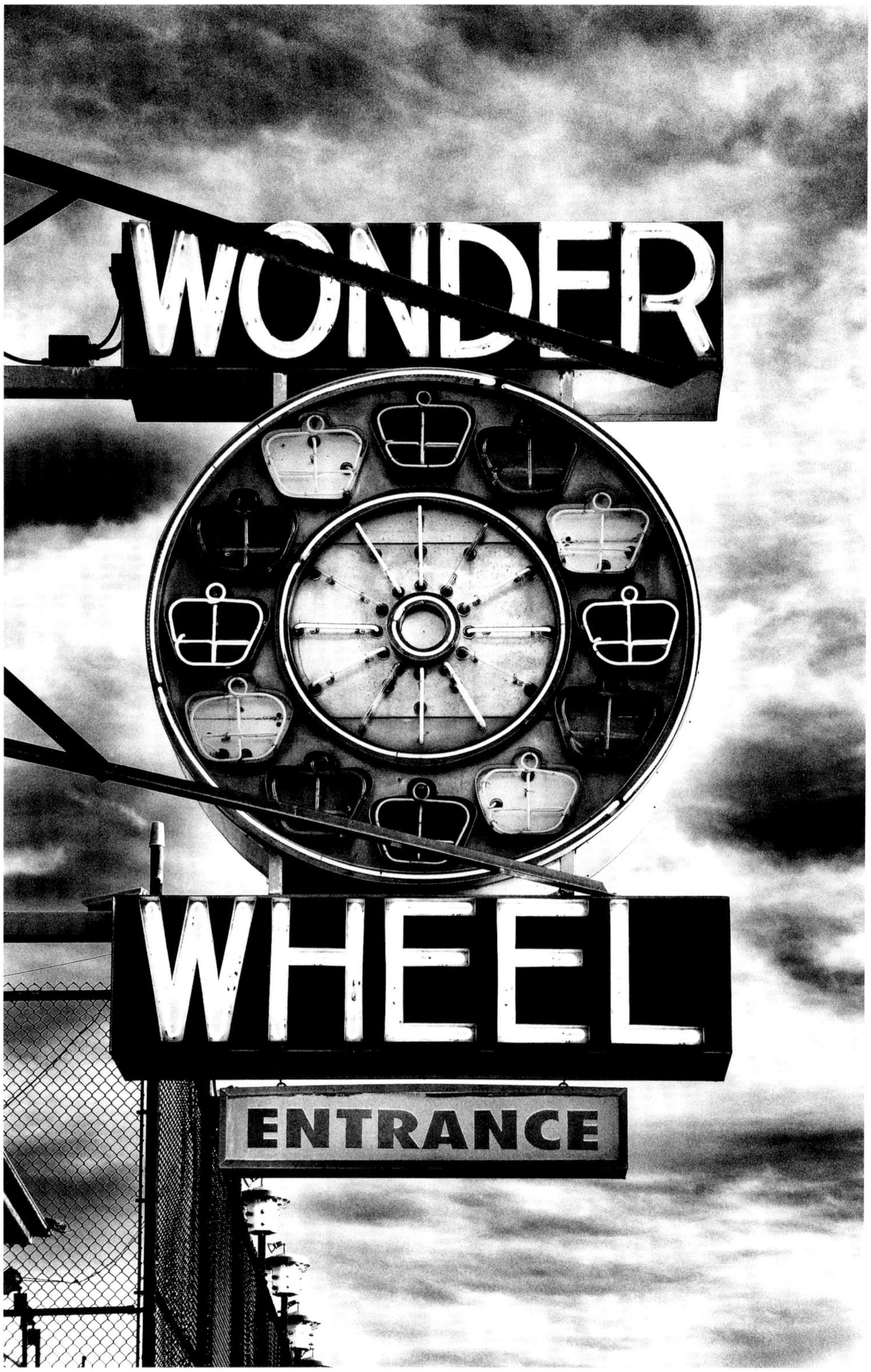
WONDER
WHEEL
ENTRANCE

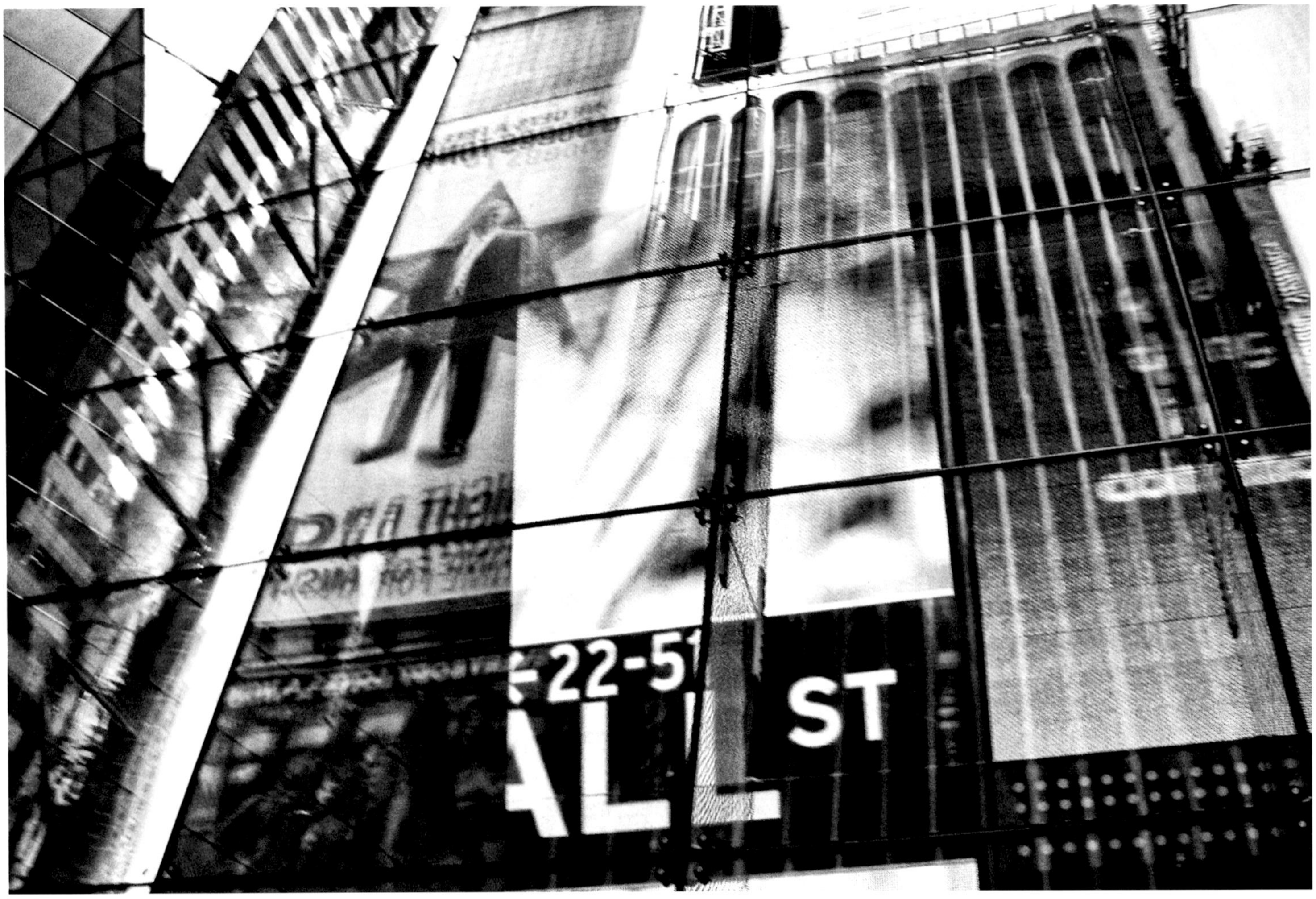
22-51
ST

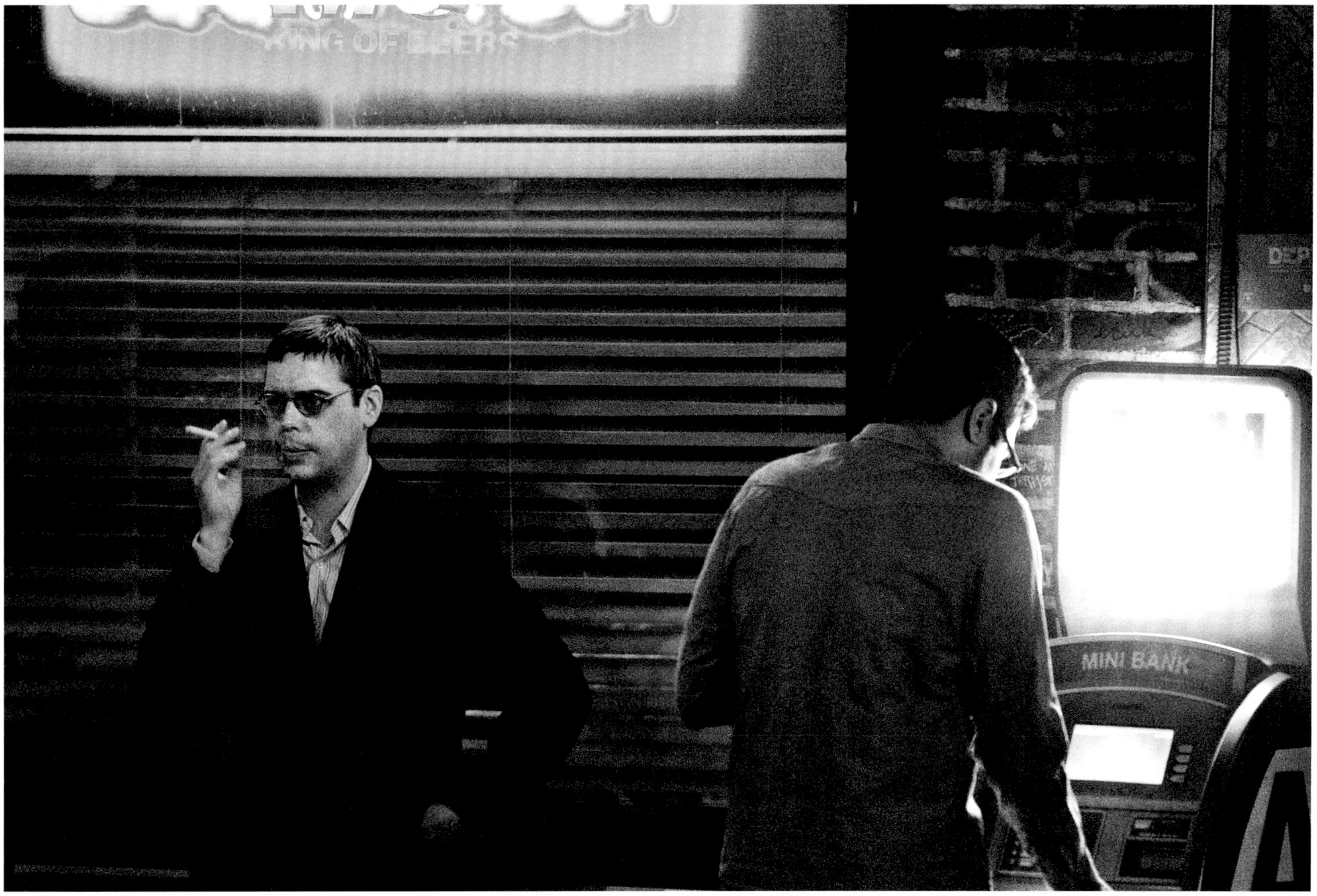
MINI BANK

3419
GROCE
COLD BEER COLD SODA - COLD CU
3417
RADIOS
RELOJES
MALETAS
MOCHILAS
TOYS
Heineken

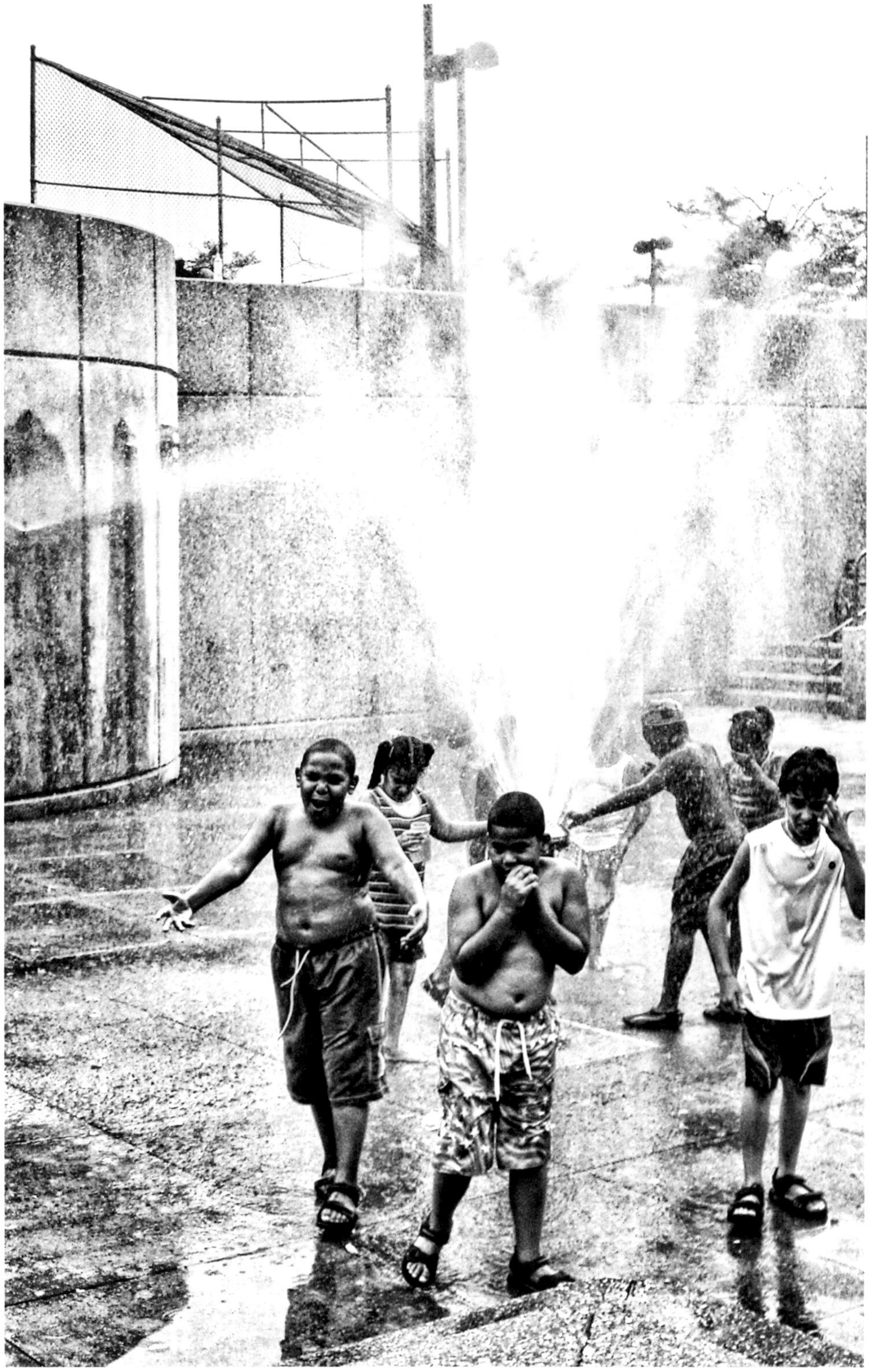

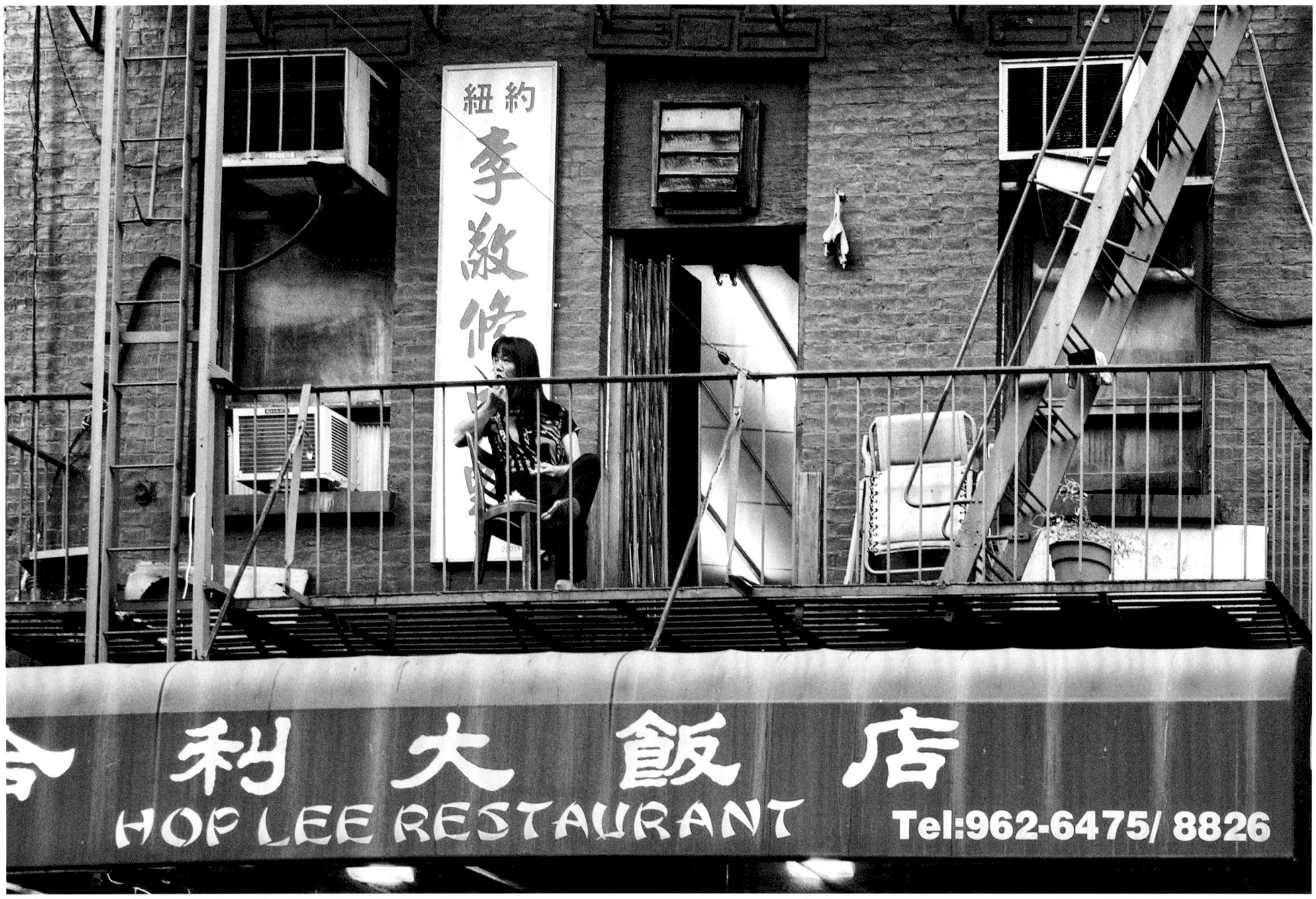
紐約
HOP LEE RESTAURANT
Tel:962-6475/ 8826

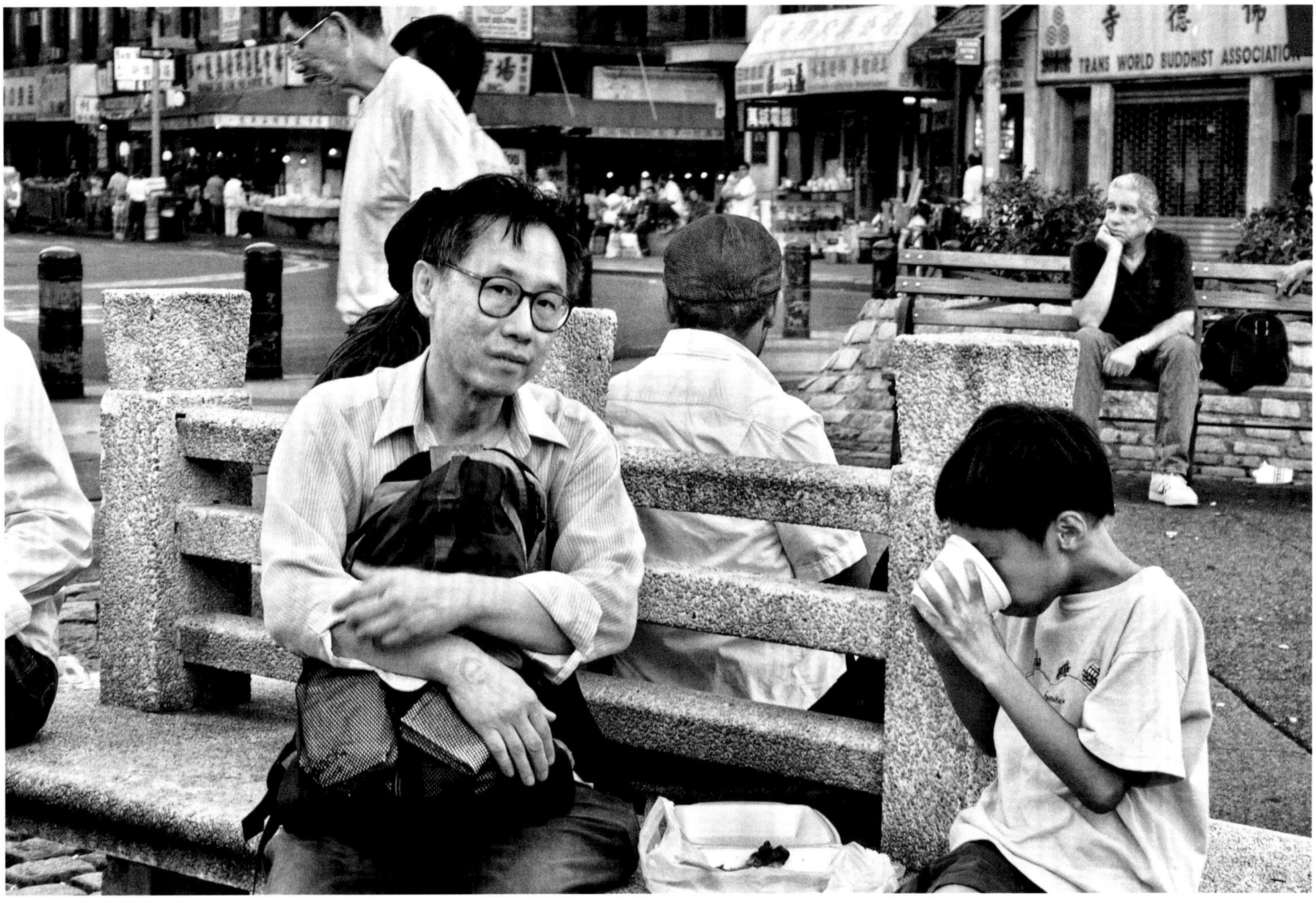
TRANS WORLD BUDDHIST ASSOCIATION

LADDER COMPAN

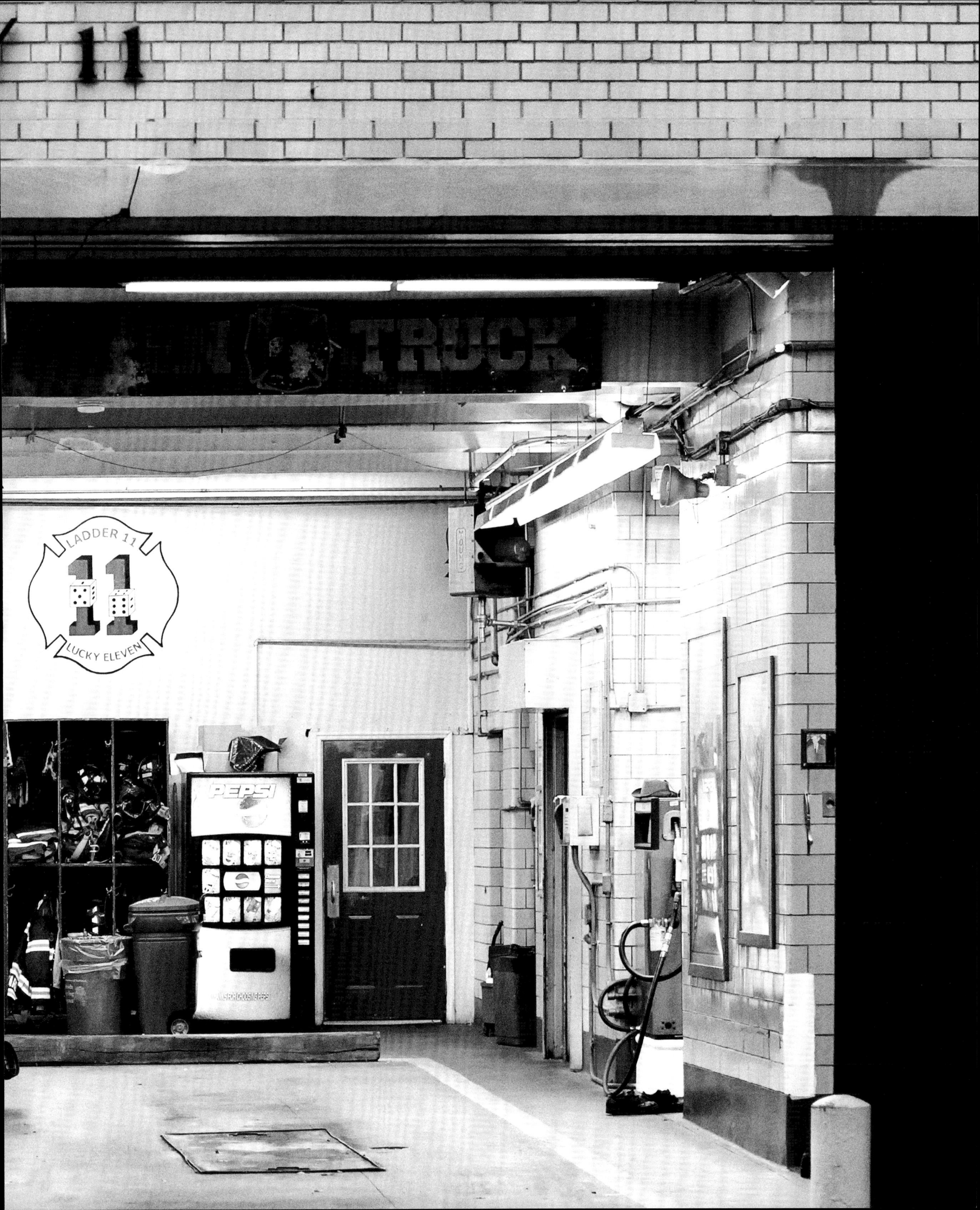
11
TRUCK
LADDER 11
11
LUCKY ELEVEN
PEPSI

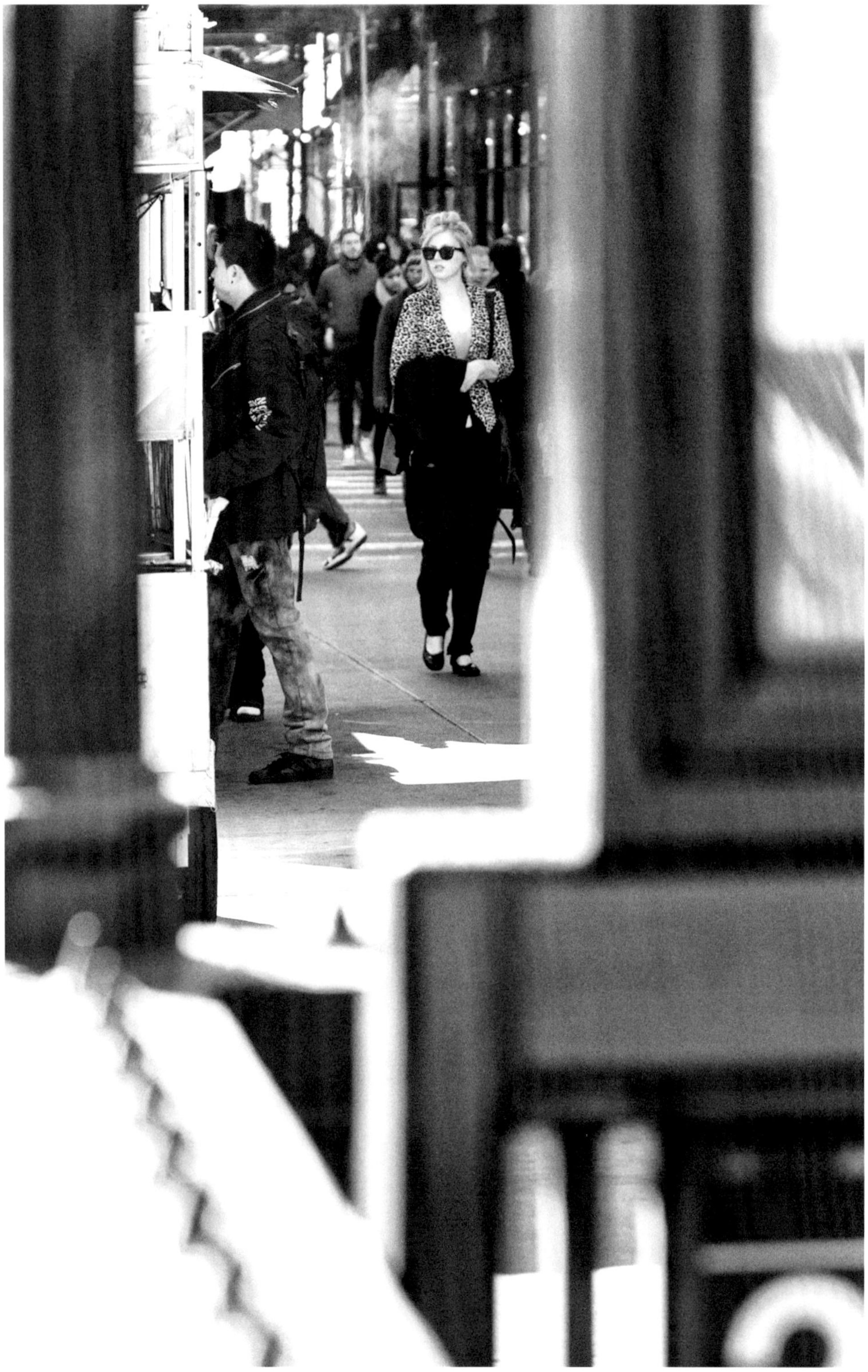

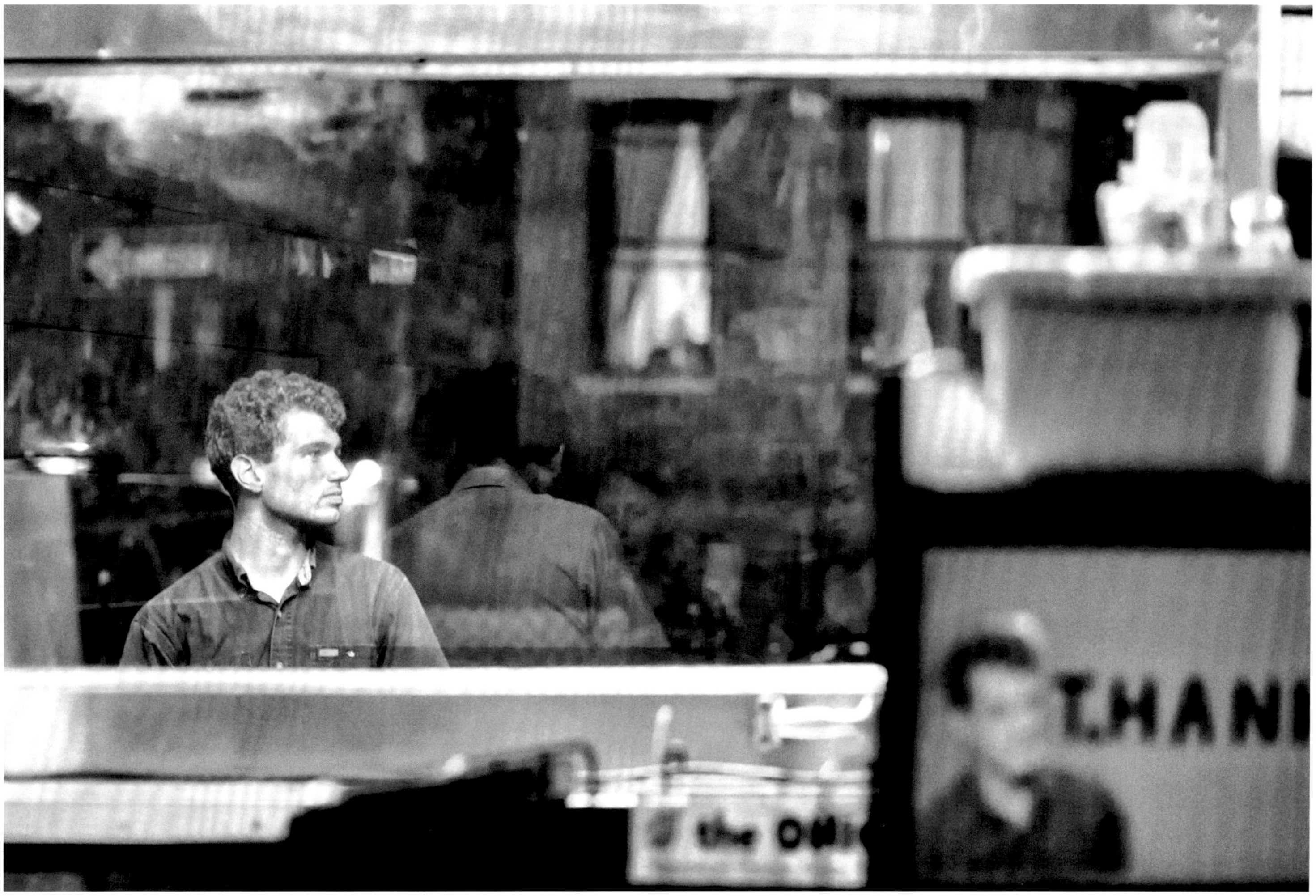
T.HAN
the OM

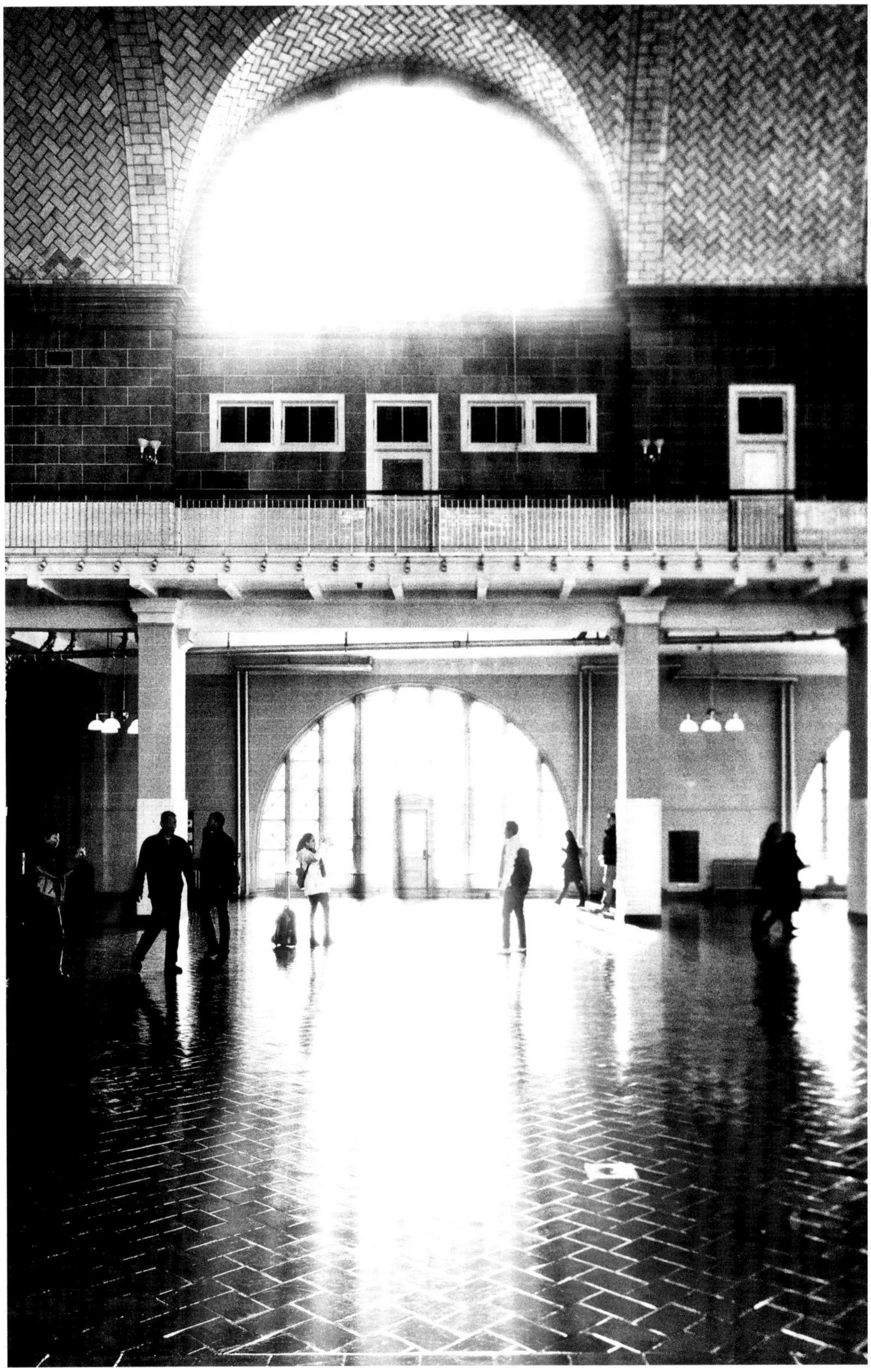

Ice Cold Beer
Sandwiches
Cigarettes
Coffee
185 Bedford Ave.
NEW YORK LOTTO
Newspaper
Groceries
Candies & Chips
Dog & Cat Food
(718) 387-8521
DELI MART
MEGA MILLIONS
Ice Cold Beer
ORNINO
718 384-6004
PEACHFROG
PEACHFROG
THERAPY for the FASHION OBSESSED
VISIT US
fashion LIQUIDATORS
Budweiser
ATM
MAVERICK
American Quality
Newport
CIGARETTES

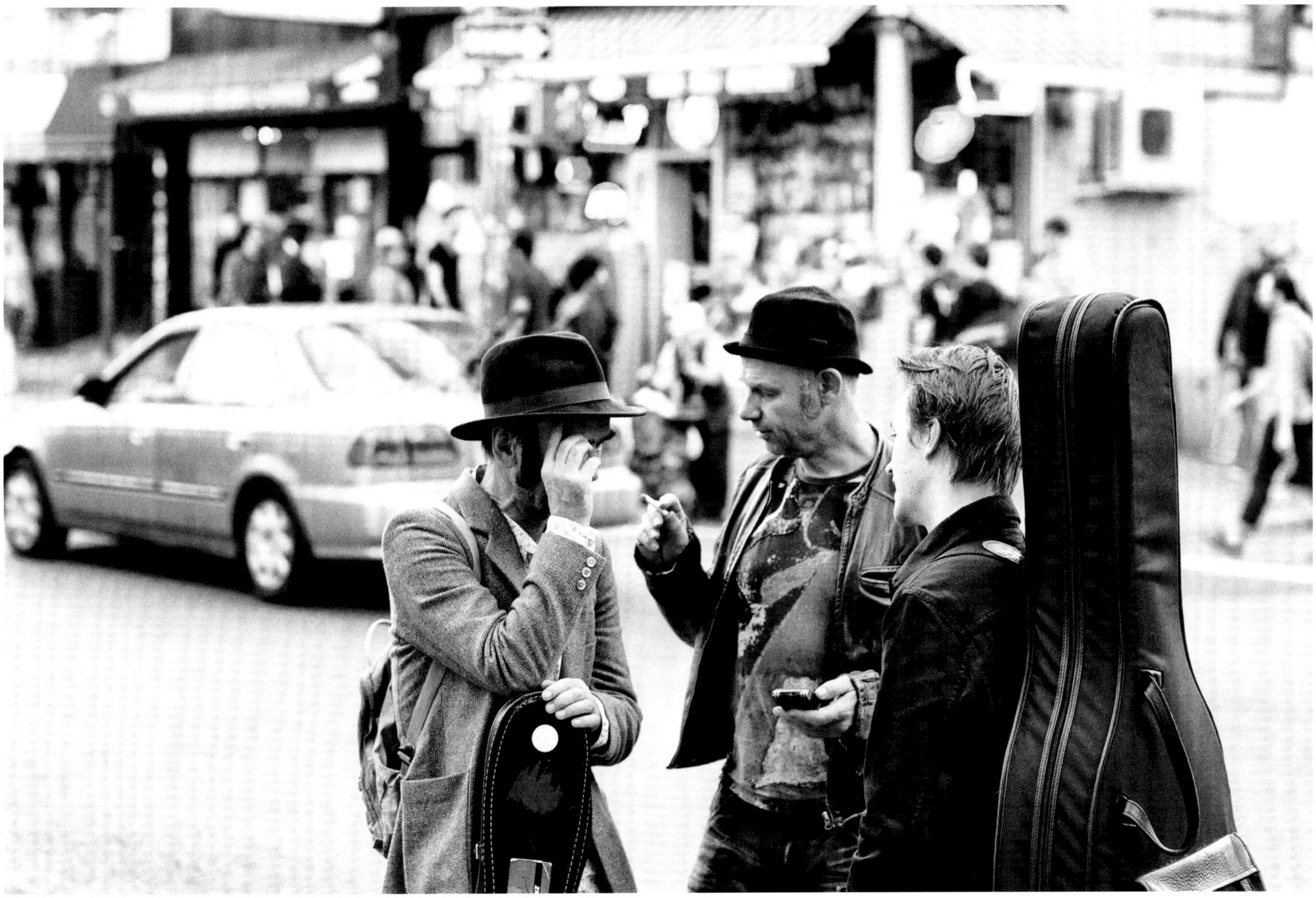

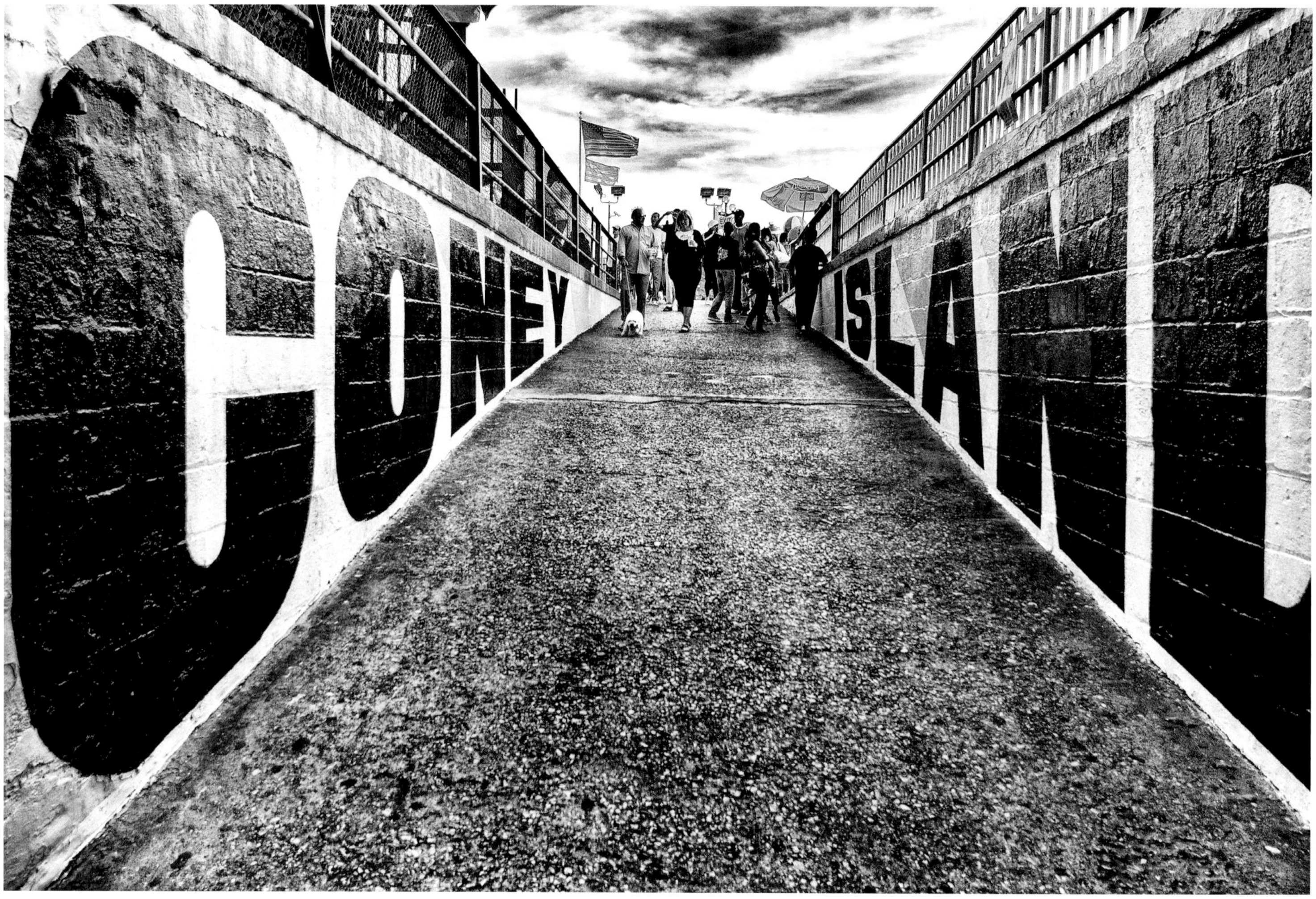
CONEY
ISLAN

Hot Knishes
HOT PIZZA
FRIED SHRIMPS
COLD CLAMS
COLD BEER
DRINKS
SEA FOOD
Paul's Daughter
Pop Corn
COTTON CANDY
ICE CREAM
HOT CORN
ITALIAN SAUSAGE
Sea Food
COLD BEER
DRINKS
FRANKFURTERS
KEEP CONEY ISLAND BEACH AND
BOARDWALK CLEAN

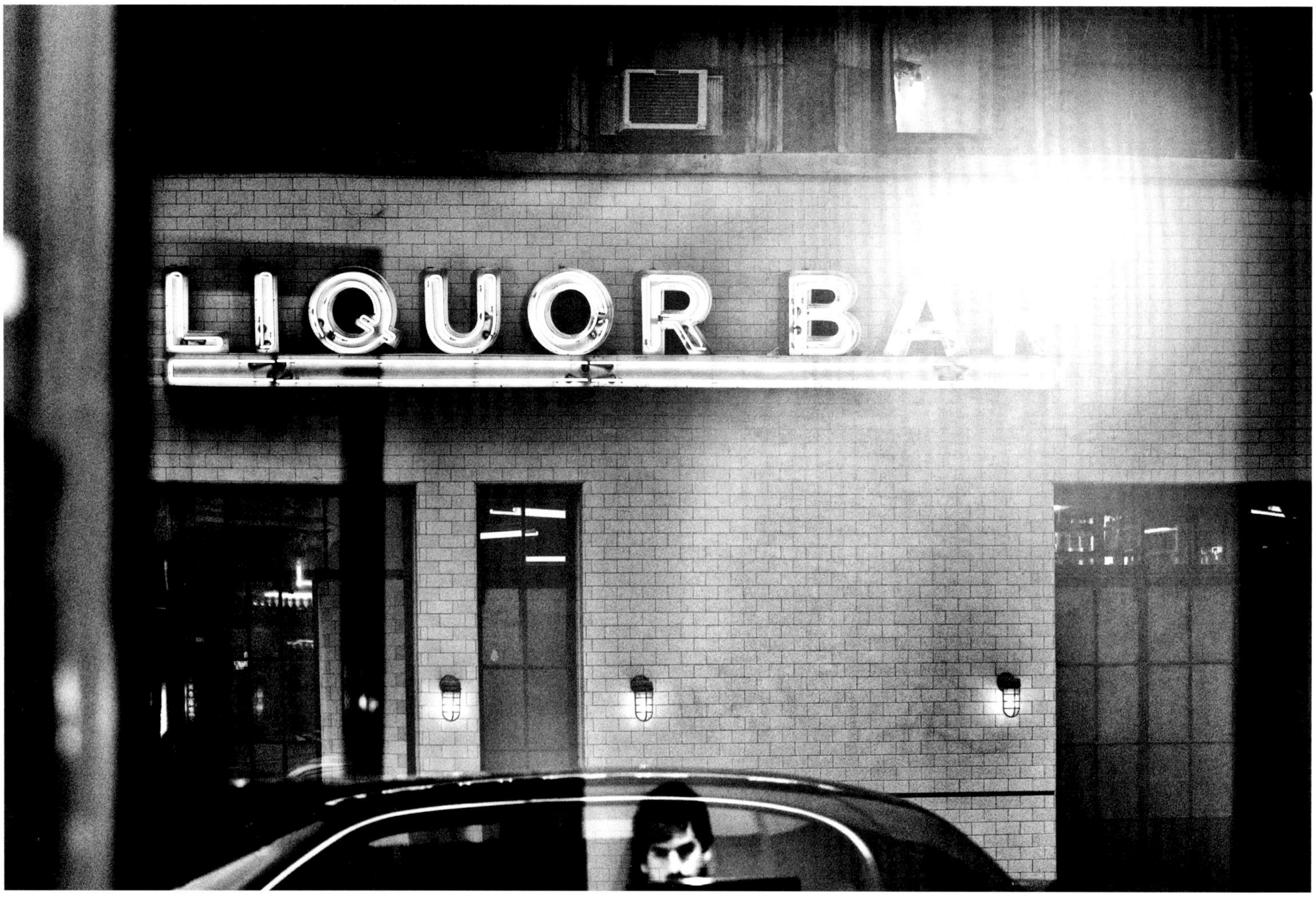
LIQUOR BA

SINCE 1983
DESDE 1983
TAX
RAPID & LOW COST
DIVORCE
BANKRUPTCY
INMIGRACION FACIL
MAIL BOXES, ENVIOS & PASAJES
Se Habla ESPAÑOL
NOTARY
TAX
DIVORCE
DIVORCIO
P.O.BOX
INMIGRACION
SINCE - DESDE 1983
212 420-1616
OPEN

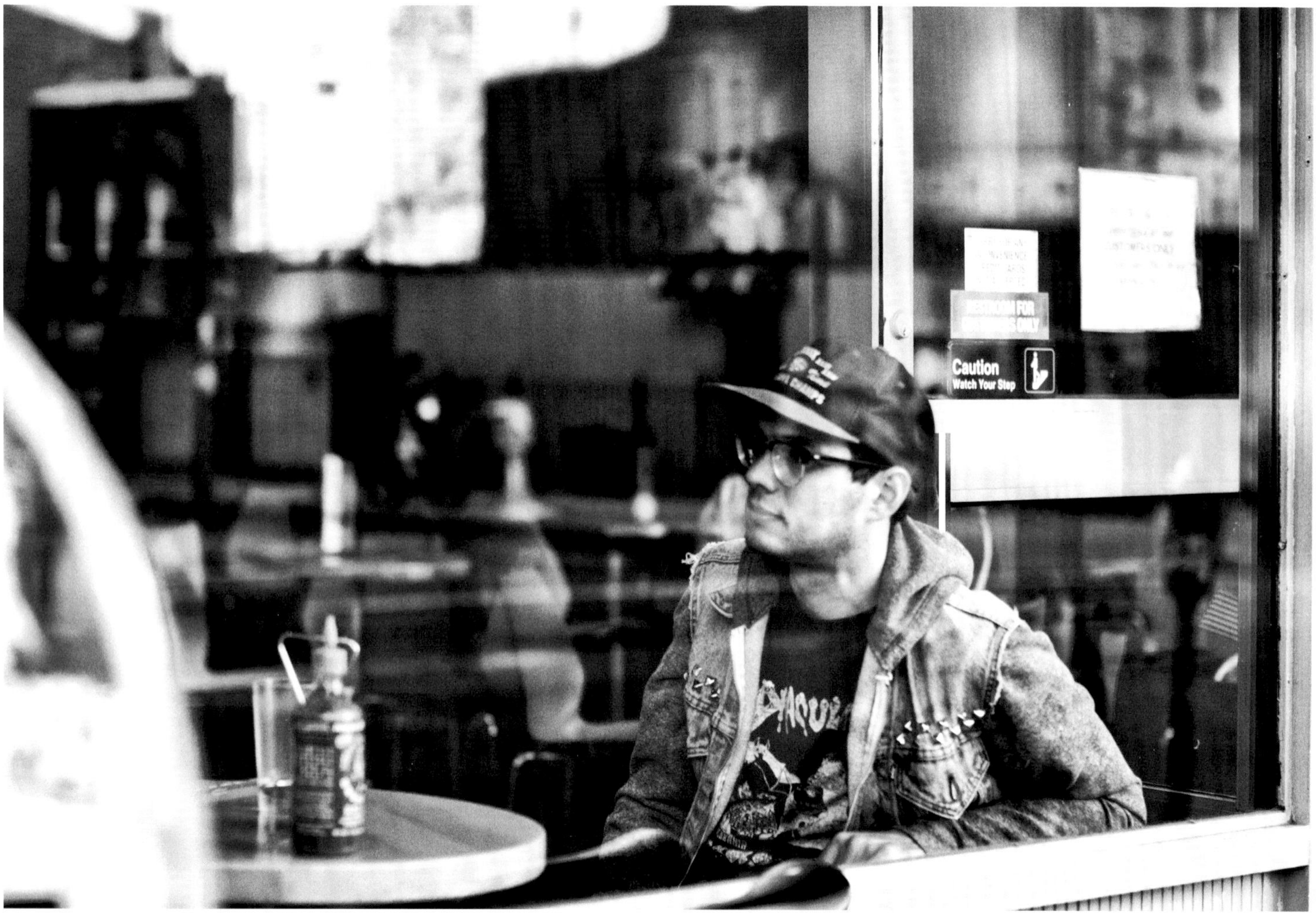
Caution
Watch Your Step

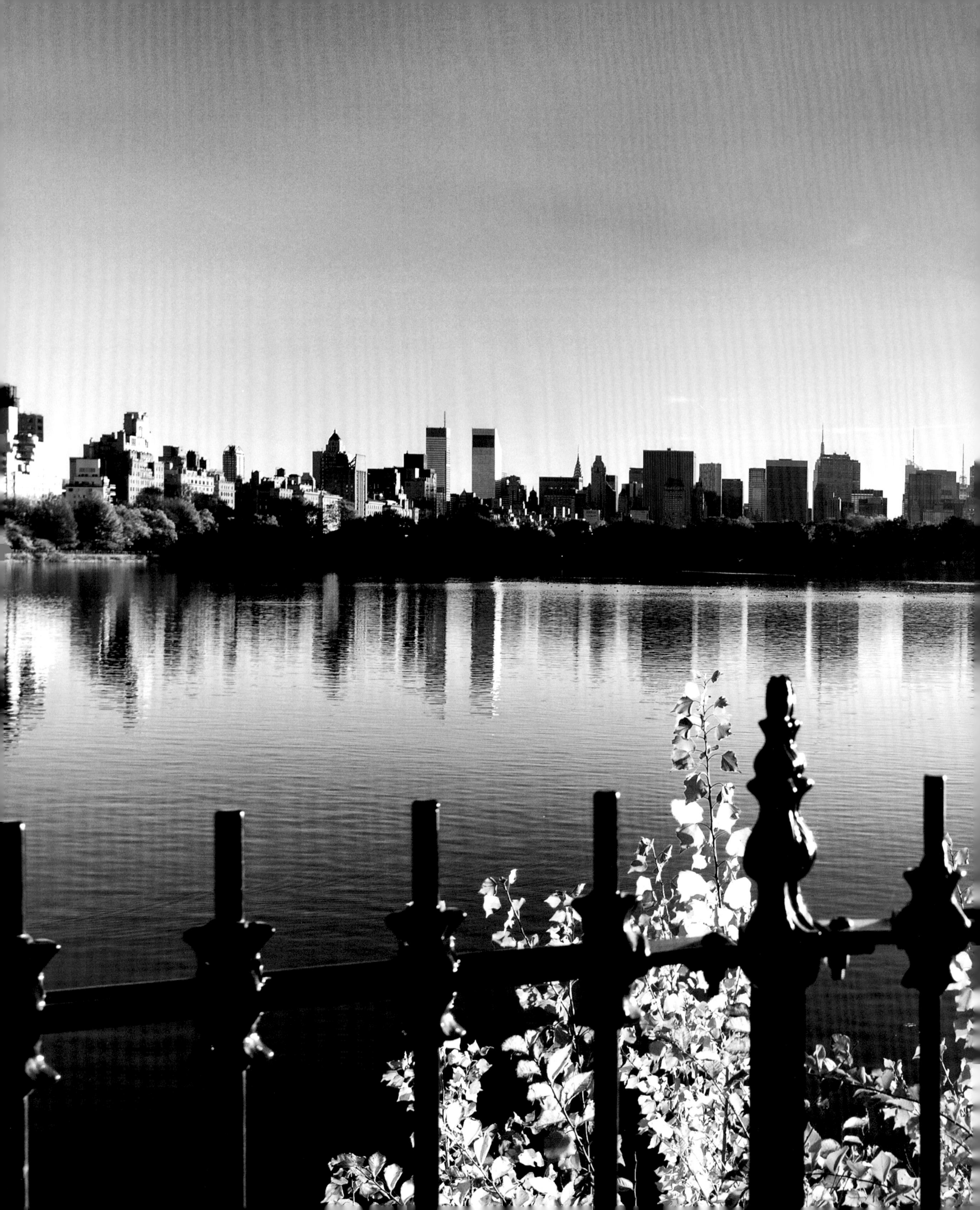

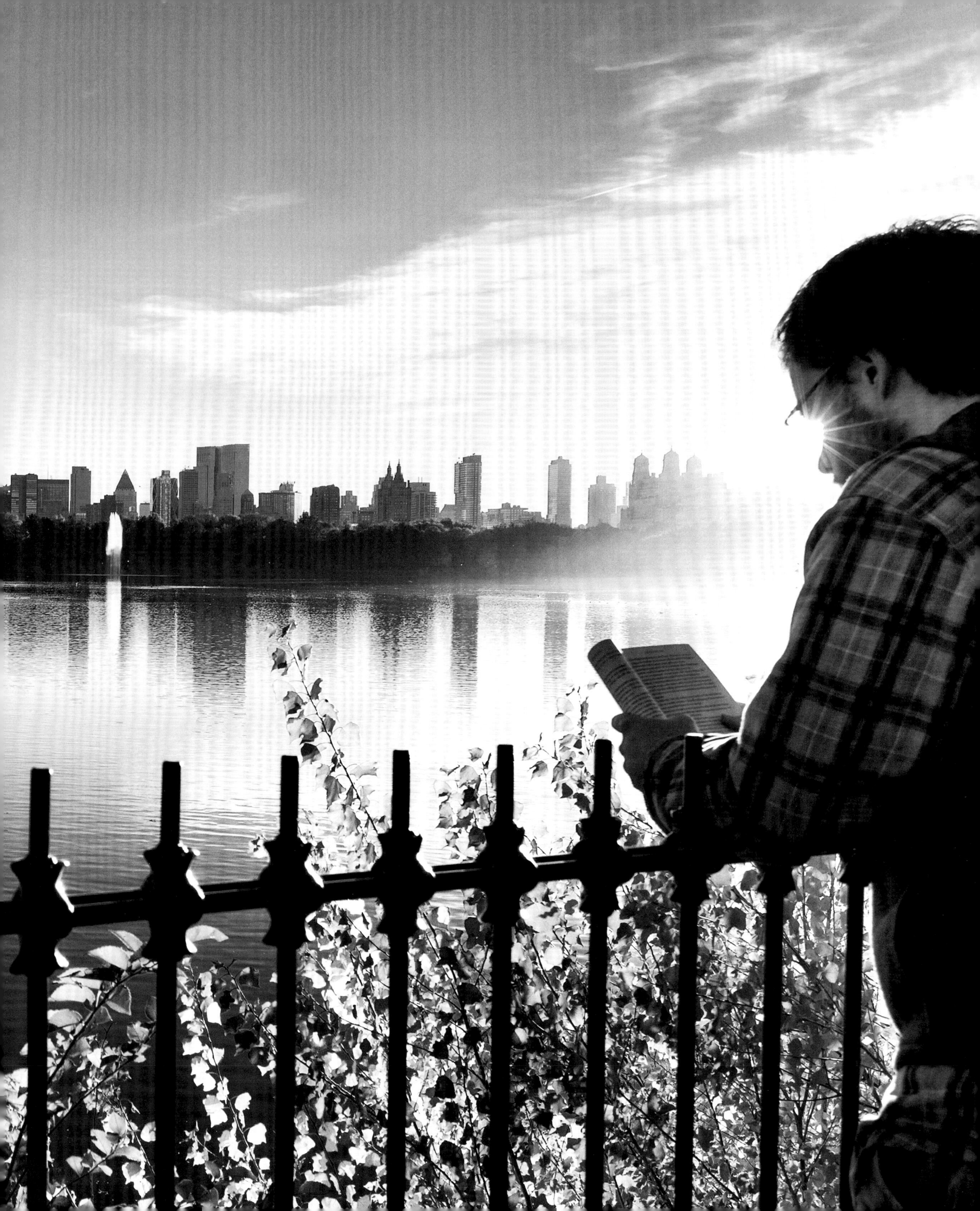

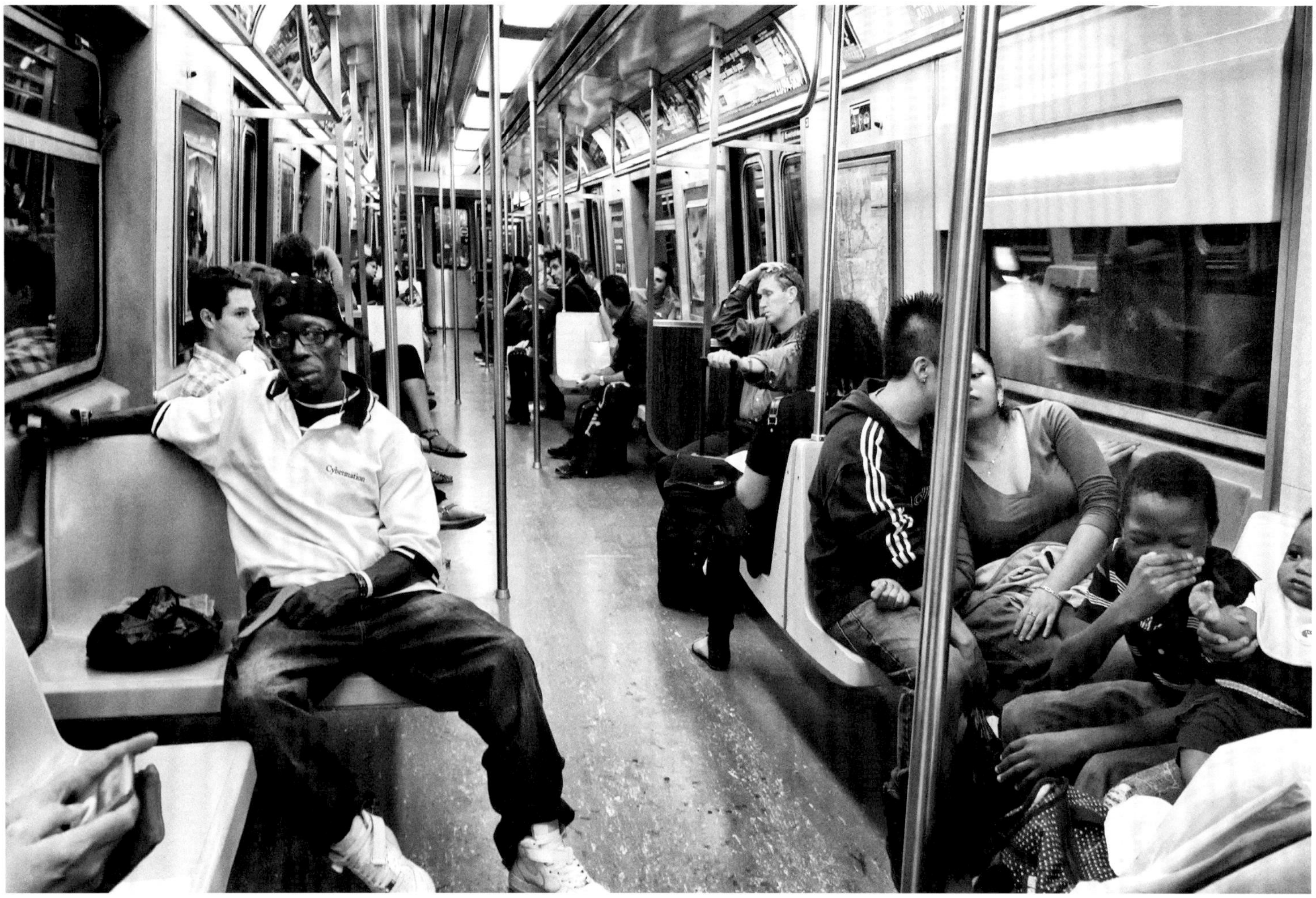

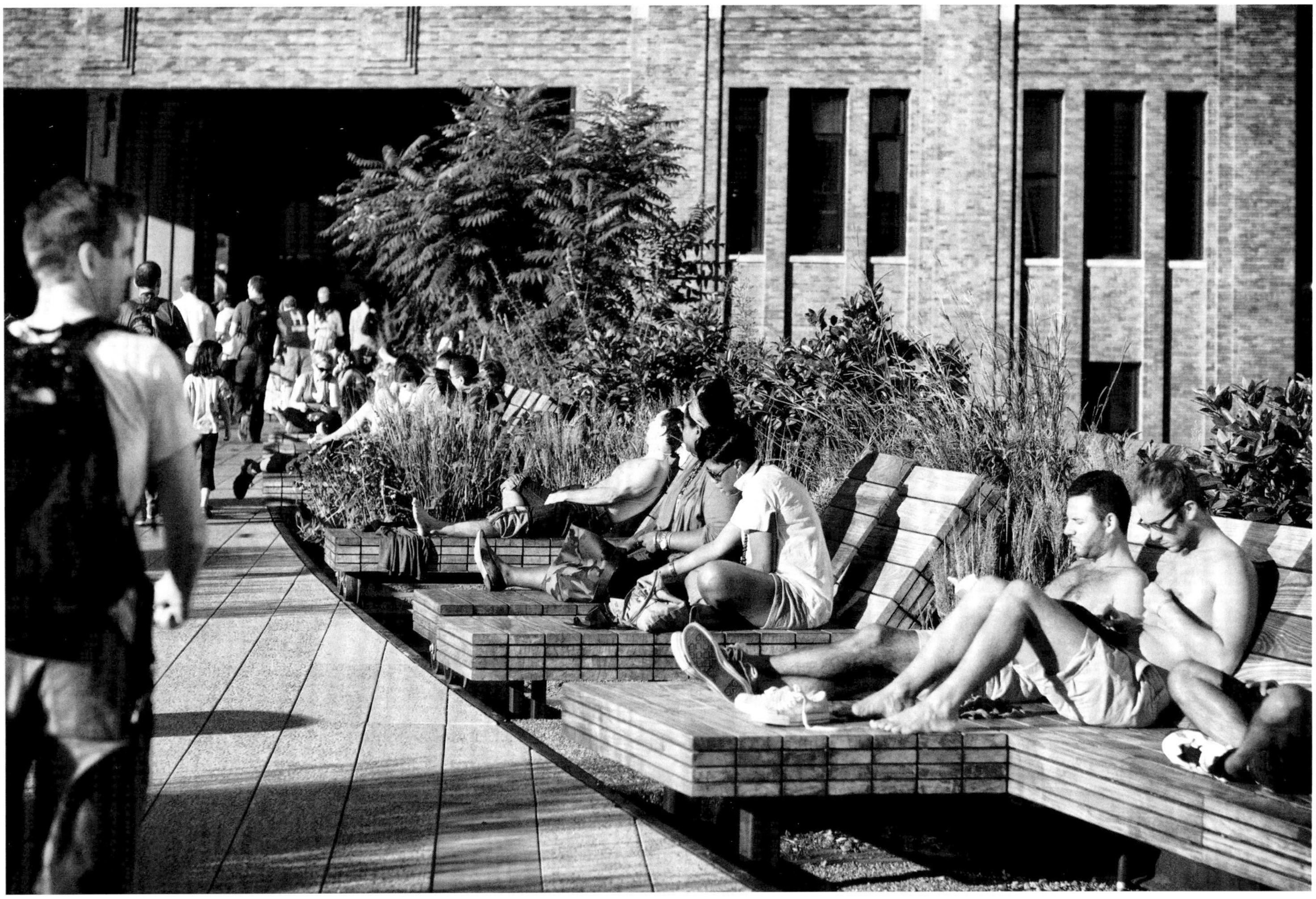

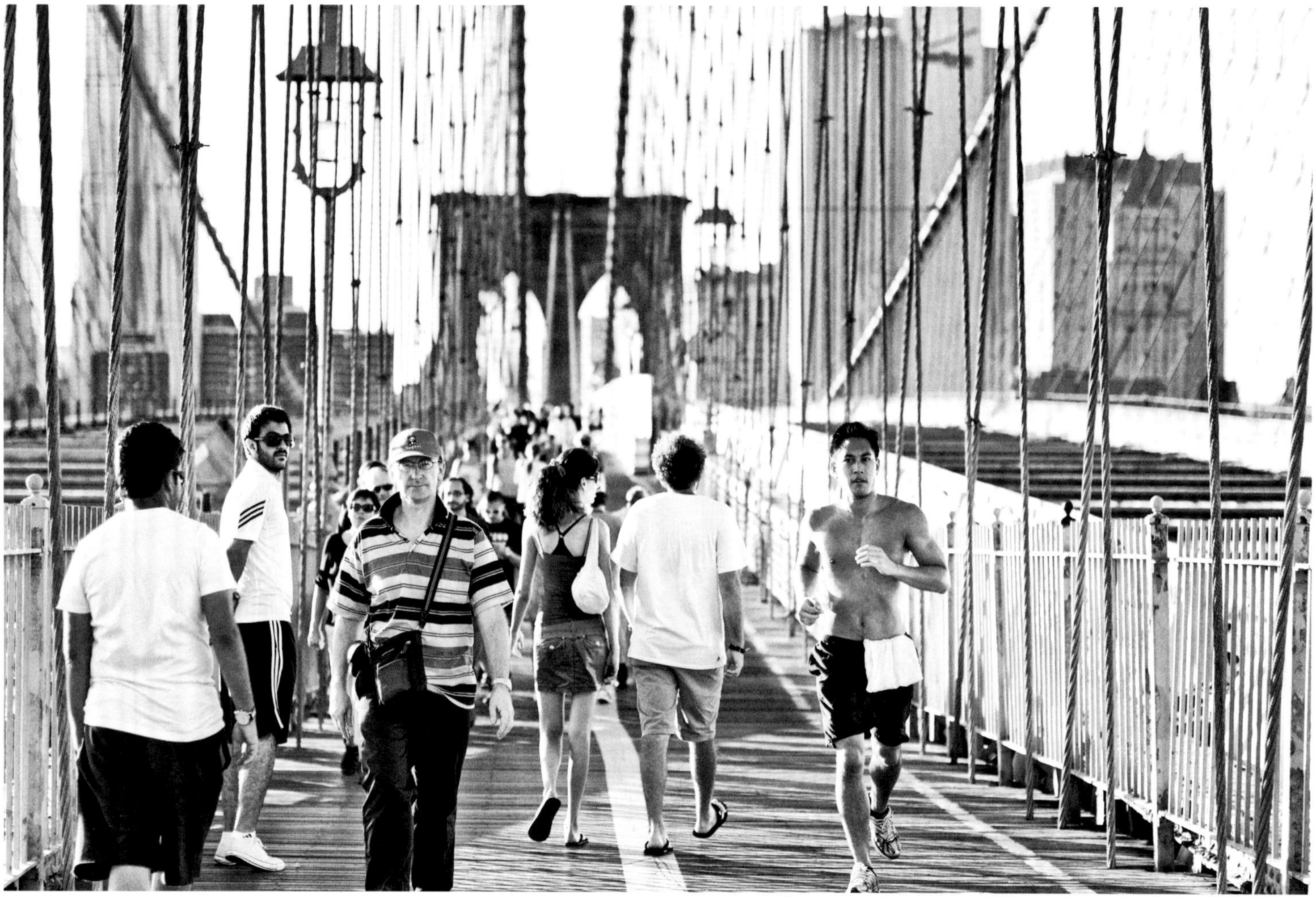

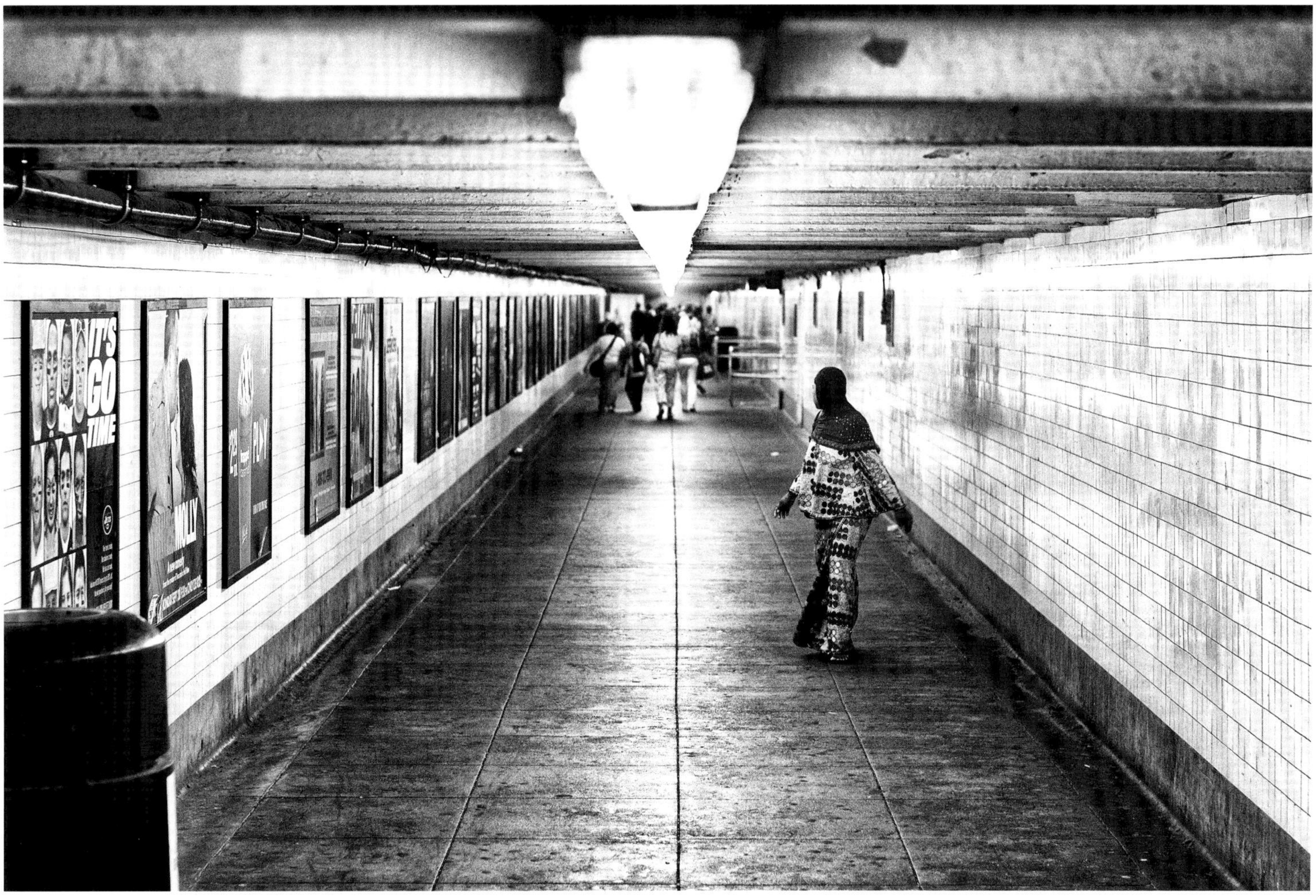

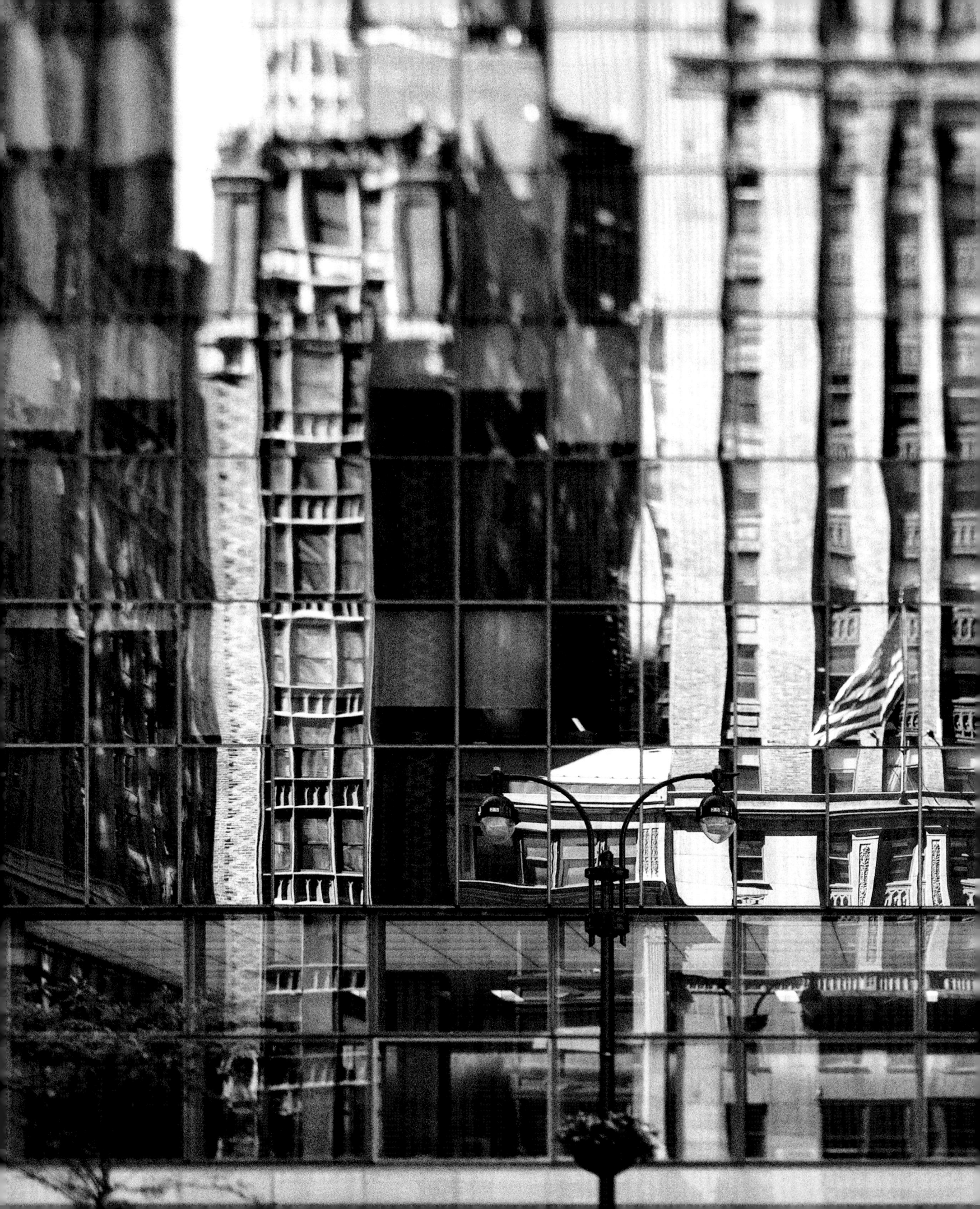

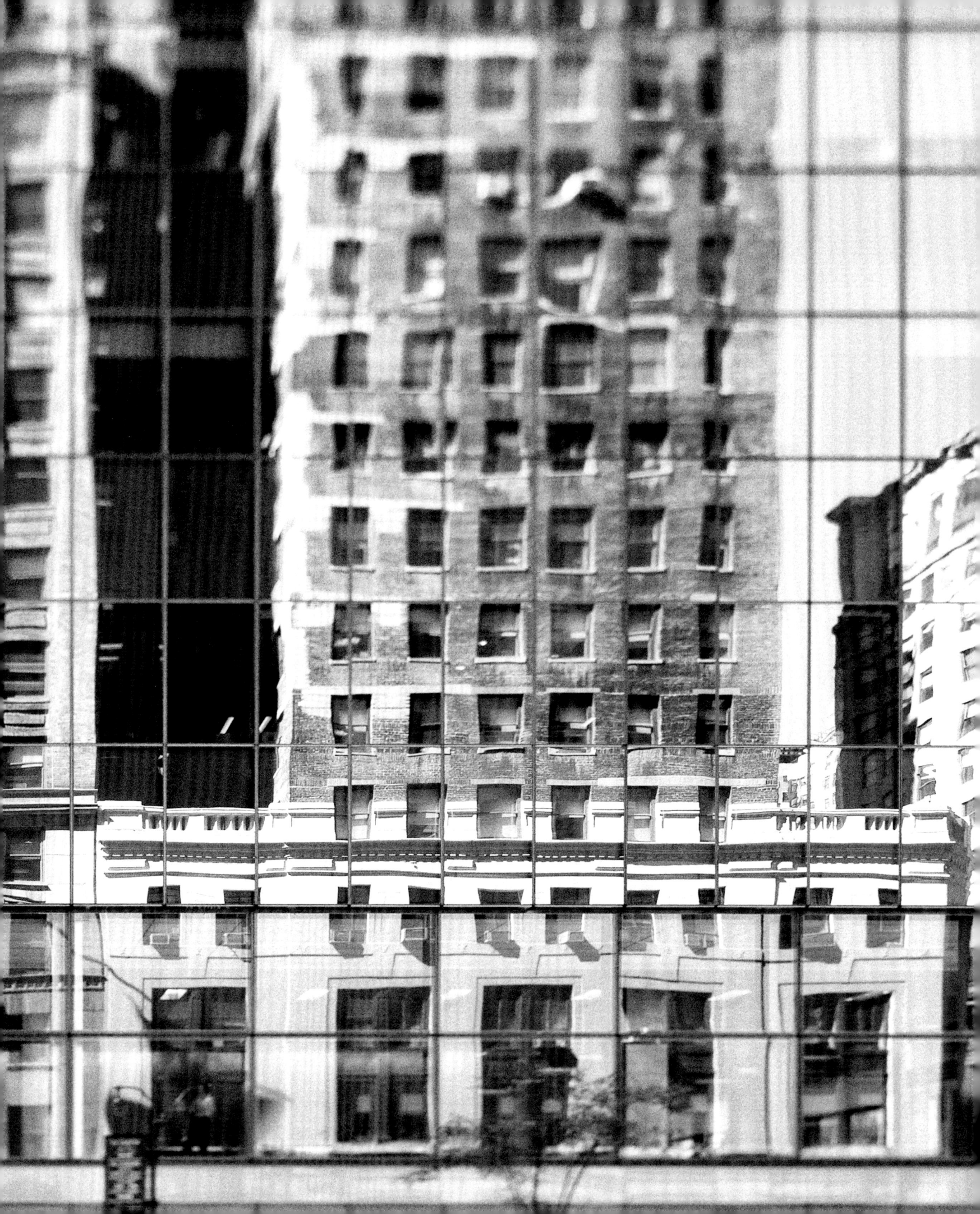

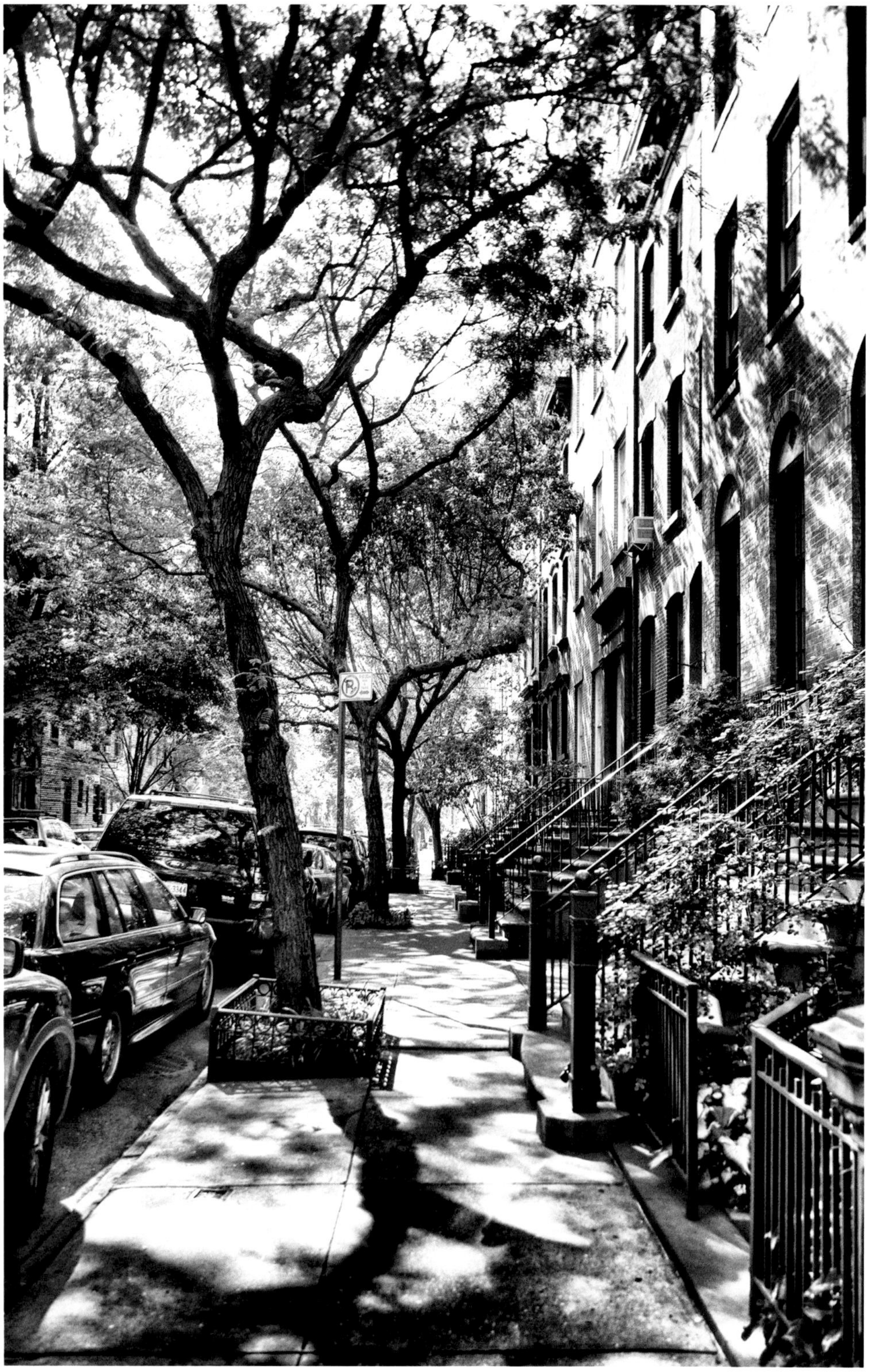

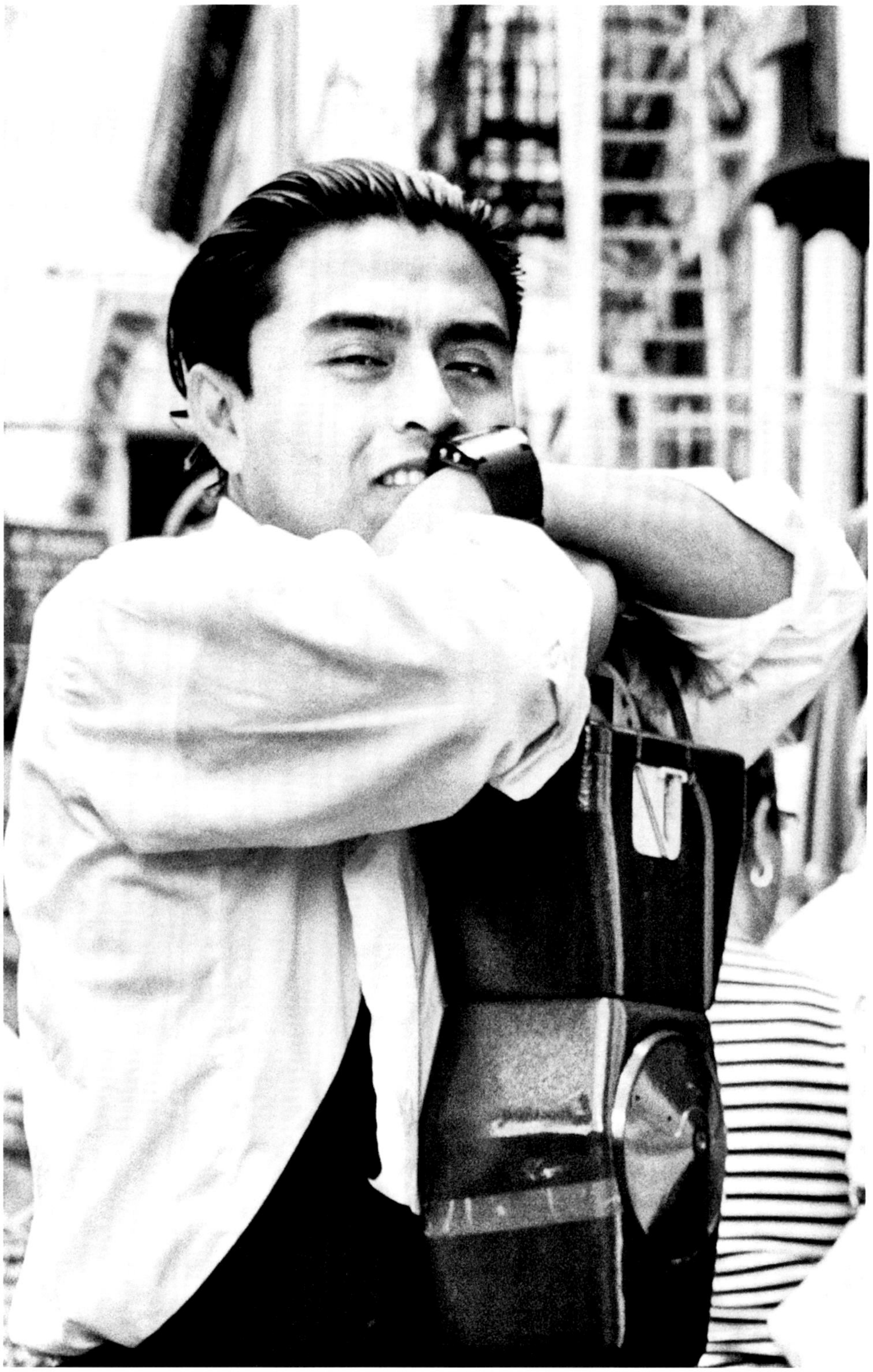

42 St - Grand Central

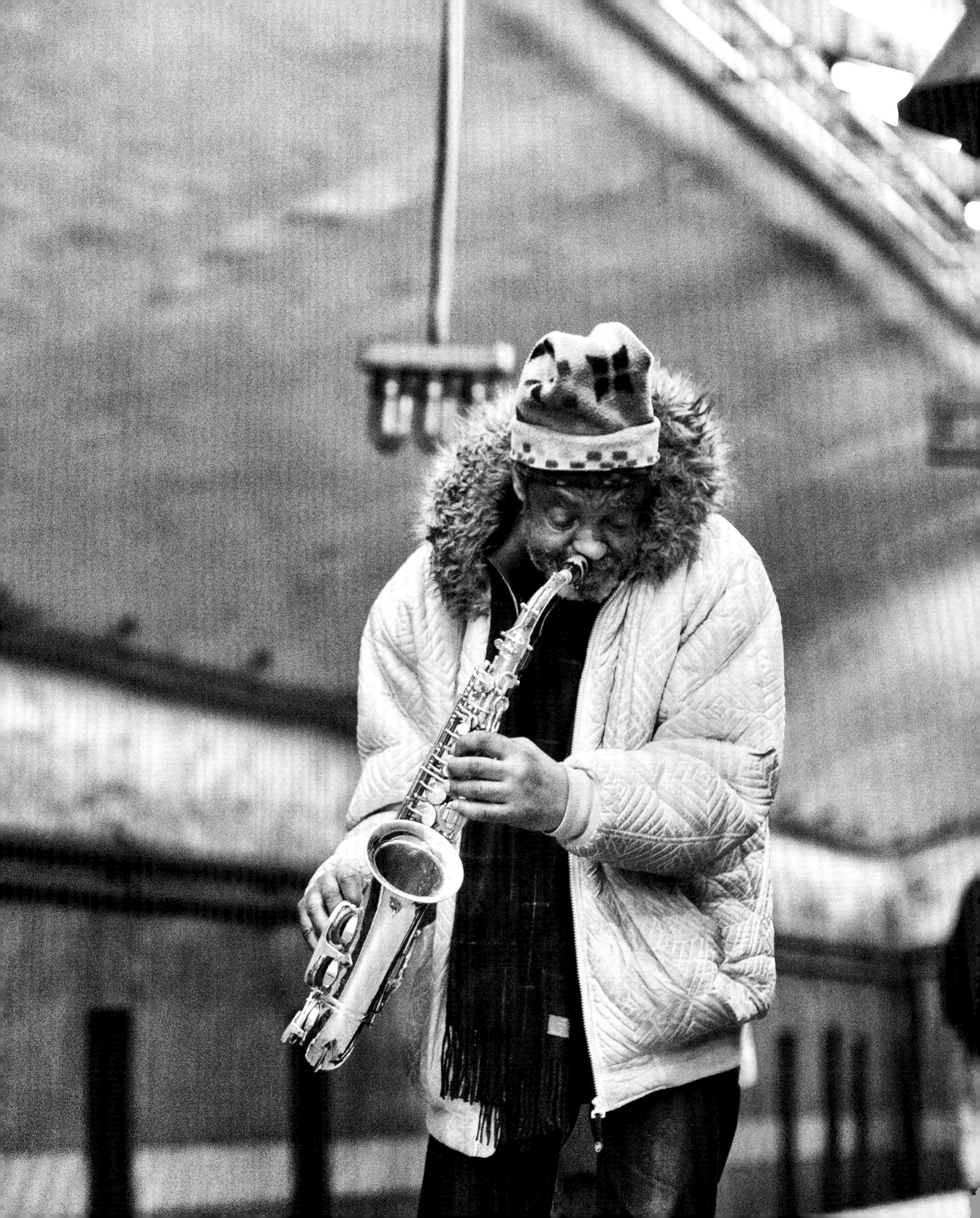

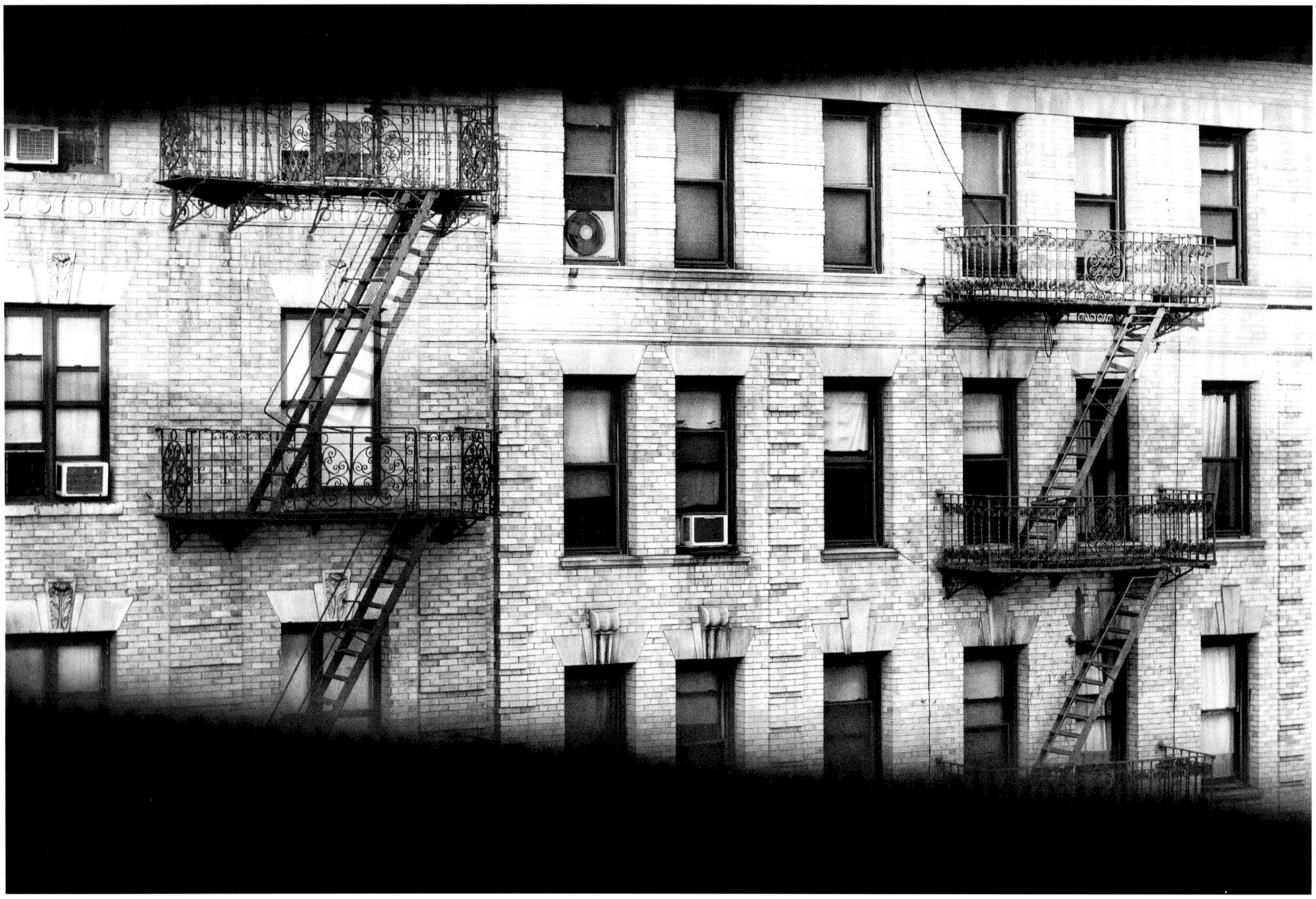

Exit
Or call...
Touch
Start
AUDIO
CREDIT/ATM CARD
CHANGE
COINS
Exit
Exit

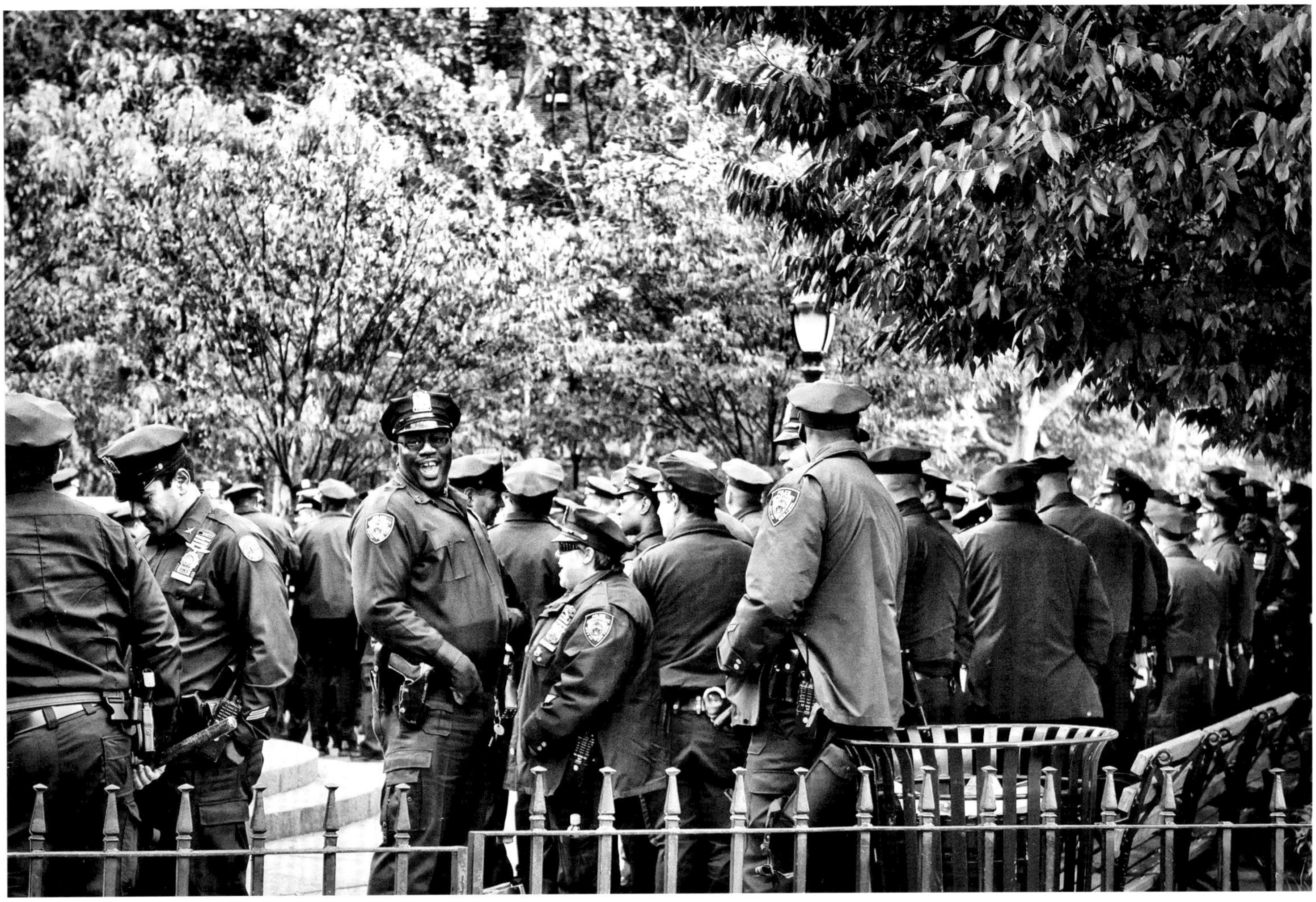

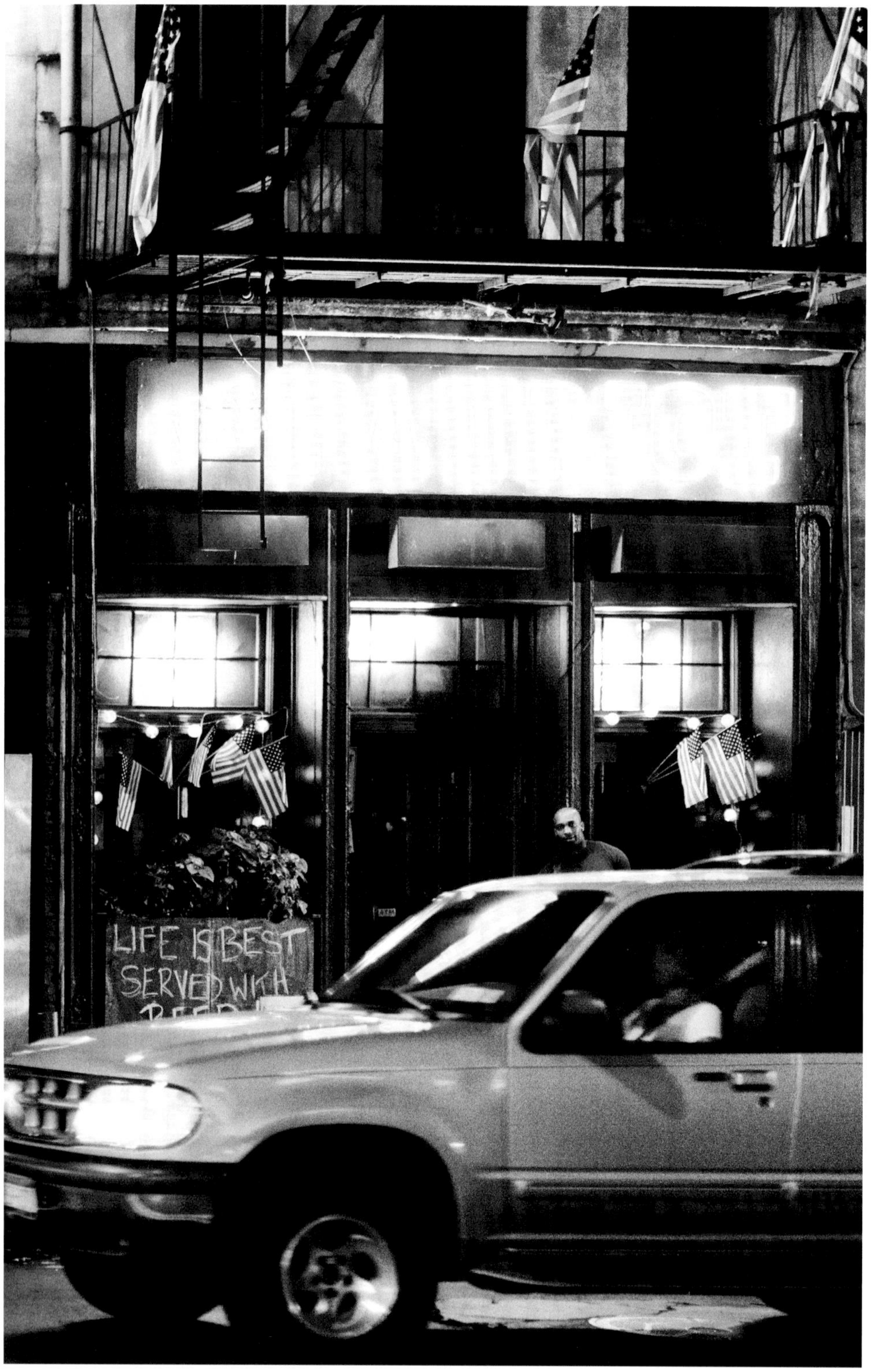
LIFE IS BEST
SERVED WITH

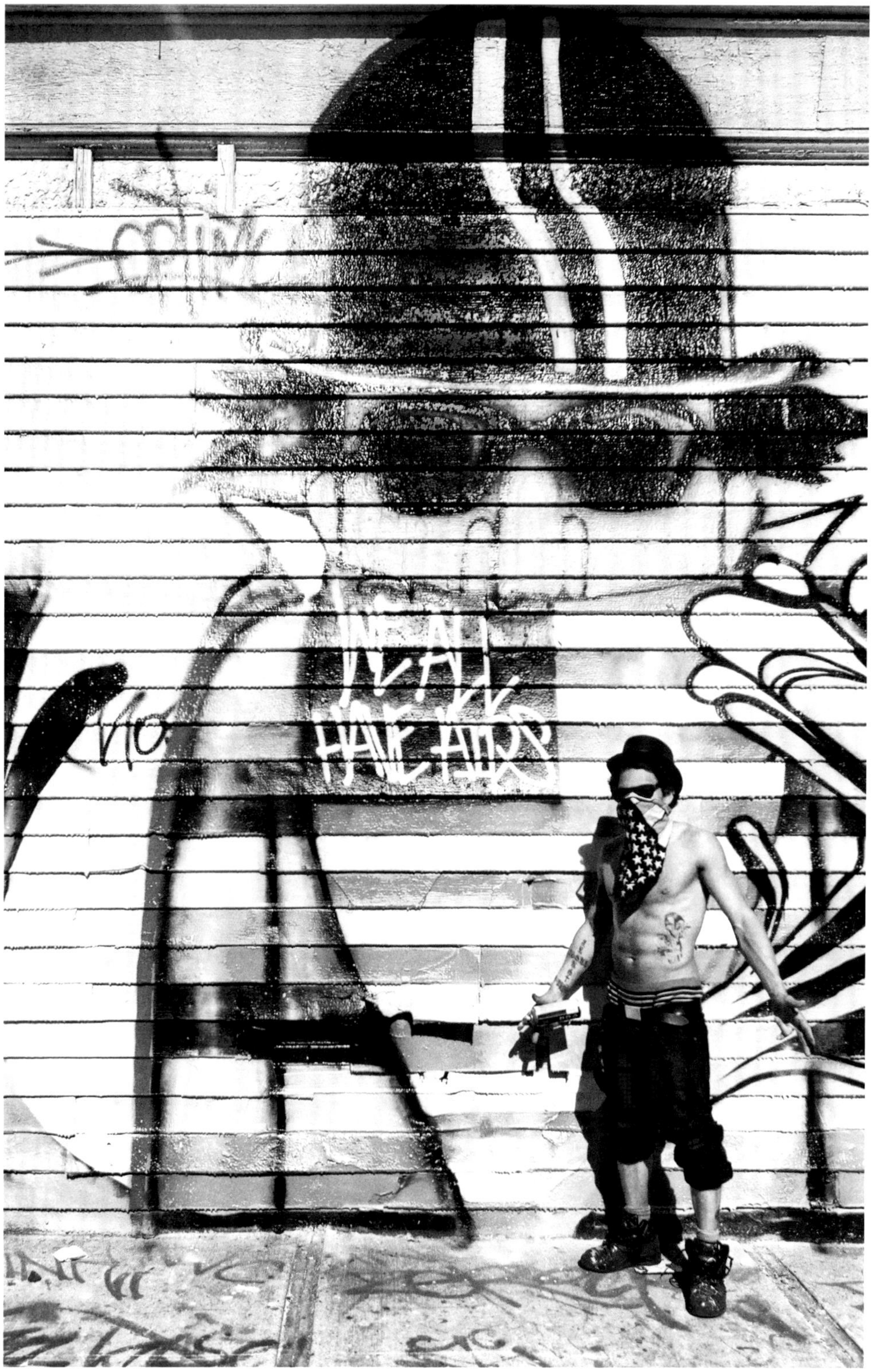

Our
DIVERSITY
is our greatest
STRENGTH
When any New Yorker is attacked for who
they are, what they believe or whom they
LOVE
it is a crime against all of us.
Keep our City strong.
LOVE LOVE. HATE HATE.
NYC
Michael R. Bloomberg
Mayor
New York City
Council
Christine C. Quinn
Speaker

Special Thanks

To the subscribers listed right: The publishing process was possible only because of your kind support and belief in its success.

I would like to express my sincere appreciation and gratitude to
ERICH JOACHIMSTHALER, RICHARD ROLKA, NICK HAHN, MARKUS PFEIFFER, MARKUS ZINNBAUER, HARTMUT HEINRICH, JOSIP MARŠAN, GIANCARLO BOZZA and JAMES BURR from Vivaldi Partners in New York, who contributed in many ways to the realization process. I am indebted to THEA BARKHOFF and NINA HEIMBRECHT for the art direction of this book. DONOVAN ORTEGA thank you for the introduction and your dedication to the project.
MARC OPGENORTH provided generous assistance during the production process. It was a pleasure to work with all of you.

Additionally, I would like to acknowledge and kindly thank Tina Müller from Henkel and Schwarzkopf Duesseldorf for sponsoring GHOST PRESS and this book.

Last but not least, many thanks to my lovely sister HELENA AZHARI and my loyal friends, SHAYNE STALEY, TILL TENHOFEN, SVEA KRELL, TYLER PETERS, ISABEL VICTORIA VILLEDA, ALI RASHIDI, ALI MOJAHEDI and JADE MOON FINCH. You are an important part of my 1440 minutes.

Book Subscriber No.:

001 ANDREAS LOHWASSER
002 DEBORAH EPKENHAUS
003 KRISTINA KLEIN
004 STEFFEN HENN
005 TILL TENHOFEN
006 JULIAN VALKIESER
007 ALEXANDER SCHULZ-FIELITZ
008 RALF SCHMIDT
009 THOMAS NEUMANN
010 HARALD FRIEDRICHS
011 LIDIA URIBE OSSES
012 SUSANNE POSTEL
013 ANNE SOEHNEL
014 INGE & HARALD KLEIN
015 FILIZ GOEZUEBUEYUEK
016 JADE MOON FINCH
017 ELKE BUESCHKES
018 ILKA SIMON
019 HELGA KLAHS
020 DIRK VONTEN
021 BASTIAN PFEIFFER
022 ANNE GOTTBEHUET
023 BRIDGET WILSON-BECKER
024 SIBEL YURTSEVER
025 DENIZ RICHTER
026 JOSE & COLLEEN ORTEGA
027 MICHELLE GARCIA
028 ISABEL VICTORIA VILLEDA
029 FRANZISKA VOELCKNER
030 STEFANIE HARTMANN
031 FLEUR ESTELLE
032 ANJA HACKSTEIN
033 HEIDI WELLINGER
034 GISELLA VICTORIA VILLEDA
035 PETER CARLSON
036 JULIA LAATSCH
037 MORITZ BAECK
038 MONICA PERKOWSKI
039 DIANE & SANDY STALEY
040 ANA CORINA ARREDONDO
041 MAREI DZIUB
042 ALICJA BERESKA
043 MARTIN ITOR
044 LUKAS GEHNER
045 NILS KRUEGER
046 DOREEN PALTAWITZ
047 NIGEL STOREY
048 SHAYNE STALEY
049 TOBY PACKER
050 HERIBERT GANGL
051 OLENA NOVOSAD
052 SASCHA PERTEN
053 MATTHIAS WINKENBACH
054 SWETLANA SLASTEN
055 ANNE WOEHNER
056 HERMINE GHERGHICEANU
057 MARCOS FERNANDEZ
058 JUAN JOSÉ VICTORIA VILLEDA
059 ANTON LARKIN
060 KATHRIN LIEBSCHER
061 ROLF FREIER
062 BEATRIX SCHMIEDEL
063 LUIS VON CZETTRITZ
064 DAVIDE ALAIN & LILLY LOUISE GALASSO
065 LINDA SEEMANN
066 MARCEL IMHOF
067 BENJAMIN PUCHE
068 JAN POULEV
069 TYLER BRETT PETERS
070 WIEBKE SCHROEDER
071 KATHRIN GEIST
072 LUTZ SCHRAMM
073 CHRISTOPHER GRUENE
074 THOMAS JOSEK
075 RAMONA JUNGGEBURTH
076 MARCO CHRIST
077 LENNART SCHLAEFKE
078 ISABEL ZETTWITZ
079 MIRJAM GUENTHER
080 PIA FREIER
081 NILS ZANKE
082 RENATE & JUAN JOSÉ VICTORIA VILLEDA
083 HELGA NOORDER-MEER
084 KATHARINA SPAHN
085 IRINA JOST & SEBASTIAN REINHARD
086 AURELIUS RUS
087 MAGDALENA BRZUZY
088 RYAN DAILEY
089 ANJA & FABIAN GREKUHL
090 KEYWAN FEIN
091 KIANA FEIN
092 CHRISTINA SCHIFFER
093 NILFUAR ANSARI
094 TIAN TIAN
095 JENS WAGNER
096 JENNIFER JONES
097 ALBAN SMAJLI
098 HOLGER KRIEGEL
099 SEMRA MIDDELHOFF
100 HELENA AZHARI

All photographs taken between 2007 and 2011

First edition 2011
© 2011 PEYMAN AZHARI

Art Direction and Design THEA BARKHOFF, NINA HEIMBRECHT
Introduction DONOVAN ORTEGA
Production MARC OPGENORTH, JUNG PRODUKTION, Cologne, Germany
Printing DRUCKEREI HIMMER, Augsburg, Germany

Printed and published in Germany

ISBN 978-3-943156-00-3

GHOST PRESS

Social Publishing
New York – London – Cologne

DE +49 221 9976 6336
US +1 347 8266 277
UK +44 20 7558 8016

ghost–press.com
mail@ghost–press.com